THE TOWN THAT COULDN'T TRUST

Denis Dwyer

High Play Publishing

To all those who help the planet

CONTENTS

CONTENTS

1

AN UNWANTED SURPRISE

Such a pristine place to fish. The early-morning sun was glittering on the river upstream but the river where Simon Hurley was standing thigh-deep was partly in the shade of enveloping bush, accentuating the sense of isolation and privacy. This was not a pleasure he wanted to share and as he cast the line and watched it dash along in the current, he sighed with satisfaction. Tumanako prided itself on its sports facilities for its 7,534 inhabitants (at last count), with numerous fields, courts, and an indoor stadium, but the best sports facilities of all had been provided by nature – rivers tumbling down from the central mountains, rippling with trout, and native bush stretching from the town to the very foothills of those mountains, where trampers, mountain bikers and hunters could indulge in as many adventures as they wished.

In his ribbed jacket and fishing gear, Simon looked bigger than he was but his outdoor lifestyle helped keep him strong and supple and his love of nature drew him into the bush and rivers at every opportunity. He peered again. There, swaying languidly just above the gravel mid-stream, was a dark, torpedo-shaped object. The sport did not provide the chat of golf but it was supreme for its mix of excitement and serenity. He cast again – an effortless sideways arc with the leader dropping lightly just up river from the trout and drifting swiftly in the bubbly current. A flick took the loop from the line and he followed the drift with the tip of the rod. Nothing doing. Perhaps he was too close, or the trout was exhausted from sex, or the water was too clear. The rivers were famed for their purity and their attraction to anglers, and the dairy farmers along the way had by and large co-operated and kept their cows and effluent out of the river; those that had not, had soon found themselves in court.

Simon took two strides back. He had fished here for thirty years, since he was a boy, and knew enough to tread carefully on the river bed's large rocks. A wrong and careless step in his waders and he could be joining the fish in a dash downstream. Care needed on the cast too – a sloppy cast might have, not a trout, but a 'bush fish' on his hook. As he repositioned himself, he looked downstream and saw something that caused his whole body to stiffen and drew a curse from his lips.

'Bloody hell.'

The near side of the river bank was a sickly yellow and as Simon gazed wide-eyed, he saw a thin stream of turgid waste ooze into the river. He knew instantly where it was coming from. Polson's. Swearing quietly to himself, he returned to his car, packed away his fishing gear and returned to take photographs of the putrid stream of chemicals winding through the bush from the factory site, glugging into the river. There it pulsed again, glug, glug, glug. Already there were two dead eels lodged by the river bank. A second later the photographs, with a note of the location, were on the way to three people: Steve Polson, owner/manager of the company responsible for the pollution, Robin Trethewan, compliance officer of Horizons Regional Council, and Felicity Spratt, reporter of *The Tararua Mirror*.

He spoke to Spratt.

'You've got to see this.'

She was there within half an hour. A slim brunette, twenty-five, with wide hazel eyes, shoulder-length hair, and pretty face, in denim jacket and jeans. In moments she had her photographs and, he suspected, her opening paragraph. Something like, 'Pollution from Polson's flowed into the Tumanako River on Saturday morning. The chemicals have already killed marine life and pose a health risk to any person or animal in the area. This is the second time in the last six months there has been pollution from the factory site. In June this year, Polson's was fined $185,000 for breaching the Health and Safety in Employment Act for a leak of contaminants on the premises.'

Simon took more photographs himself. He would use them in *Help the Planet, Aotearoa*, the monthly publication he owned and edited. It would not be the lead story – he preferred something positive – but it would give a timely jolt to page three. He expected, though, that the story would be the lead in *The Tararua Mirror*.

'What a shocker. It's horrible isn't it,' Felicity Spratt said, when she had finished taking her photographs. She brushed strands of hair away from her face and winced. 'You'd think they would have learnt after last time.... You've told Polson's and the council, haven't you?'

'Yes.' His insides shrivelled as he said it. He thought of Rosemary, his fifteen-year-old daughter, now in a wheelchair with spina bifida. Simon and his wife Patricia suspected the spina bifida was caused by exposure to toxic chemicals when Patricia was pregnant. They had been living at the time on a property adjoining Polson's that they suspected was contaminated with dioxin, possibly from fugitive emissions from the manufacture of the herbicide 2,4,5-Trichlorophenoxyacetic acid at the factory years before. There had been another case of neural tube defect locally and the child's father had worked at Polson's. Nothing could be proved in either case and it hadn't helped that Patricia was not at first aware she was pregnant and was not taking supplements of folic acid. That was when Ray Polson, Steve's father, was running the factory. Ray Polson said he had been assured the site had been cleared of contamination before it was leased to the Hurleys.

Rosemary's neural tube had failed to close completely during the first few weeks of embryonic development so that when the spine formed, the bones of the spinal column did not close around the developing nerves of the spinal cord. In New Zealand, about one in a thousand pregnancies are affected, making it the most common central nervous system birth defect. In Rosemary's case, the spina bifida was higher on the spine resulting in paralysed legs and the need to use a wheelchair. She had an occasional problem with bladder and bowel control.

'How's Rosie?'

It was as if Felicity could read Simon's thoughts. She was a family friend of the Hurleys, especially good mates with the older children Daniel, twenty-two, and Charlotte, twenty-one, who had been contemporaries at school.

'She's good. Always better for your visits.'

'Sorry I haven't been round for a while. Down to two reporters now, most of the time. I can't be sure what I'm doing next. My gigs could be fire, police, ambulance, council, or cattle yards. I hope I can catch up with you all on Saturday at the mountain biking.'

'Rosemary wants to talk to you about the story you did on pest control in the native bird sanctuary.'

Rosemary did not have the learning problems often associated with spina bifida. Indeed, she had an exceptionally high IQ, especially her verbal IQ, and she had no trouble concentrating.

'Fine. Any time. I'll drop in and see her.'

Daniel and Charlotte Hurley shared Felicity's passion of hurtling through the bush on the mountain bikes, just about the most dare-devil thing you could do in Tumanako, apart from the four-wheel drive club, but most of the mountain bikers considered that outfit stark raving mad. Simon wondered if it was usual for people like Felicity with edgy jobs to also have edgy pastimes. Surely some chilled out on the mild side, not the wild, doing crosswords or jigsaws or making soap. Felicity was one spunky young woman. Simon and Patricia took turns themselves to ride at the weekly mountain bike meets, but it was on the more sedate trails while the other sat with Rosemary. Afterwards the whole family shared a picnic lunch.

'You got the notice about our meeting on Wednesday night?'

'Yes, I did thanks. I'll do my best to make it.'

'Won't be all doom and gloom Felicity. I try to make it as constructive as I can. It's important people feel they can make a difference.'

The slam of the door of a vehicle drew their eyes in that direction. Moments later Steve Polson himself appeared. He was around Simon Hurley's age, also of average height, but more solidly built and with hair much thicker, though more grey than black. His sharp blue eyes glared on the yellowish discharge and his shoulders slumped. He turned to Felicity Spratt.

'Not you, already.' A nod acknowledged Simon Hurley. Polson gestured towards the discharge. 'Tony's dealing with it. He's at the source of the leak now. He'll update me any minute.'

Tony Gillard, chief engineer at Polson's, was a grizzled veteran who had worked for Steve Polson's father.

A nerve twitched beside Simon's right eye as he gazed at the sickly-coloured discharge. 'It's not good enough Steve. That's the second breach in six months. Look at the damage it's done to the river.'

'I'm doing my best here Simon. Tell me one outfit that's one hundred percent perfect in its operations. Things wear out, things break, people make mistakes. Sometimes nature knocks us around. Give me some slack here. We've got on to it straightaway, right?'

'Mr Polson, what guarantee is there against another breach?'

Felicity Spratt had never had a problem asking the difficult questions. Polson's lips pursed and he visibly controlled himself for a moment.

'As much guarantee as you have, Felicity, that your car won't let you down one day, out of the blue. We have a maintenance programme and that seal was ticked off...You can say that the factory is undergoing a rigorous check and that I have contracted a crew to clean up the discharge.'

'Does that include the river?' Simon Hurley was thinking not just of the fish and other aquatic life but of those who swam in the river and drank from it.

'Yes. As much of it as they can.' He turned again to Felicity as he thought of something else. 'You might like to remind the readers that Polson's provides most of the jobs here and that the well-being of the town is at the heart of everything we do.'

At that point his phone rang and he moved away from them to take it in private. When he turned back, anger had replaced anxiety.

'The breach was deliberate. It was not a faulty seal. It was sabotage.'

His next call was to the police.

There was the sound of another vehicle. Robin Trethewan, compliance officer of the regional council, appeared. He greeted them curtly and began to take photographs. Polson moved away to talk to him.

Simon Hurley had no interest in resuming fishing upstream from the discharge. He felt nauseous from the sight of the dead and dying fish and from the thought of other damage the noxious chemicals would be doing. He suspected the discharge contained copper chromium arsenic. It effectively preserved timber but was deadly to life. The incident brought all his anguish back. Why would some maniac now be deliberately releasing deadly chemicals?

While Felicity Spratt lingered to have another word with Steve Polson and Tony Gillard, and check the arrival time of the clean-up gang, Simon made his way back to his Tesla Model 3 car. Its purchase had taken a fair chunk from their bank balance but he and Patricia had considered it the right thing to do. He was better informed about vehicles than he had ever been as vehicles would feature in the next edition of *Help the Planet, Aotearoa*. He had discovered that world-wide, vehicles accounted for thirty-three percent of carbon emissions. And he had read with envy of a vehicle powered by a hydrogen fuel cell that had zero harmful pollutants, emitting only water vapour. The hydrogen was carried on board and the oxygen came from the atmosphere. He presumed there would still be tyres, though, producing pollution in their manufacture. He mused wryly that in an ideal world he would be vehicle-less but had to concede that would make life too difficult.

Voices drifted to him from the river. 'The clean-up gang,' he said to himself. 'At last, thank God.'

He did wonder, though, what use they would be. The damage had been done and the effects would linger. The fish would ingest arsenic particles when they fed on the invertebrates in the river and they would also be exposed to the toxic compounds both in the water itself and in the stream sediment. His own conscience was salved that he had done everything he could to let people know what had happened.

On the drive home to their lifestyle block by the river, he thought about Steve Polson and the dominant role of the factory in the town. Polson had been born into his position as third-generation owner/manager of the firm and had cleaned the place up a lot from what it had been in the rough old days when, unknowingly, all sorts of nasty stuff was lying around. He had seen first-hand that Steve and Stephanie Polson were loving parents as their daughter Polly was close to his own children, often living at much at their place as at home. Simon never lost the feeling, though, that Steve Polson saw him as a nutter, a conspiracy theorist even, excessively alarmed about global warming and causing many of the people of the district to be excessively alarmed along with him. Polly had said as much. But Simon was too deeply committed to his cause to worry about that. He never saw himself as in the least eccentric. Nothing like his good friend Hector Dunwoodie.

The memory of the poison oozing into the river put him, temporarily anyway, on the same side as Polson and for the first time he wondered if that earlier breach had been deliberate as well. As if the breaches were not enough to worry about, there was also Patricia's problem to deal with. It frequently disturbed his waking hours and even sometimes his sleeping.

2

HECTOR AND BERTIE

As Felicity drove to the office, she considered who might have sabotaged the factory. She prided herself on knowing Tumanako and its inhabitants but couldn't think of anyone with that sort of grudge against Steve Polson and the factory. The sabotage had shaken her. She had never covered a case of sabotage before. Simon and Patricia Hurley hated the chemicals at the factory because of Rosie and because of their green beliefs in general. And when she thought about it, Simon had been first on the scene. But she could not in a million years think he would release the chemicals he loathed, and into a river he treasured. No. And how galling, she thought, the incident would be for Steve Polson. There would be fear now that the saboteur could strike again. That other breach would be re-examined. Polson had made it clear there would be a cost to it all. Security would have to be upgraded. For the first time she had sensed a loss of faith in Polson. He had looked badly shaken. He had lived through the eras of his grandfather Harry and father Ray and there had only ever been growth. Would he be the first to lay staff off and retrench?

Job losses would mean people and their families leaving town and that would impact on everything. Her own father Lionel, as owner/manager of Tumanako Realty, would immediately feel the effect. There would be properties to sell but in a depressed market and the takers would mostly be out-of-towners looking for something functional and cheap. If the job losses were heavy, it could result in a downward spiral. She loved this town and she loved her job reporting its activities.

Her father knew all the top bosses at Polson's, and many others there too through the Cosmopolitan Club. Lionel Spratt was one of the first to know when people were coming and going and he was not backward in coming forward. Assertive. Forthright. Bullying even. She shuddered as she recalled certain car trips when she was growing up, her mother at the wheel when her father had one of his bouts of gout and couldn't drive.

'Hell's bells! Look out! You're going to kill us!' he would shout, or, 'For God's sake! Mind what you're doing!'

Once, her mother had stopped before a pedestrian crossing where an elderly couple were waiting to cross and her father was completely oblivious to them and had been urging more speed. Sometimes it was nothing spoken but the more subtle sudden gasp, shudder of fear, imaginary foot stop or agitated hand movement, with a constant stream of advice about hazards present or future and reminders about near misses in the past. She knew it was nothing to do with her mother's performance but everything to do with her father's need to be in control. Like the person standing by the cook telling them how much salt or sugar to use. If her mother listened to his agitations long enough, even the lamp-posts standing so still and silent could seem a threat.

It had been good to get away to journalism school for a year and she had been lucky to get a job back in her home town.

Soon after her return she had moved out of the family home and into a flat with secondary school teacher Melody Gilmour. Melody had welcomed the company. Felicity could understand how a teacher would need adult input after days spent with students.

With the thoughts whirling, not least about the story she was going to write, the problem with the car did not at first register. But when the car started to dip and veer left, she realised she had a puncture. Blast! She pulled to the side. What was it Steve Polson had said? 'As much guarantee as you have, Felicity, that your car won't let you down one day, out of the blue.' But that had been before they knew the breach at the factory had been sabotage. Then she noticed a large nail in her tyre and looked at it suspiciously – was someone getting at her? She crinkled her face resignedly – after all, there was all sorts of debris on roads and she had had punctures before. She had to concede the factory sabotage had got to her a little.

◆ ◆ ◆

'Felicity, the pollution breach story will take the front page, with a jump to the bottom of page three. The lead story on page three will be your story of the sponsorship by Polson's of the Young Achievers' Award. People will be sympathetic towards Steve Polson and the factory, and some will be worried. And mark my words, fingers will be pointed.'

Editor Colin Trainor ran a hand through his thinning hair and shrugged his shoulders. The factory nearly always featured prominently in *The Tararua Mirror* and the sabotage would be talked about for months. There was no industrial unrest that might have triggered a loose cannon to commit such a crime. It had come out of the blue and the factory and town would be on tenterhooks over it.

A long-distance runner with a hyperactive temperament, Trainor had a lean, mean build and decisive gestures. Now, he turned to his two colleagues, Pru Hardacre, administrator and sales manager, and Felicity Spratt, reporter, and swept an arm wide.

'Steve Polson has had to put up with a lot. Bashed by the greenies and blamed for everything that goes wrong in the town. We could fill the newspaper every week with letters to the editor about dust, damage to roads and excessive noise, but the whiners need to get a grip and accept the factory was here first. The town, as we know it, followed. It's like people moving to the country and complaining about the country smells, or people buying beside the airport and complaining about the noise of the planes. We must remember that Polson's is the guts of the town.'

All three were aware that Polson's regularly took display advertising for its building products and its staff provided a hugely significant percentage of the newspaper's subscribers.

'The pollution was bad Colin. There were dead fish in the water. The greenies should be worried.'

'Okay but not Polson's fault. We must be careful we don't get into a mindset of 'factory bad' in the way some media hammer the hospitals. That can start to put people off the hospitals altogether. Not to say the hospitals don't have their problems.'

'Like my uncle,' said Pru Hardacre. 'Fell over and was reluctant to go to the hospital for a check-up. Turned out he had smashed his hip and needed an operation.'

They all knew how important it was to talk freely amongst themselves. They shared most roles as necessary to get the paper out on Thursdays, including managing the online version of the paper. By sharing their news and their thoughts they reckoned they had a good handle on Tumanako and could step in whenever one of them was absent. Their catch-cry was local – if people wanted national or international, they could go to Google or the *Herald*.

Felicity paused on the keyboard.

'Can I float an idea?'

'Go for it. Float away.' Some of their most talked-about stories came from such off-the-cuff starts.

'What about a series of stories about local identities.'

The suggestion hung in the air so long that Felicity began to think it had fallen flat. But Colin and Pru had been looking at each other and seeing the interest in the other's face.

'Oh yes,' said Pru. 'I can give you half a dozen characters straight off.'

'Good idea,' said Colin. 'Go for it. Mind you get a good mix of people.'

'Don't worry I will.'

Felicity was happy to give herself the extra work. It would help give structure to each edition and take the pressure off digging up new stories. She already had someone in mind for the first story and he was a good mix of people all in himself.

Hector Dunwoodie was a single man of sixty-two, a former government scientist, who lived with a parrot, Bertie, on a lifestyle block at number 6, Shambles Line. One third of the property was an embryonic wetland adjoining the dairy farm of Barry Fitzwilliam, long-established regional councillor and failed National Party candidate for the area (which was saying something as Tararua was usually as blue as the sky in a drought). Felicity was aware the two rubbed uncomfortably up against each other for not only was Dunwoodie an organic regenerative farmer while Fitzwilliam was traditional, but Dunwoodie was to the left of Che Guevara while Fitzwilliam was to the right of Marine Le Pen. A 50-foot-high fence between the two properties being impractical, Dunwoodie insisted that Fitzwilliam aerial spray only when the wind was from the south, minimising the risk of drift onto his property.

As she approached Hector's property, Felicity glanced skywards. Hector was rumoured to have his own microsatellite in a low orbit, circling the Earth sixteen times a day, delivering data to his computer. But as she looked around, there was no indication of a launch pad or anything that might propel a satellite into space. Perhaps the microsatellite was on his wish list and Hector had spoken about it in a manic phase of his bipolar disorder, or someone else had launched it for him. She knew very well, from their mutual membership of Forest and Bird, that Hector could talk 'big' when he was in the manic phase and you couldn't get a word in edgeways. Especially when he had been on weed or his Elderberry wine. But from what she knew of Hector and of bipolar disorder from her dip into the world-wide-web, she would never underestimate him. He was in good company – Vincent van Gogh, Virginia Woolf and Ernest Hemingway were said to be bipolar.

He was standing in his doorway when she pulled up in her car, thin as a stake with a smile splitting his face. She knew he had been working in his garden for he was wearing the body suit that recycled the sweat from his body and at the end of the day provided a nutritious drink full of protein. He was promoting it to endurance athletes and was only sorry that more people were not trekking the Sahara or rowing the Atlantic. When they hugged, she looked into the most alert eyes she had ever seen on a human being.

'You've been slaving in the garden Hector.'

'Not slaving Felicity. Loving every moment of it. How can you not when you have your hands in such beautiful soil as mine.' He stepped forward, crouched, and plunged his hands into the dark soil. It spilled over his hands. 'Just look at this. Gorgeous. Regenerative farming Felicity. Rich in organic matter, drawing down carbon and reversing climate change.'

'You're sucking greenhouse gas from the air?'

'That's it. I am. And another thing – the crops produce far less nitrous oxide than farms using synthetic fertiliser. I try not to disturb the soil too much because that releases carbon to the atmosphere. I add high-quality, natural compost. It's all about the soil. When I got rid of the old banger and bought an electric van to deliver the produce to the market, I became carbon-zero here. I'm always learning. My aim is to be significantly carbon-minus.'

She gazed over his acre of vegetable garden. Beyond was an orchard with native trees around the boundary on all sides except for the wetland on Fitzwilliam's side. She noticed an unfamiliar, striking-looking plant amongst the familiar ones. It looked more like a hothouse plant than a field plant, with enormous leaves and fruit that was glossy, purple, and teardrop-shaped, like eggplant, but much larger than any eggplant she had ever seen.

'What on earth are those, Hector?'

He laughed with satisfaction. 'They are my latest experiment, Felicity. I call them aubers. They are a cross between the eggplant or aubergine, and a plant I found growing wild in Peru. Very exciting indeed. The hearty texture inside can be a substitute for meat.'

Felicity had to wonder what Barry Fitzwilliam would make of that and she had her own doubts – the 'meat' of an auber instead of a juicy chop or sausage done to a turn!

As they walked back up to the house, Felicity remarked on what looked like a Second World War landing barge on Hector's property, except the sides were lower. There was a motor at the rear.

'That's my amphibulator, my emergency response craft,' Hector said. 'With all the floods and fires round the world nowadays, you'd be mad not to have one.'

When they went inside, there was a raucous screech and a 'Give us a kiss!' from Bertie, Hector's blue-fronted Amazon parrot, in his enclosure that took up a good twelve-metre length of the vast living room. Classical music was playing softly in the background. Hector wiggled his fingers and touched the parrot on the head and Bertie lowered his head and fluffed his feathers.

Felicity noticed the firmly closed catch on the enclosure door. She understood that parrots were as intelligent as a four-year-old child and were notoriously clever at opening cages.

'He's a happy chappie. I let him out for three hours a day. Got to make sure the windows are shut. Two crusty old bachelors, company for each other.'

He gave her a peek in his workshop out the back. She had never seen anything like it. It had everything from what looked like a particle accelerator to a petri dish. It could have been the set of a mad scientist film.

'I'm working on a faster charger for an electric vehicle.'

Hector noticed that a tube of yellowish liquid had caught Felicity's eye.

'Yes, it is what you think. Using pee to charge a mobile phone.'

THE TOWN THAT COULDN'T TRUST

She made notes as he showed her round, amazed that a scientist would speak so freely of his projects in their embryonic stage. When she questioned him on this, he said he didn't mind if someone beat him to a patent because knowledge was best shared.

In one corner there appeared to be the beginnings of a robot. Hector paused there, as if surveying his work to date and envisaging the finished product. Felicity could see a gleam in his eye. This was clearly something of special importance to him.

'My exoskeleton. Based on exoskeletons in nature,' he said. 'Many invertebrates have such a skeleton. Hard and stiff but with joints allowing for easy movement.'

'Who would use such a thing?' Felicity asked.

'Anyone without the structural strength to stand,' Hector said. 'And what use would it be to stand without being able to move. This is for people confined at present to a wheelchair.'

Felicity knew he was talking about Rosemary. She had seen the bond between the two of them at meetings of the mountain bike club. The manic ageing scientist, constantly active, and the girl with the brilliant brain, trapped in the wheelchair. Felicity shook her head in wonder. For a moment, she herself visualised Rosemary walking in her exoskeleton.

They finished the interview in the dining room to occasional interjections from Bertie such as 'Time to play!' and 'You're a genius!'

As Felicity was leaving, a familiar SUV emblazoned with 'Tumanako Realty' pulled up outside.

'Dad.'

'Felicity. Hector.'

Lionel Spratt towered above the two of them. He was a large florid man with a prominent nose and sparse hair.

'Hector, I've been talking with Fitzwilliam next door. He's asked me to run something by you.'

'All right. Come in.'

As Hector led the way, Lionel Spratt murmured to his daughter, 'Silly old bugger' before following him inside.

Outside, Felicity heard Bertie's verdict on the visitor. 'Don't like the look of that! Give me a kiss!'

3

THE MAYOR REFLECTS

'There's somebody there but all I'm getting is the blur of movement. I can't distinguish anything about the person.'

Bethany Callendar, fifty, mayor of Tumanako, was with senior sergeant Rowley Rowlands and Steve Polson peering into a CCTV camera at Polson's.

'A shame there's not a better picture Steve,' Callendar said. 'The town's quite jittery about it. Marjorie Flett stopped me in the street this morning and told me I needed to do something.'

Rowlands, Maori, thickset, with frank, discerning eyes, shuddered. Hoary veteran though he was, the name Marjorie Flett brought his lips together in a thin straight line.

'She's given me three names of suspects already,' he said.

Callendar turned away from the fuzzy picture and straightened. Built like an elegant liner, solid fore and aft but sleek, she wore a smart, gray trouser suit which set off her striking blue eyes and earrings.

'Can't see a thing,' she confirmed.

Rowley Rowlands, as always, was straight to the point. 'You must upgrade your surveillance system Steve. This is just not doing the job.'

Polson nodded glumly. Callendar could read his mind. More expense on top of the probable fine and the cost of repair and clean-up.

'There is some amazing new surveillance stuff available Steve,' she said. 'The council has upgraded along Main Street and some of the cameras can even pick up number plates. The usual complaints of course from those you would expect about invasion of privacy.'

'No law against it and a big help to the retailers and us,' said Rowlands. 'The cameras are like honorary constables on the beat.'

Callendar and Rowlands were relieved when Steve Polson said he would install a system with night vision that covered every inch of the place. Callendar said that would go a long way to calming the fears of the town. She would let the council and *The Tararua Mirror* know.

As she drove away, she checked her watch and became aware yet again that the life of a mayor is not day to day but hour to hour, sometimes minute to minute. She had a meeting in her office in half an hour with Simon Hurley about the Save the Planet demonstration the coming Saturday. Rowley Rowlands would be there too. Reaction to the first demonstration had been mixed and neither she nor the police wanted the shouts of scornful hecklers to morph into something more serious. Such passion now about environmental issues.

She would have to concede that town sometimes came before family. Not that husband Paul and son Rob were not frequently on her mind. Paul was busy himself as a self-employed accountant, often working late, and Rob, a delivery driver flatting on the outskirts of town, worked all hours. She determined to have Rob home with them for Sunday lunch for a catch-up.

◆ ◆ ◆

'Simon, we are both very concerned that the demonstration might get out of hand. Some of that heckling – from both sides may I say – was very disturbing at the first one.'

Bethany Callendar, Rowley Rowlands, and Simon Hurley were seated informally in easy chairs in front of her imposing mayor's desk. Callendar was never one to foist herself unnecessarily on people, flash her mayoral regalia, or make people feel subservient. Her previous position as co-ordinator of social services had shown her how much more could be achieved by co-operation and a few words over a cup of tea or coffee than by the heavy stick of officialdom.

'No holding up the traffic like last time,' said Rowlands. 'That can only lead to trouble.'

Simon Hurley smiled wryly. Tumanako was hardly Auckland or Wellington – three cars waiting was congestion.

'Toni Dalzell. Yes,' Hurley said. 'Her enthusiasm sometimes does get the better of her. Devoted to the cause. A green warrior you might say.'

'Tumanako does not need a green warrior Simon,' Callendar said. 'Indeed, I believe the town is generally sympathetic to the green cause, provided it doesn't impact on jobs.'

She briefly considered her own green initiatives since taking office – the electric car fleet and the increase in the number of chargers, solar power in the new annex, LED lights in council buildings, encouragement of cycling, council support for Plant-for-the-Planet, and the annual environmental awards.

'Toni Dalzell. Perhaps I should have a word with her.' Rowlands made a note of the name.

'I don't think that's necessary Rowley,' Simon said. 'Let me have a word with her.'

Callendar looked inquiringly at Rowlands. Was he thinking of the demonstration or was he thinking of the sabotage at the factory?

'Toni will be fine unless she's hugely provoked,' Simon said. 'It's the climate-change deniers who worry me. Like Lionel Spratt and Barry Fitzwilliam. It's very important we hold a demonstration. Silence is complicity. There are a lot of people with their heads in the sand who don't want to know.'

Bethany Callendar shook her head in bewilderment. Barry Fitzwilliam, a climate-change denier and a regional councillor. It seemed a contradiction in terms but she herself had been forced to listen more than once to his theory of natural cycles and his belief the climate problem was overstated. 'The voice of reason' he had called himself in the lead-up to the regional council election. To her astonishment, he had polled the second-highest number of votes.

Simon Hurley continued.

'How on earth can they put themselves above the Intergovernmental Panel on Climate Change? The IPCC has said the next few years are critical if we want to limit global warming to 1.5 degrees centigrade.

'Don't worry about that lot,' Rowlands said. 'Just keep your own crowd in order.'

As Callendar saw them out, she confirmed to Simon Hurley that she would take part in the Tui Walking Club's bush outing on Sunday. She wished she could get Paul and Rob out as well but Paul had been strangely lethargic in the mornings recently and Rob had given up bush walks long ago. She wondered if Paul was ailing from something. She would encourage him to see the doctor.

Paul Callendar was putting the final touches to the spaghetti bolognese when Bethany arrived home. They shared the cooking.

She kissed him on the cheek. 'Smells delicious dear. How was your day?'

'Quite an eye-opener,' he said, pouring a glass of wine for each of them. Tall and solidly built, he had the same majestic carriage as Bethany. They were an impressive civic leader and partner for Tumanako. His face, long and tapering surmounted by a great shock of fair hair, was strikingly sheeplike but the eyes were anything but ovine. Indeed, they were sharp and astute, befitting someone immersed in a world of imputation credits, allowances and expenses, disposals and disclosures. Bethany Callendar was more of a broad-brush person herself and would have hated the minutiae of his job.

'I worked on the accounts of the Black Stump Bar and Grill today. They run twelve gaming machines in their back room. Would you believe it? Those machines brought in close to half a million dollars over twelve months and there are six times that many in the town. There are some dedicated gamblers out there.'

Bethany grimaced. 'You'd think people could get more excitement and benefit in their lives than using the one-armed bandits. I saw the effects up close in social services.' She had a flashback of shouting matches, broken relationships, and food coupons.

How was your own day?'

'Meeting after meeting. I've got another one tonight.'

When Rob left home, Bethany seconded his bedroom as her personal study and prominently on the wall was her appointment diary. It ruled her life. She ensured there would be no slip-up by having the diary on her phone as well. The appointment diary on the wall allowed Paul to track her movements easily.

Bethany let a sigh escape. Her first weeks in the job had been testing but tremendously exhilarating as well. Now, some months down the track, there were times when she wondered if she had done the right thing, by herself and by Paul. At this moment she would have liked nothing better than to stay home, watch a film and have another wine with him. Instead, she would be embroiled in a community consultation meeting over road maintenance. Few things, she mused, could get up people's noses more than pot holes. She would much rather the meeting were about the proposed new recycling centre.

'I am definitely taking this weekend off. What about joining me with the Tui Walking Club on Sunday morning? Rob's coming round for lunch afterwards. It's ages since we've seen him.'

'Thanks, but not after golf on Saturday... Are you sure he's coming round?'

'He texted me he would.'

'Good. He's been wired to a different clock than us since he took on that delivery job.'

With a wine in hand and no meal to cook, Bethany could feel herself begin to relax. She looked gratefully at Paul. They were a good team. She was proud to have him by her side at official functions, so gentlemanly and so well dressed and groomed. Even now, at home cooking dinner, he looked immaculate in smart casual. That's accountants for you, she mused, everything had to be right to the last detail, no room for error, no surprises. She welcomed that balance in that part of her life.

4

NATURE CALLING

When Polly Polson knocked on the Hurleys' door on Saturday morning, Daniel was ready and waiting and within five minutes he, sister Charlotte and Polly were on the road on their mountain bikes heading for the outstanding circuit in the bush at the back of Tumanako. It had something for all abilities. Simon and Patricia would meet them there with Rosemary in twenty minutes. The Hurleys' electric vehicle was modified to take Rosemary's wheelchair.

Daniel and Charlotte had their parents' dark hair, sharp features, and slim build while Polly had honey-blonde hair and was rounder in the face and more stockily built. The road had little traffic but it was narrow. Daniel and Polly biked side by side with Charlotte tucked in behind. The three of them had grown up together in Tumanako, attending the same district high school, and there was much unspoken understanding. The bond had been a major factor in Polly choosing to do her business management degree at the University of Canterbury. Daniel was doing his engineering degree there while Charlotte was at Lincoln College studying horticulture. They were in separate flats but saw a lot of one another.

'I'm a bit worried about dad,' Polly said as they biked into a head wind. One frequent advantage of mountain biking was no wind – they were often so deep in the bush that tree roots were more of an encumbrance than wind. Daniel waited for her to elaborate.

'The sabotage has got to him. More than the first time. He's quieter these days and not sleeping as well. I know mum's worried.'

'Who would want to damage the factory and the river as well?

Charlotte, tucked in behind, missed the odd word but got the drift of the conversation. 'Does he have his own suspicions?' she asked.

'If he has, he hasn't said…I heard somebody at the factory say it could be a greenie who got carried away.'

'Your dad must feel he's carrying the town on his back.' Daniel was grateful to Steve Polson for his holiday job at the factory. He earned good money assisting chief engineer Tony Gillard, and it would look good on his CV as well. Polly also had a holiday job at the factory, in the office, while Charlotte had a holiday job at the local Planters and Growers.

Polly winced. 'Ironic, isn't it. He's doing more and more to make the place environmentally friendly but the way things are, it will never be enough. I get the feeling the place would have to be knocked down and started again.'

'It would be good if they could replace the preservatives,' Daniel said. 'Despite what some authorities say, the CCA is not safe.'

Polly said nothing.

Daniel continued. 'The ingredients don't decompose. The heavy metals leach out of it, polluting soil and water.'

Charlotte changed the subject, suggesting they ride the Spur Track, an especially challenging route. Polly's heart leapt at the thought of the Spur Track. Its sharp bends and sudden dips and rises would give her something else to think about. It was enough for her now to feel their support for her.

Soon the club members were assembled in a clear patch of grass where there were sign posts to various tracks and an information board. Polly was pleased to see Hector Dunwoodie there. She hugely admired his commitment to living the life he preached. He was just about the most interesting person she knew. Hector was the oldest active member and had declared his intention to still be riding as an octogenarian. He had a mere eighteen years to go. Polly was aware his modified mountain bike was his secret weapon. He had installed an ingenious suspension system that eliminated most of the shock, sparing not just his backside from a pummelling but his entire body. Hector seemed to float through the bush as light and free as a dandelion. She had urged him to patent it and he said he would when he had time.

Polly exchanged smile and greeting with Felicity Spratt. Polly felt an empathy with Felicity. She wondered if it was partly because they both had a connection with her father. Steve Polson might moan about the media at times but Polly knew he respected Felicity for the fairness of her reports. For both Polly and Felicity, the mountain biking was a welcome relief of pressure.

When the group of three arrived, Simon was activating the wheelchair hoist to lower Rosemary and in moments she was happily surveying the buzz of activity beside a rug which Patricia had laid out, along with a few picnic boxes. Polly immediately went to Rosemary and struck up a conversation. She was six when Rosemary was born and she vividly remembered the grief of the Hurley family at the time and the dismay of her own parents. But Rosemary had since brought so much joy into the world. Dark-haired, small, neat, and smiling, she was happy by nature, and delighting in the company.

Polly changed her mind about the Spur Track.

'Actually Daniel, I've decided to stay and talk with Rosie.'

Daniel looked disappointed. 'Are you sure? Mum or dad are happy to stay with her.'

'No, I would rather. Really.'

Simon and Patricia saw the delight of Rosemary and, pleased at the unexpected opportunity, joined Hector Dunwoodie to ride one of the easier tracks.

Within minutes the mountain bikers were gone along with the bustle and banter, and just Polly and Rosemary remained. For a while they played a game of identifying the bird song around them. The bush was virgin, full of magnificent ancient tawa, rimu, totara, matai and other native trees, each tree home to birds and other small native creatures such as weta.

The Hurleys and Polly Polson were actively involved in a Forest and Bird programme here to trap introduced pests such as possums, stoats, ferrets, weasels, and rats and the prolific bird song was testament to its success.

'No mistaking the tui and the bellbird,' said Polly. 'What's that one?'

They couldn't see the bird, but the sound was close at hand, loud and persistent, as if the bird was summoning their attention.

'Piwakawaka,' said Rosemary. 'Fantail.'

Such a noise for such a little bird.

Another bird got their attention not for its music but for the loud beat of its wings in the bush canopy. As they peered, the kereru appeared on a branch, superb with its broad white breast and red beak. The precious kereru – the only bird large enough to spread larger seeds for the regrowth of some native trees. From bird song, they turned to identifying trees and other plants around them. Polly assisted Rosemary in moving her wheelchair along one of the bush paths so they had the benefit of sight and texture and even smell and taste when they crushed some leaves. If they were really stumped, Polly used the app on her phone of Flora Finder, the digital device of the University of Otago that enabled eighty-seven of the most common New Zealand native trees and shrubs to be identified, based on an image of the leaf and the user's data on shape.

There was one small tree with heavily serrated and heavily veined leaves which Rosemary thought was makomako but

Polly wasn't sure. On checking, she found Rosemary was right.

'Such a versatile plant,' said Rosemary. 'Also known as wineberry. Maori boiled the leaves to treat burns and infected wounds and the berries could be squeezed to make a thick, sweet drink.'

Rosemary loved the bush and nature and already had a strong foundation of knowledge of the natural world. She intended to study botany, probably nearer to home at Massey University.

Soon after, Polly became aware that Rosemary had gone quiet. When she looked closer, she saw that Rosemary looked distraught. Her face had gone pale and her knees were tight together.

'Oh Rosie.'

Rosemary looked as though she was going to cry. Polly's heart went out to her. Usually, it would be Simon or Patricia helping her when this happened.

'Come on. Let's get changed.'

Rosemary had slumped in shame and Polly pushed the wheelchair back to the clearing, got the change of clothes which Patricia had left, and helped change Rosemary.

When Rosemary was dry and could get her breath back, she murmured, 'I feel like a baby.'

'Cleverest baby I know,' said Polly. But Polly had had an inkling of the challenge facing Rosemary if she moved away from home to study at university.

There was an unofficial arrival back time of eleven thirty and happy riders began to arrive soon before, ravenous for their sandwiches and drinks. When Patricia and Simon returned, Patricia took one look at Rosemary and knew what had happened. She said nothing, simply hugged Polly and Rosemary. Daniel and Charlotte, on an adrenaline high, recounted some of the high points of their ride but came back to earth when they looked at Rosemary, quiet and shaken.

Before the group dispersed, Simon got everyone's attention and reminded them of the Save the Planet demonstration in town that afternoon.

As Polly left with Daniel and Charlotte, she noticed Hector talking animatedly with Felicity.

5

THE GREEN WARRIOR

C ould someone get 'Coal Cooks the Climate'?

Simon was marshalling the demonstration on a convenient section of High Street. Not only was there a large patch of grass in the middle of the street but also a controversial totara tree, earmarked for felling by the council. Bethany Callendar had had the last word at the relevant council meeting: 'A shame to fell the old tree but large, bright tiles would cut down on maintenance, smarten the look and improve visibility for motorists.' As patron of the Forest and Bird Society, she had felt conflicted about it but she believed it was the right thing to do.

The submission of Forest and Bird to retain the tree for its ecological, aesthetic, and cultural value vanished into the council's archives.

'Could somebody please bring me my rucksack!'

The request came from the base of the tree where Hector Dunwoodie was conspicuously tied with thick rope, leaning against a cushion so as not to damage the bark. Polly Polson obliged and Hector drank deep of a water bottle.

Casual observers from out-of-town might have been surprised that a town so far off the main grid as Tumanako would exhibit such passion on a global issue, but it was testament to the commitment of the Hurleys and a handful of others. Simon himself was delighted at the turn-out. They had been lucky with the weather. The wind was brisk but that was all the better as it made the banners flap and billow. 'Coal Cooks the Climate' was now fluttering freely, competing for attention with 'Time is running out!', 'Solution not pollution', 'I speak for the trees', 'Make Planet Earth cool again' and 'Wake Up!' He frowned at the banner held by Toni Dalzell and a female friend: 'Hot climax not hot climate', but stopped short of banning it as it was garnering attention, which was the point of the exercise. Dalzell had her own hairdressing salon and was her own best advertisement with her superb chestnut hair spilling to her shoulders.

Their group was disparate, to say the least. Besides Hector Dunwoodie and Toni Dalzell, it included regional councillor

Wiremu Ratima, fish shop proprietor Bac Nam Nguyen, school teacher Melody Gilmour and a group of her students, Polly Polson, the rest of the Hurley family, including Rosemary, and others who had been mountain biking that morning. Most of the thirty or so held a banner while some distributed pamphlets. One demonstrator was dressed in plastic and wore a vast hat that replicated a packet of biscuits. Between each biscuit was a huge wad of plastic. That idea had come from Simon himself. He had recently bought such a packet of biscuits and was still shocked at the deception and future pollution. Bad enough to buy a packet only half full of product let alone be lumbered with all that plastic as well.

'What a useless bloody shower!' snarled Lionel Spratt. 'Rent a mob if ever there was one.'

The great bulk of him, in suit and tie ('Every day is a business day,' was his mantra) was standing under the awning of his shop, opposite. Beside him was Barry Fitzwilliam, fifty-five, paunchy with close-cropped dark hair, in light-brown jacket and matching corduroy trousers.

Fitzwilliam cast a disapproving eye over them. 'Most of them wouldn't know which side their bread was buttered on. We can't make money without using nature to everyone's benefit. What would be there if my farm wasn't there? Bush, that's what. No wealth there, unless we cut it down and mill it. No meat and milk unless we have animals.' He chuckled. 'I wouldn't mind betting most of them love cheese and yogurt and a nice beef steak or bit of bacon.'

Spratt nodded. Then he peered closer and jerked his head. 'My God, that's bloody old Hector. He's tied to the tree. That's just the sort of silly bloody thing he would do. Sooner that tree's gone the better. I put in a submission for the tree to go. Got Cindy to sign it too.' Then he flinched. 'Felicity refused. Said the tree was beautiful and anyway, she had to keep her professional impartiality. Bloody rubbish.'

Simon Hurley was delighted with how things were going. The occasional car was tooting its support and some of the passers-by were happily accepting the pamphlets. Hector appeared to be at ease, enjoying the attention, feeling good about himself and the cause. Hurley gazed up at the totara tree with appreciation. It was here before the factory, when Tumanako was nothing more than a scatter of houses, and deserved to live on. It had survived decades of passing traffic and he was one of many who saw it as an icon of the town.

Simon Hurley could see Lionel Spratt and Barry Fitzwilliam looking at them and could imagine what they were saying. He smiled to himself. Further along the street he could see Cindy Spratt, wife of Lionel and mother of Felicity, looking at them and smiling. Felicity Spratt was hovering near her mother, taking everything in. She had already taken photographs. And Stephanie Polson had come to have a look but Steve was not with her. Simon suspected that Steve Polson might have feared the factory would be vilified. Stephanie, or Polly for that matter, could report back that that was not the case.

Hurley was heartened that the spectators included many who even weeks before would not have given the demonstrators a second look. He believed the green cause was making progress. There were now dairy farmers planting native trees and fencing off their waterways, and townies understanding what carbon footprint meant and looking at purchasing an electric vehicle or hybrid. 'Green' was now less cranky and outlandish.

Simon also saw Bethany Callendar observing proceedings. She was on her own. From her sauntering manner, she could have been out for an afternoon's shopping or a cuppa at a café. But he could see she was vigilant, occasionally turning to look, and as she came closer, she stopped and stared closely at the group and their banners before moving on.

Simon turned his attention back to his group. Some had started a protest song, but the words were indistinct and some of the notes were badly off key. People were looking at them and then at one another in bewilderment. A few spectators were laughing.

He hurried to the group and urged them to stop. 'Well done but you'd better stop. We're losing ground.'

When the song stopped, chanting started and became quite hypnotic, gathering more attention to them. But you can only chant 'Save the Planet' for so long before it becomes an earworm and it died of its own accord. Perhaps, if their numbers had been greater, another rousing chant might have started up, but Tumanako on a Saturday afternoon was not a throbbing metropolis. The demonstration might have ended there and then if senior sergeant Rowley Rowlands had not ordered Simon to release Hector Dunwoodie from the tree.

'There is no need to involve the tree,' Rowlands said. 'That is a separate issue and is only likely to inflame the situation.'

Simon could see that Rowlands was edgy and hyper-vigilant. The demonstration had disrupted the town's placid Saturday afternoon.

'It's only symbolic Rowley,' Simon said. 'We'll release him when we wind things up in half an hour.'

'No. Release him now Simon. There are many people want the tree gone and I do not want the situation inflamed.'

Hector had become agitated. 'The tree was here long before us. We must save the tree from the axe.'

Simon could see that Hector was becoming aggressive under the stress. His eyes were darting and the cords of his neck were taut. Simon gestured to Daniel and they moved as calmly as they could towards Hector to untie him.

'No,' Hector said. 'If we give way on this, where will it end?' He glared at them and folded his arms over the rope, challenging them to keep away.

Simon motioned for Daniel to stop but moved forward himself to sit with Hector and reason with him.

It was Toni Dalzell who changed everything. Impelled by either passion for the cause or heady from the excitement of the day, she had seized the banner 'I speak for the trees' and was now climbing the tree. Simon called to her to come down but, lithe as a monkey and a national-class rock climber, she was already ten metres up and getting higher by the second. Soon, she was in the topmost branches and attracting attention like nothing before, her chestnut hair radiant in the mid-afternoon sun. She jammed the banner between two branches and perched proudly beside it, as relaxed as if in a deckchair at the beach.

The other demonstrators now surged across the street from their grassy sanctuary in the centre, to get a better look from beneath the shop awnings. Toni Dalzell waved gaily to them from her treetop eyrie. In the sudden exodus, Rosemary, to her frustration, was momentarily left behind. Daniel came to her assistance and manoeuvred her into a prime viewing spot on the opposite side.

'For hell's sake,' said Rowley Rowlands. Turning to Simon, he spluttered, 'You promised to keep them in order.'

'I didn't know she was going to do that.'

'Untie me,' demanded Hector, realising he had been made irrelevant and wanting to have a look himself. Simon swiftly obliged and Hector rose stiffly and followed the others across the street.

And so it was that Tumanako raised its eyes that Saturday afternoon to the heavens. Rowley Rowlands gazed in vexation, Bethany Callendar in chagrin, Felicity Spratt in personal and professional joy, Lionel Spratt in outrage, Hector Dunwoodie in admiration, and Simon Hurley in mingled embarrassment and approval. Even Rob Callendar paused in his distribution of small, illicit packets to have a look and Paul Callendar, who had arrived in town from golf, gazed in stupefaction.

Toni Dalzell was by now a traffic hazard. Vehicles were slowing and two had even stopped in the middle of the street for their occupants to get out and have a look. Bethany Callendar bustled up to Rowlands and Hurley. There was a fury in her eye that took Hurley aback.

'I am totally incensed Simon. How on earth did you permit that woman to do that!'

Husband Paul trailed after her, eyes glued above.

Simon Hurley splayed his arms wide in helplessness. 'What could I do? She was up there in seconds.'

They peered wordlessly for long seconds at Dalzell who was peering happily back at them, occasionally waving to the other demonstrators. The iconic totara tree and its 'I speak for the trees' banner was sending perhaps a final message and for some, no doubt, it was a poignant moment. But not for Bethany Callendar.

'Simon! Do something!'

Rowley Rowlands grimaced. 'I'm tempted to call out the Fire Brigade and charge her for it. Make it clear she's disrupting traffic and causing inconvenience.'

'Good idea,' said Bethany Callendar.

Simon Hurley stepped into the street and bellowed skywards for Toni Dalzell to descend. Rowley Rowlands also gestured.

Toni Dalzell's zeal had run its course anyway. She let the banner loose and it fluttered to the ground. Then, nimble as you like, she descended amid gasps and exclamations at her dexterity. She was on the ground in seconds. Severe admonishment by the tongue of the law followed but Simon would not have been surprised if her aerial jaunt had boosted her hairdressing business. The protestors returned to the central grassy area to retrieve belongings and banners. But, as the last of them departed, a crack like a rifle shot rang out and a large branch of the iconic tree broke away and crashed to the ground. If Hector Dunwoodie had still been tied to the tree, he would have been crushed.

'Bloody hell!' said Simon Hurley.

'Shit a brick!' said Rowley Rowlands.

'Thank the Lord!' said Bethany Callendar, no doubt relieved Dunwoodie was uninjured but perhaps pleased as well that the tree was now an obvious menace.

Gazing round, Simon Hurley saw Patricia had disappeared. Then he realised with sinking heart where she was.

6

DESTRUCTION FROM WITHIN

'It's a difficult time but you must keep things in perspective Steve.'

Bethany Callendar was walking and talking with Steve Polson around his factory.

'Justice is all askew Bethany. Here I am being prosecuted for something that was not my fault.'

She pulled a long face. 'Well, the river was polluted by chemicals from the factory. The court will want to ensure safeguards are in place. But surely there would have to be diminished responsibility when an outside agent caused it.'

She took in the strained face, the throbbing vein on his temple, the slump of his shoulders, and was reminded of her late father Chester before the ghastly day he had taken his own life. There was scarcely a day when she didn't have flashbacks.

He ran a hand down the back of his neck. 'Look Bethany

I've done what I can. Since the incident we've checked our leak detection devices and overflow controls, strengthened our diversion berms and revised our spill response. Those things are within our control. We've also tightened security.' He gestured upwards at a camera. 'We have CCTV throughout the factory and a security officer on the premises twenty-four seven, supplementing the mobile, night-time patrol. I can't do more than that.'

'That's good. The court should be impressed.'

'I hope so. We can do without a damaging fine. The balance sheet's a bit fragile. Jobs could be on the line.'

It was Bethany Callendar's turn to look dismal. Lay-offs could really hurt the town, put a strain on social services.

'Isn't it time to be proactive,' she said. 'You have nothing to be ashamed of and a lot to be proud of. I for one am grateful for what you do for Tumanako. Why not have an Open Day and showcase the factory and all the products you produce?'

Their stroll stopped and he turned to her with the first smile she had seen that day. 'You know, that's not a bad idea.'

That evening, Blake Thomas, security officer, was settling down behind a pallet at Polson's to have his first fag of the night. He had checked he was out of sight of a camera and that had taken some trouble as the cameras seemed to be everywhere. Thomas had been grateful for the position. He had been between jobs, depending on his occasional role as a runner for Rob Callendar to make ends meet. He had known from the moment he had walked in for the interview with the security firm that the job was his. He had seen the heads jerk back and the eyes open wide at the sight of his 1.9 metres and 120 kilograms. He was relieved to have passed the police check. Well, the stuff they had caught him on had been minor and some years previous. In the darkness and the quiet he relaxed and within minutes his head lolled back, the cigarette slipped from his fingers, and he slept. If Blake Thomas had been a sentry in the First World War, there would have been a court martial with imprisonment and hard labour at best. But there was no one to find him sleeping at Polson's and he dozed on. A goose on a leash would have been better.

As it was university holidays, Bethany Callendar was greeted by Polly Polson on the Open Day. Both Polly and Daniel Hurley had been seconded this day to show visitors around the complex. The guides had a prescribed route to use as they were showing visitors around a working factory. Polly had a group of ten which was manageable if they stayed close together.

Surveying the scores of people coming through the gates, Bethany Callendar had to wonder if they included the saboteur. This would be an unrivalled opportunity for whoever it was to become fully acquainted with the factory and its vulnerable points but she was sure the advantages of the Open Day far outweighed the disadvantages. A jolt of positivity was needed, not just for the factory but for the town itself, especially after the fiasco of the recent demonstration and the mad woman scaling the totara tree. She shuddered at the memory of it. Who was that woman? A hairdresser somebody said. They could be thankful she hadn't fallen with that branch.

Bethany knew none of the others in her group of ten. She was impressed when young Polly asked the couple on sticks if they could manage stairs. They said they could and hopefully that was true. This was a day of celebration and there should not be a toll of injured at the end of it. Polly led them by the lumber yard, through the sawmill where the logs were scaled, debarked, sorted, sawed, and trimmed, by the drying kiln, by the CCA pressure-treatment plant and planer mill, by the lamination department and upstairs through administration, finishing in the showroom. Bethany was surprised at the range of jobs in administration. She supposed that reflected the complexity of Steve Polson's operation. Steve was assisted by a logistics manager, procurement manager, sales manager, IT and systems manager, account manager, production co-ordinator, production manager and chief engineer as well as, no doubt, their assistants.

'I can remember when the office was a secretary,' Polly said.

Bethany loved the dynamism and sense of order in the sawmill, everyone brisk and working as a team, and she loved the smell of the freshly cut timber. In the show room, she revelled in the sight and smell of the finished products and the feel of the wood; products of surprising range and surprising shape for furniture as well as construction, hand-crafted products, posts and beams, lintels and fascia, crib walls and laminated products. Polly reminded them all, too, that wood is one of the only renewable construction materials and that the manufacture of wood products consumes little energy compared to similar products and structures made of other materials.

When Daniel Hurley arrived with his group in tow, Bethany noted with interest how Polly's face lit up. She saw, too, his rolled eyes and momentary look of dismay and Polly's hand sympathetically touching his arm. What was that about?

Bethany was not one to remain needlessly in the dark. She had seen Daniel confide in Polly when their groups had time to look around the products before leaving and Bethany raised the matter when thanking Polly.

'It's fine. No one was hurt,' Polly said defensively. 'Well, just a little. Lionel Spratt and Barry Fitzwilliam were in Daniel's group and were so immersed in their own conversation they wandered off the pedestrian crossing into an area where a forklift driver was operating. Barry Fitzwilliam took a slight knock. A lot of shouting. A bit of bruising. Unfortunately, Daniel will have to write an incident report. It was not his fault.'

Bethany agreed there are some people you cannot tell.

That evening Bethany phoned Steve Polson to say how much she had appreciated the tour and what a great job Polly had done. Stephanie answered the phone and said Steve was still at the factory. Bethany hesitated a moment and then she saw the face of her father she had loved so deeply, and remembered the pain of his passing, and the pangs of anguish she had felt ever since.

'Stephanie, I feel awkward saying this but you are both dear friends and I feel I must. I've seen the pressure Steve is under and I've been worried about him.' She recalled the strain on

Steve's face. He seemed to be ageing before her eyes.

There was silence before Stephanie spoke. 'I'm worried myself Bethany.' The voice was low, hesitant. 'But you know Steve. He won't slow down.'

Just like Chester, Bethany thought. She recalled how he had become withdrawn, drinking more, smoking more, not getting enough sleep, but pushing on regardless.

Stephanie continued. 'Thank you for calling Bethany. I'll keep working on him. He does need a break but if it's anything like last time, he'll cut it short and go back to work.'

Bethany asked for her congratulations on the Open Day to be passed on and hung up. She wanted to suggest counselling for depression but felt that might be stretching her relationship with Stephanie too far. Perhaps later.

◆ ◆ ◆

Bethany's Sunday lunch with Paul and Rob left her with more questions than answers. Such a striking difference between father and son. Where Paul was always smartly dressed and well groomed, taking even more pride in his appearance as he aged, Rob had really let himself go. His clothes were shabby, he had lost weight, his eyes were bloodshot and, though she was reluctant to admit it, he smelt.

'Why don't you move back home for a while,' she suggested.

His face fell and his moustache quivered. 'Hell no, please, don't suggest that. The job has me delivering on different shifts, as required. My van would be up and down the drive all hours, disturbing you.'

'You've got to eat better Rob,' Paul said. 'Your flat turned out good meals as I remember. Robyn is a chef, isn't she, and Jason enjoys his food.'

'They moved out. It's Harry and Sophie now...We share the cooking.'

Bethany and Paul exchanged a look. They had both liked Robyn and Jason. Harry and Sophie they didn't know.

Bethany left it at that. But in the following week she called round twice to the house Rob was renting. The grass and front garden were unkempt and there was a dilapidated utility vehicle on the lawn. Despite the presence of the vehicle both times, there was no response when she knocked on the door. She noticed cameras covering the front and sides of the house. When she saw a small plastic bag in a shrub, her worst fears were confirmed. She felt as though someone had reached into her chest and crushed her heart.

Her third visit was at ten on a Saturday morning. Again, she knocked on the door and got no response. She drove away, went round the block, parked up the road where she could see the front door of the house, and waited. Some twenty minutes later a late model Chevrolet Camaro pulled up outside and a young man with a beard, dressed in jacket and jeans, uncoiled himself and strode to the door. His knock was answered immediately and he disappeared inside.

Bethany sat frozen amidst the sounds of her town stirring into life – nearby a motor mower roared into life, and soon a power tool, and someone emerged in the distance and began washing their car. Gradually, her heart steadied and her body loosened, but her eyes hardened. Rob had had every opportunity. He had been a good all-rounder at school and had even started a science course at university. For five minutes she stewed in frustration and then drove to the house and knocked on the door once more. She knocked so hard she could feel the blood pounding in her forehead. One minute and then two and still no response. She turned and started to go towards the back but when a furious barking broke out and a great mongrel of a dog began leaping at the high wire fence halfway down the side of the house, she retreated to her car.

What options were left?

7

BEACH CLEAN-UP

The beach clean-up was Bac Nam Nguyen's idea. the Vietnamese proprietor of the Number One Fish Shop in Tumanako, ran his own fishing boat from a tiny harbour fifty-five kilometres to the west of Tumanako and it was the pollution he saw in the sea and on the beaches that impelled him to join the local branch of Forest and Bird. Simon Hurley had been delighted by Bac Nam Nguyen's suggestion and was even more delighted when Bac Nam Nguyen offered to sponsor the clean-up.

Bac Nam Nguyen was short and wiry with a moustache and a much-creased face that broke readily into a smile. His face became sombre when he spoke about the pollution.

'Terrible mess Simon. Very terrible. You would not believe how terrible. I see it every time I fish.'

He spoke of bottles in his nets, shopping bags, food wrappers, all manner of plastic, even cigarette butts that had made their way through storm drains to the coast. Much of it swirled around in the ocean while some heavier items sank to the bottom and lighter items washed up on the beaches.

'Chemicals too,' he said. He told Simon of the strange discharges from outlet pipes he sometimes saw, viscid and oily, garish yellows and reds.

Simon knew some of the chemicals would be run-off from the land. But that sort of glutinous waste would be discharge from factories by the coast. Whichever way the chemicals flowed to the water, the result would be algal bloom from the excess of nitrogen and phosphorus, and algal bloom was toxic to animals and harmful to humans.

'Yes, truly terrible Bac Nam Nguyen.'

Simon felt deeply for Bac Nam Nguyen. He was working hard to give his family a good life in their new country but pollution caused by the greed and carelessness of others was affecting his livelihood. Simon knew that plastic does not biodegrade like many other substances but will photodegrade on exposure to the sun into ever smaller pieces and these microplastics have been detected in plankton and whales. When small organisms are eaten by fish, the microplastic enters the food chain. As hard as it was to believe when you looked at the size of whales and at the size of some shoals of fish, scientists were saying that by 2050, at the current rate, plastic in the sea would outweigh all fish.

Simon toyed with the thought that if so much plastic would inevitably end up in river or sea, should not Consumer Affairs insist all plastic be safe for human consumption. The matter of flavours could be left to each company.

It was a gloriously still, clear morning when the members of

Forest and Bird gathered on the beach. The water was like glass and the surface glittered so brightly, Simon wondered if the sun shone on water or plastic. As usual, banter flew. The Hurleys were all present along with Polly Polson, Hector Dunwoodie, Toni Dalzell, and Melody Gilmour who had a dozen students with her. To Simon's surprise, Stephanie Polson had turned up with Polly and Paul Callendar had arrived, saying he was representing Bethany. Felicity Spratt was there to cover the event and take part herself. When all thirty or so were assembled, Simon thanked Bac Nam Nguyen for his provision of the jute rubbish bags of all sizes and his funding of the disposal of the waste material. Bac Nam Nguyen beamed from ear to ear and so did his wife and three children, all eager to help clean-up.

The volunteers had been told to bring thick gloves and it was just as well as some of the plastic waste was sharp and could cut, and the occasional syringe was found. Hector was responsible for sorting the rubbish - some objects he put aside for recycling – and Rosemary was responsible for recording the different sorts of items. Soon the volunteers were spread right along the beach. When somebody came across a seagull entangled in twine but alive, Hector was summoned and set it free.

Simon and Ban Nam Nguyen had both been acutely aware of the problem but both were staggered by the amount of rubbish collected, mostly plastic. A great heap of it arose. There was a sense of competition in the air, collectors returning with a full bag, emptying it, and racing away to get more.

Then suddenly the even tenor of the day was shattered. Simon saw two people down the beach waving their arms in agitation and heard faint cries for help. A trapped bird or animal?

Medical event? Someone caught in wire? He was the one with the spade and he ran for all he was worth, closer to the sea where the sand was firmer. As he approached, he saw panic on faces and followed the eyes to the soles of feet protruding from under a dune.

'It's Toni. She was hauling out a large piece of plastic when the sand collapsed on top of her.'

Simon set to with the spade, shovelling frantically but mindful he must not strike her with the sharp steel cutting edge. Others, too, were clearing away sand and two others each had hold of an ankle. As he dug, the world stopped. A life was in the balance. Simon knew of children who had been digging in dunes and been suffocated. He felt dizzy as he plunged his spade in again and again. Would life be literally smothered out of her? Would desire to do good result in death?

In moments that seemed an eternity, the lower part of her body was cleared and the helpers could pull her free. Her lips were tinged in blue and she was ominously silent and still. Then, with CPR about to start, she shuddered, coughed, spluttered, and gasped in rapid, life-saving breaths.

Bystanders hugged, cried, and smiled. While her airway was checked and she was put in the recovery position, Polly explained what had happened.

'There was a hollow in the sand dune and Toni saw plastic there. She crawled in to pull it out but instead pulled the sand down on top of her. It was just luck I had been working nearby with mum and I saw her go in.'

Paul Callendar had also helped dig her out. 'Just as well she's an athlete,' he said. 'Her fitness would have helped her come through.'

And Simon agreed that was true. Toni Dalzell's predilection for risk had put her in that hazardous situation and her lung capacity had helped her survive it. The glorious chestnut hair so evident at the top of the totara tree was now almost indistinguishable, caked with sand.

Polly and Stephanie saw to Toni's recovery on the beach and then Stephanie drove her to Tumanako Hospital for a check-up while Polly followed in Toni's car.

The incident provided an arresting paragraph for Felicity's report. She stressed, though, the sheer amount of plastic garbage collected. Rosemary provided her with a useful summary of objects found. They included five syringes as well as several of the small plastic bags favoured by drug addicts.

◆ ◆ ◆

Driving the family back from the beach, Simon noticed the familiar real estate sign of Lionel Spratt. It was advertising several hectares of undeveloped land for sale a couple of kilometres from the coast.

'Dolly McMurtrie's land,' he said. 'Tom must have put it up for sale after Dolly died.' He could see Dolly as if it was yesterday, small but indomitable, a fixture on any activity of Forest and Bird. She must have planted more trees than the rest of them combined. Many of those native trees were on that land for sale, and thriving in the rich soil. Dolly had always said that land would never be sold in her lifetime as it was too valuable. Simon knew she meant too valuable as an ecological treasure.

'Just a minute,' he said. He parked by the sign and swung over the fence. The amount of rubbish along the beach had shocked and dismayed him and the near catastrophe with Toni Dalzell had shaken him deeply. The walk now across the field helped ease his tension. The ground was soft and he could see a small stream winding through it to the coast, and pools of water glinting in the morning sunlight. A strutting, purple-blue pukeko of the long red legs and red beak, emerged from a patch of reeds and a pair of paradise shelduck flew away as he proceeded. The scores of trees that Dolly herself had planted were providing shelter for countless birds and animals.

'He can never sell this,' Simon said.

He had thought he was talking to himself but Daniel and Charlotte had joined him and all three gazed in wonder at the extent of life around them. There were spur-winged plover, white-fronted tern, oystercatchers and dabchicks and Daniel saw a kereru in a kahikatea tree. No doubt the stream would have eels, invertebrates, bullies, smelt, shrimp, and other aquatic life.

'We have to speak up for Dolly,' Simon said. 'She's gone but we must try to save what she created.'

All three knew that not only would those creatures be gone, but the value of that area of land as a carbon sink would be gone as well. Any interference with it and the three greenhouse gases that contributed the most to global warming

– carbon dioxide, methane, and nitrous oxide – would be released.

Simon dropped the others home and went to have a chat with Lionel Spratt. His wife Cindy, a slightly built woman with short black hair and kind brown eyes, was at reception and greeted him warmly. When Simon said he wanted to speak with Lionel, Cindy disappeared into an inner office and Simon heard him swear, protest he was busy, and swear some more. Then the man himself was coming through the door, his hair brushing the top of the frame, arm extended for an insincere handshake.

'Simon, good to see you. How can I help?'

'I've come to check about that land of Dolly McMurtrie,' Simon said.

'Tom McMurtrie,' Lionel Spratt corrected.

'Well yes,' Simon conceded. 'I'm surprised it's being advertised for sale.'

Simon saw Spratt's face grimace and behind him he saw Cindy Spratt flinch.

'Has Tom got the necessary resource consent to sell the land?'

Simon could see he had hit a nerve. Spratt straightened and glowered and Simon could see the white of his knuckles as he clenched a fist.

'I don't think that's any business of yours Simon. You need to take it up with Tom.'

'I can understand Tom being ignorant about a resource consent but I can't understand you not knowing.'

Cindy Spratt vanished into a back room.

Spratt advanced uncomfortably close to Simon and raised his voice. 'That land should be drained and turned into productive pasture. It's just bloody swamp as it is. Good for nothing. It could be earning Tom thousands of dollars a year. Who are you green earbashers to tell everybody what they should be doing? If it was left to you lot, this town would be nothing. We'd all be living in grass huts chewing on lentils and bloody brussels sprouts. It's Tom and people like him who put food on your table.'

Simon could see there was no point in staying longer. Lionel Spratt did not want to hear about ecological value let alone a cultural impact assessment. As he left, he could hear Spratt shouting for his wife and wondered how Felicity could be the daughter of such a man.

The following Monday, Daniel had some news from the factory. A security guard had a broken collar bone and cracked ribs from a fallen pallet of wood. It appears he had been sleeping on the job and had made a cosy 'bivvy' for himself, but he must have shifted his position in the middle of the night and brought the heavy pallet crashing down. Polly said her father was very disappointed but at least there was no question of compensation.

8

FELICITY BEGINS INVESTIGATING

'It's not good enough Colin. Front page for that fiasco of a demonstration. A pack of greenies disrupting the town, running across the road, holding up the traffic. As for that that bloody mad woman climbing the tree. She should have been arrested. Instead, she's being celebrated as though she's a hero.'

Felicity was sitting at a far desk at *The Tararua Mirror* but she could hear every word of her father's telephone call to Colin Trainor. She anticipated what he would say next.

'I put a lot of money through *The Tararua Mirror*. Thousands a year. And I think I have a right to say what I think.'

Felicity was reminded how grateful she had been to move out of the family house and into a rental property with Melody Gilmour. She had been grateful her father had put a roof over her head but the more she had learnt to think for herself, the more distant she had become from him. She did worry though about her mother. His browbeating manner had dented her confidence and dimmed her fun-loving personality. Why on earth did her mother become the office receptionist? She immediately knew the answer to her own question – to save him money. Living with Melody had its own challenges, Felicity reflected, but it was Shangri-La compared to her father's household.

She became aware Colin had put the phone down and was looking sideways at her.

'His lordship,' he said.

She nodded. 'I heard. Par for the course.'

Pru Hardacre chipped in. 'It's a fine line we tread.'

All three loved their work and the camaraderie they shared but they knew that the future of *The Tararua Mirror* could not be guaranteed, at least in its present form. A few years back it would have been inconceivable that a town of 7,534 would not have a newspaper of its own but with the rise of electronic communication, the media landscape had changed immensely in recent years. Most of the young ones now were turning to their cell phones for news. At least the *Mirror*'s digital version showed willingness to adapt.

'Bloody good front page,' said Colin. 'That photograph of the woman in the tree helped sell about two hundred more papers Felicity. Well done.'

Felicity smiled. She didn't let on that she'd taken another photograph of the same woman at the beach clean-up, recovering from an encounter with a sand dune. Page three had been prominent enough for the story, with the mountain of plastic garbage the main point.

Later that day Colin Trainor congratulated her again, this time on her personal profile of Hector Dunwoodie that included a striking photograph of Hector and his parrot. Interviewing a personality had become Felicity's favourite part of the job. She had discovered she had a knack of putting people at ease and having them reveal themselves. She remembered, too, some words of her mother before she started at the newspaper. 'Always respect. You don't know what someone has gone through.' That had helped ensure that with the power of her pen, she did not take advantage of people.

"I'm thinking Bac Nam Nguyen would have an interesting story to tell. He and his wife came here as refugees with nothing and now have two children, a house, and a business. He sponsored the beach clean-up at the weekend.'

'Good. I think it's important, at least at the start, to keep clear of the obvious worthies like the mayor and business leaders. Mix them up so readers don't know who to expect next. Show we are a paper of the people.'

'That's what I want too,' Felicity said. 'Any suggestions welcome.'

Felicity decided to raise another idea with Colin. She had been toying with it for some time, excited but nervous.

'Colin, there's another thing.' She went over and sat by his desk. 'I want to investigate the drugs scene in Tumanako.'

He looked at her in silence. She saw a range of emotions playing in his face – surprise, intrigue, disquiet. Was he considering things he had heard or seen? Was there something personal there? Did he know people involved?

'I don't know Felicity. Maybe we're too small. Too close to anything if you see what I mean.'

She had considered that factor. In some ways, it would be easier and safer to write about the drugs scene in Auckland or Wellington than in Tumanako. She could write in more general terms there and not point the finger. In Tumanako everybody knew everybody.

'We could find ourselves being sued if we weren't careful,' Trainor said.

'Drugs are a very real issue in the town. They're right in your face. We found several discarded syringes and drugs packets even at the beach. Melody pulled the students back from them; she didn't want anyone touching them. Go to the pub and you can probably score something any time if you want.'

'They can be cheeky beggars,' Pru said. 'I know an elderly woman here who didn't know she was next door to a meth house. Young people renting. One weekend they asked if they could tap into her electricity and she obliged because she wanted to be a good neighbour. A few weeks later she discovered they had disappeared and soon after that the landlord visited and there was a cleaning firm there and a pile of carpet at the end of the driveway.'

Colin Trainor pondered some more. 'Keep the personal profiles going Felicity and get some background on the drugs scene if you want. Have a chat with Rowley Rowlands. And run everything by me.' He grimaced as he recalled some Scum Dogs gang members he was acquainted with. 'We don't want a bomb through our window.'

That evening Felicity and Melody Gilmour joined two guys and two women – teaching colleagues of Melody – for a quiz night at the pub. They were 'The has-beens', courtesy of one of them in his sixties. There was the buzz of greetings and a busy bar. Felicity's team got their drinks individually as their drinking varied hugely – some nursed one drink all evening while Melody would be at the bar after every round of questions. The bar's red house wine was her favourite. Aged twenty-eight, with an appealing face and blonde ringlets, and smartly dressed in blue jacket, skirt, and ankle boots, she looked every inch the high-achieving young professional. She did not, though, look happy with her drink.

'Talk about tight. Look at this – the tide's out.'

'That's how they do it,' said a friend. 'Half full.'

'Half empty more like,' said Melody.

Felicity knew that back home in the flat, Melody's glass would be full to the brim and there would be no need to go to a bar for more; the bottle would be right beside her. She would binge drink, especially at the weekend, and finish up sweaty and shaky, even retching sometimes. Felicity knew of at least one relationship the drinking had destroyed. It worried Felicity more than she let on. She recalled Melody's reply just the previous weekend when Felicity had told her she was drinking too much.

'I know, I know. I'm going to cut down. I'll finish what I've got and I won't drink any more.'

As if that was going to work. It was a worry and a pity as Melody was great company when she was sober, and a well-respected teacher who cared about her students. Felicity was in a quandary. Should she contact Alcoholics Anonymous herself on Melody's behalf? But Melody would know who was behind it and might leave the flat in a funk.

Soon the crush at the bar eased and the patrons were poised.

'Play fair,' the MC said. 'No phones.'

Felicity had heard of such vile behaviour.

'How many of Henry VIII's wives were called Catherine?' A testing question for the opener, Felicity thought. Heads leaned forward as team members did their best to frustrate any flapping ears of neighbours. Despite protestations, Melody was adamant the answer was three and that was recorded. Melody reeled off the next three answers as well – on Denmark's currency, the smallest planet in the solar system, and the legendary surrealist artist famous for painting melting clocks – but by the second round her speech had slurred and her answers had dried up.

The team finished a meritorious third, just pipped by The

Dodgy Rogers, a jolly team of retired veterinarians. With honour salvaged – it was always a risk for a team of teachers to compete – they merrily farewelled one another and began to disperse. Except for Melody who went to the bar. Felicity joined her there, anxious to see her safely home.

'You don't have to stay with me. Honestly, Felicity, it's like my mother keeping an eye on me.'

Felicity turned to go but became aware of a young man in denim jacket and jeans by her elbow. She knew him from school. Rob Callendar. He had been in the same year, one of the cool boys but good at his classwork too. She and Rob had even been an 'item' for a time. He would only be mid-twenties but the years between had taken a toll. His hair was untidy, his eyes were bloodshot, and he was thinner than she remembered. Felicity was certain he was on drugs. As he settled in a seat at the bar, she became aware her story on the drugs scene in Tumanako had just come to her. She sat back on her seat between Melody and Rob Callendar.

For ten minutes they chatted of this and that and Felicity wondered how she could steer the subject to drugs. But she didn't have to wonder. When the bar man was occupied, Callendar flashed a small packet before them. Felicity knew he was taking an almighty risk as conviction for dealing and possessing for supply meant a serious sentence, but drugs were clearly his lifestyle now. She and Melody must have seemed likely targets.

'How much?' Felicity asked. She heard Melody gasp.

Rob Callendar gave her a price, asked for their address, and said he could drop some off any time they wanted. Felicity could see he was sweating, his right cheek had a tic and his pupils were heavily dilated. He asked if they had anything he could write on. She never went anywhere without her notepad, and produced it, and a pen. He wrote his phone number. She had a barrage of questions to ask, such as where he got his drugs from, how many he supplied to regularly and whether he had any involvement with local gangs, but she realised it was not the time. Already she had confirmed it was dead easy to obtain illicit drugs in Tumanako.

Soon after he slid off his seat at the bar and was gone. Usually, Melody would sit until closing time but did not object when Felicity said they should leave. Felicity could see Melody was still shocked that Felicity had asked 'How much?' Both knew now that a supply of methamphetamine was but a phone call away.

9

A BRAVE NEW WORLD

'Polly put the kettle on,
Kettle on kettle on
Polly put the kettle on
All have tea.'

Polly Polson and Daniel Hurley clutched each other in helpless laughter as Bertie welcomed them to Hector's home. The 'Polly' lyrics had been one of Bertie's first ditties and Polly knew instantly that Hector had done it for her. She and Hector had always clicked. She noticed now that he looked with interest and, she thought, approval, as Daniel and she hugged.

When peace was restored and Bertie had had his head rubbed and was contentedly murmuring to himself on his gumtree perch, Polly and Daniel mentioned Felicity's story on Hector in the latest edition of *The Tararua Mirror*.

'It's a cracker. So interesting,' Polly said.

'Really? I haven't seen it.' Hector didn't get the newspaper. He always said he had enough to be getting on with without other people's troubles. Daniel offered to drop a copy off but Hector told him not to bother as he would pick one up in town later.

'Can we see the exoskeleton?' Polly had been intrigued to read of this. She had been thinking a lot about Rosemary recently. Could the exoskeleton be a first step towards giving her more control over her body?

They followed Hector to his workshop as Bertie started up another ditty, 'Polly come too Polly come too,' sending Daniel and Polly into hysterics once again.

As Hector explained his projects, Polly and Daniel were captivated. Polly realised that while she was looking at Hector's creations as a lay person, Daniel was looking at them as an engineer, marvelling at the man's incredible vision and inventiveness. He had told her more than once that Hector was a genius.

The exoskeleton appeared to Polly like something from a science fiction novel – metal in the shape of a person, attached together in a variety of ways, with some obvious flexible joints. It took her breath away and at first, she couldn't speak. She tried to visualise Rosemary inside it. Daniel, meantime, was running his engineer's eye over it in silence. At last Polly found her voice.

'How would Rosemary get into it?'

Hector stepped forward, undid a latch, and opened the pelvic region of the exoskeleton right up.

'Rosemary could be lifted into this inner chamber and from then on, she would be the one in control,' Hector said. 'She would operate the arms and legs electronically. She would simply have to push the buttons in the control panel.'

All three continued to gaze. Polly realised it could be a glimmer of the future but it was also stark testament to the enormous challenges ahead for Hector, and for Rosemary.

'Just like she can control her descent and rise into the rear of the van,' Polly said.

'Exactly. The mobility van enables Rosemary to get around and about, even in the outdoors, and the exoskeleton will give her a wider range of movement wherever she may be.'

Polly relived the mountain biking incident. 'Would Polly be able to change herself in the exoskeleton?'

Daniel nodded. He knew all too well Rosemary's problems with bowel and bladder control.

Hector had clearly not considered that scenario and paused. 'I would have to work on that,' he conceded.

Hector brought them up to date with other projects. There was his work to turn plastics and discarded electronics into paving material for roads. Hector was convinced that the crushed computers and suchlike could be melded with plastic waste to form an impermeable road surface that could take heavy weight.

'Technology can be a villain but it can also be a saviour,' he said.

Daniel's admiration needed no words.

Hector acknowledged he was often adapting someone else's idea and that progress was seldom alone. 'Knowledge is for sharing,' he said, with his customary disregard of patents.

They moved on to Hector's working shower that recycled its water, with the water cleansed along the way. The water was pumped through a filter in a closed-loop system.

From the workshop, he led them outside to the front garden and to saplings in a corner. Their bark was unusual, knobbly like that of a ginkgo tree, but they were clearly not ginkgo trees.

'I've bred these trees in the laboratory,' he said. 'They are an amalgam of eucalyptus and fir. They have an unusually thick bark which makes them less likely to burn and very likely to grow again quickly after fire.'

Polly recalled the images on television of the fires that had raged through forests in the United States and Australia, causing immense destruction of plants, animals, and housing.

Her thoughts were interrupted by a car pulling up beside their own. Felicity Spratt. Felicity exchanged greetings with everyone. She had several copies of the newspaper under her arm.

'Thought you might want some extra copies for family and friends.'

'OK. Thanks. Put them on the table inside.'

'How you going?' Bertie asked when she entered the living room.

When Felicity returned, a frown had replaced her smile. Then she appeared to push whatever it was to the back of her mind and turned to Hector.

'What was dad so intense about when he visited you the other day Hector?'

Polly had seen Felicity in action before and knew she was never one to beat around the bush when she could go in with a machete.

'An expression of interest, as he called it, from Barry Fitzwilliam.' Hector waved his arm towards the neighbouring property. 'Fitzwilliam's got his eye on this part of my land, across the road from his own.' The four of them gazed over the several hectares of low-lying land. It was in scrubby grass intermittently broken by trees and bush. By the road itself, were broken slabs of concrete and bricks, the scattered foundations of buildings that had once been on the site. 'I want to turn it into proper wetland. No doubt he wants to drain it and turn it into pasture.'

'Can't blame him for that, I suppose,' Daniel said. 'A farmer wanting to increase his stock.'

Polly knew Daniel was committed to green values, like the rest of them, but he had an empathy with people and an ability to see things from their point of view. Daniel was usually the family mediator in any disagreement.

Hector shifted uneasily. 'Matter of fact, I'm considering it. The money would be very handy for my research.'

Polly looked at the land under consideration again. This time she didn't see a wetland crammed with bird and aquatic life but Rosemary manipulating her exoskeleton.

'We'll see,' Hector continued. 'I've got to think about it. Yet another change for that patch of land.'

'What was there before?' Felicity asked.

'An abattoir,' Hector said. 'Back in the day. This is Shambles Line remember. "Shambles" means slaughterhouse. The Shambles was an historic street in York, England. To be more exact, The Great Flesh Shambles. Some thirty butchers' shops at the end of the nineteenth century. Underneath the scrub down there is the old concrete floor of the abattoir and the remains of some of the old tanks it used.'

Polly realised she always came away from Hector knowing more than she had before.

'Better to live in Shambles Line than Schitt's Creek,' Felicity said as they dispersed with a laugh.

◆ ◆ ◆

'Tough decision for Hector,' Polly said as she and Daniel drove away.

Daniel agreed, and then, thinking about money, brought up a concern of his own. 'I think things are pretty tight at home too.'

He explained that his father's monthly publication, *Help the Planet, Aotearoa*, was increasing in circulation and advertising revenue but that its profit was still modest and Simon was making as much from selling his garden produce at the weekly town market. His mother, Patricia, was on a regular wage as a data collection specialist working at home for Statistics New Zealand, but he had heard her many times quietly asking Simon for money.

'Dad's starting to get tetchy about it,' he said. 'Mum wants a joint account but dad is reluctant. They both need to see a budget advisory officer if you ask me.'

Polly had seen up close how careful Daniel was with his own money. Polly's parents were paying her way through university but Daniel and Charlotte were funding themselves. She knew how grateful Daniel was to her father for the holiday job at Polson's. With that and the student loan from the government and part-time work in Christchurch at an engineering firm, he was paying his way.

'Never knock money Polly,' Daniel said. "We will never reduce greenhouse gases unless we find solutions that will make money. And there are some solutions here already.'

The subject was his passion and the floodgates opened. He cited Neocrete, a natural additive for concrete that reduces the amount of cement required in concrete.

'Concrete is the second-most used material in the world after water and cement is its key ingredient,' he said. 'Globally, five billion tonnes of cement are produced every year, causing eight percent of the world's total greenhouse gas emissions.'

He said Neocrete's additive reduced the embodied carbon by up to fifty percent, besides making the concrete more durable. He also cited 3D concrete printing and cross-laminated timber as other initiatives that reduced greenhouse gases while making money, but he must have seen Polly's head already swimming over the concrete additive and didn't elaborate.

Polly arrived home amidst a taut conversation between her father and mother.

'I've half a mind to pack it in,' Steve Polson was muttering as Polly entered the room. 'Sell the whole outfit and go and live on the coast.'

He stood slumped, gazing out a window towards the factory.

Her mother explained there had been a spillage of adhesive liquids at the factory and sabotage was suspected, despite the extra cameras and the replacement of the security officer who had slept on the job.

Polly's heart went out to him. Lately he seemed to be visibly ageing. She feared he was in depression. Now she went to him and enveloped him in a hug. Polly sensed that his distress stemmed partly from being seen by green extremists as a villain. But she knew he wanted to do good and cause least damage and she continued to take pride, as she had ever since she was a little girl, that he was the owner/manager of the town's biggest business.

She learnt later that the spillage had been of phenol-formaldehyde and urea-formaldehyde, substances used as adhesives due to their high weather and water resistance. She went to the world-wide-web and found that when they were completely cured, they were regarded as non-toxic and safe but that they could, prior to that, damage the eyes, lungs, and liver. Fortunately, the spillage had been small and had been confined to the factory. Nevertheless, the incident would still have to be reported and investigated.

That evening Steve Polson said a valve in a storage tank had been found to be faulty. There were indications of interference. There was scarcely any damage but Polly could tell from the look on his face that there was an unspoken nightmare – what might happen next?

10

BACKLASH

As Felicity drove away from Hector's property, she wondered if Rob Callendar's network included 6 Shambles Line. When she had returned from putting the newspapers inside, on Hector's table, the frown had not been caused by her father's earlier visit to Hector but by the sight of Callendar's phone number on a notepad on the table. Since the night in the pub, the number had seldom been far from her mind.

Her probe of the drugs scene in Tumanako had barely started but it was already beginning to change her view of the world. Was the eccentric, kindly, brilliant Hector a customer of Rob Callendar? She had always attributed his tireless focus and occasional manic episode to his bipolar disorder, but perhaps it was as much due to taking illegal drugs. She had seen wild mood swings even during a Forest and Bird meeting, Hector placid one moment and the next on his feet agitated and talking like Bertie on speed. She had a weird, random thought that Bertie could lift the lid on Hector if only he could compose his own lyrics.

Felicity had an appointment to see Rowley Rowlands the next day and ran through some questions in her head. She had also arranged to see Bac Nam Nguyen for the next personal profile.

It was heartening that 'Spotlight on...' was already popular after just one article. Then, with a jolt, she was reminded there was possibly a grimmer side to Hector's story. There was a meeting, too, of the regional council to cover, the AGM of the women's guild, and the annual school sports day. *The Mirror* was, after all, the life of Tumanako in a weekly nutshell.

◆ ◆ ◆

'Felicity, you said you wanted to run an idea past me, get my opinion on it. What can I do for *The Tararua Mirror*?'

Felicity knew that in Rowley Rowlands she had a pool of goodwill to tap into. The newspaper always responded readily to requests by the police to help locate missing persons and help identify offenders by publishing photographs caught on CCTV. The police stories were always compulsive reading with just their bare facts and did not need any embellishment. They were often the lead story, such as the ramraid of the jewellery store the previous week. A grainy photograph in the newspaper had led to family handing the offenders in.

'I want to do a story on the drugs scene in Tumanako, Rowley. Not just a skim-the-surface but in some depth. You have said yourself that drugs are behind a lot of the other crime in Tumanako – the burglaries, vehicle thefts, and assaults. There are the occasional arrests for dealing and using, the rumours about the role the gangs play, the rumours about out-of-towners. I think there would be a lot of interest in it.'

As she spoke, Felicity could see his attitude shift from benevolent to hostile.

'You stay out of it Felicity. You don't know what you would stir up, who you would be dealing with. You would be putting yourself under a lot of risk and for what? A story in the newspaper. You don't think you would solve the town's drugs problem on your own, do you?'

He was not just alarmed, but angry. But she had questioned her motive herself and she was sure it was not vanity behind her project. She knew of partners assaulted because of drugs, families going hungry, young people's prospects ruined. She had hoped Rowley Rowlands would be an ally, providing background information and details on arrests.

Now she would have to do it all herself.

◆ ◆ ◆

When Felicity got back to the flat later that afternoon, a car she didn't recognise was disappearing into the distance. When she walked into the living room, Melody looked up as startled as one of her students caught in the act of cribbing.

'You're early.'

'I brought some work home,' Felicity said. 'I've got a meeting at seven and didn't want to be at the office all day.'

The objects on the dining-room table were more than a little incongruous. A pile of students' exercise books for marking, a bottle of wine, two empty glasses of wine, and a sachet of white powder.

Felicity stood in silence, staring at the sachet.

'You haven't?'

Melody averted her eyes, and then tossed her head and gazed at Felicity defiantly. She looked tired, guilt-ridden.

'Why shouldn't I live a little? The phone number was for both of us.'

'The phone number was for me. For my story on drugs use in Tumanako.'

'I'm sure if you asked Rob he would not agree.'

'Rob is it now? You're mates already? Melody, seriously, you've got to look at yourself. The drink's bad enough without getting into the drugs.'

'Felicity, you can really piss me off. What's wrong with having a glass or two to wind down at the end of a busy day. Are you so perfect you can tell me what to do? Give me a break.'

Felicity felt shattered. She cherished her friendship with Melody who was probably the most compatible flatmate she had ever had. They had so many laughs together and there was never an issue with sharing the costs equally. But some nights Melody's drinking had soured the atmosphere and one night Melody had binge-drunk until she had keeled over and retched. Now, there was the issue of illicit drugs as well. Felicity was tempted to wash the contents of the sachet down the sink.

Melody must have read her mind for she quickly reached out, grabbed the sachet, and took it into her room.

Felicity realised their flatting arrangement and friendship was hanging by a thread.

With the drugs issue now starkly personal, Felicity became deeply committed to her research. Her work colleagues had long recognised Felicity's bloody mindedness – when barriers were put in her way, she redoubled efforts until they were swept aside. She acknowledged Rowley Rowlands' objection but pushed it to the back of her mind. Personal danger when probing a sensitive subject was an occupational hazard. It would have been less risky for a reporter from a national newspaper to delve into the drugs scene in Tumanako, but Felicity had not become a reporter to simply cover monthly meetings of councils, guilds, and sports bodies, as much as she enjoyed most of that. No, she had always craved to probe a weighty subject in depth and provide insights that would change people's lives for the better.

In the early evening the next day, she went to a different pub. The Club Hotel was on a corner of the roughest part of town. It was the drinking hole of the Scum Dogs motorcycle gang and Felicity noticed three motorcycles parked outside as she approached. An ugly-looking dog was tethered beside them. It stirred as she passed and she edged away. She was dressed as plainly as possible, in jacket and trousers, with her hair tied back, but still drew attention when she entered the bar as the only woman amongst a dozen or so men. She regretted not having her usual social companion, Melody, with her. Surely their fall-out would not be permanent. They had avoided each other as best they could that morning.

She sat on a stool at the bar. She would at least have the companionship of the bar man. Thin and wizened with a moustache, he looked at her quizzically. She ordered a glass of the house red wine.

Felicity had no clear plan, just the wish to be in a likely haunt of drugs dealing where useful information might fall into her lap. She would get nowhere sitting in the office or at home. All she knew was that she had to put herself out there. Whatever followed, followed.

Moments later, a huge man thumped down on the seat beside her.

'What's this pretty lady? Can't have you drinking on your own.'

Felicity turned to look at the massive bearded man in a gang jacket, holding a glass of beer. His eyes were kind and she saw humour there.

'I thought a friend of mine would be here but he must have got held up.'

'If I may give you some advice, you don't want to hang around here too long on your own.' He took a long drink of his beer. 'It can only lead to trouble.'

Felicity could see the bar man looking their way, nodding.

'One of the boys would make a move on you and then someone

else would get jealous and have a go and it would be all on. Half of them are out of their bloody minds on P.' He tapped his right hand against his head. He could see the question in her face. 'Why do I bother to tell you? Well, I've got two sisters. I wouldn't want them here.'

'Good advice,' said the bar man abruptly. 'Best to go.'

Felicity heard the roar of motorcycles outside and the excited barking of the dog and then five more Scum Dogs gang members surged inside. The man beside her gestured and she followed his lead, quickly finishing her drink, sliding off her seat, and walking beside his massive form to the door and outside. He stood and watched until she got into her car and drove away. She had to wonder if he was under cover or just a good guy.

She arrived home to a box of chocolates and a 'Thank You' card.

'Sorry Lise. You were right. As usual. I was bloody silly to phone Rob Callendar.'

Melody was looking contrite. No sign of the drugs and not even a glass of wine.

'Now you're making me addicted. You know nothing comes between me and a box of chocolates. But thank you.' Felicity hugged her.

Felicity told her of her visit to The Club.

'Might have been a good thing I wasn't with you. Twice the

trouble.'

As they chatted, Melody conceded she did find it difficult to stop at just one or two glasses of wine and surmised she might have an addictive personality.

'I don't think so,' Felicity said. 'Honestly, I think that's too easy to use as an excuse. That's saying you have no control over your life. But you do have control. You're so determined in other ways. In your job. In sport.'

Melody was quietly reflective.

'Alcohol hasn't been good for our family,' she said eventually. 'There's a line through my father's side of the family. My grandfather couldn't drink and neither could my father nor my brother. One sniff of the cork and they were off their heads. Judgment gone and dangerous behind the wheel.'

Felicity was buoyed by Melody's insight and admission. 'I'll go teetotal in the house too. It will do me good to dry out for a while. I'll settle for a couple of chocolates a day.'

'There is one problem though.' Melody was looking concerned. 'The drugs I've bought.'

She and Felicity both knew that if someone dobbed them in and there was a raid that minute, even possessing a pipe or utensils for smoking could be a year in jail, and possessing for supply could be a life sentence.

11

A MOTHER'S
TORMENT

Bethany Callendar, for no apparent reason, donned the mayoral chain in her office and fingered it uneasily. For the first time she regretted standing for the position. Was she happier now than when she was running social services? No. Was she temperamentally suited to being mayor? Possibly not – she took things too much to heart, she suspected, spread herself too thin. Was her family better off since she had become mayor? Her brow creased and her knuckles tightened on the chain. Hardly. Her husband scarcely saw her some nights and her son was slipping away from them.

But soon other thoughts rose to the surface and her face reflected the sense of purpose which had prompted thousands to vote for her. She took off the chain before her secretary might appear and reached for the telephone.

Late that afternoon, at home, Bethany was relieved when the doorbell rang. It had been so difficult to get in touch with Rob lately. She realised what she was doing risked losing him altogether but her worry about him was affecting her health and her job. It had been gut churning to knock on his door for no response, and to visualise him looking at her through the security camera fearful of letting her into the house where she might see or smell things she didn't like. She recalled others she had seen in the course of her work at social services, emaciated, angry and paranoic.

She hurried to the door, welcomed him, and hugged him, aware again of his weight loss and torpor. In the living room another visitor awaited, a man of around thirty years of age with trim dark hair and stubble. She had known Raymond Proctor well when she was co-ordinator of social services and admired his skill and dedication as senior drugs counsellor.

'Rob, this is Raymond. He was one of my colleagues at social services and has come round for a chat...Will you have a coffee? Help yourselves to the biscuits.'

After initial greetings and appraisals, Rob sat on a settee facing Raymond Proctor and regarded him with suspicion, eyes darting. The two of them lapsed into silence. Bethany jollified the atmosphere as much as she could, bustling round the kitchen, making drinks for them, and finding chocolate biscuits to offer as well. But when she looked anew at her son's haggard face, lifeless eyes, and spare form, she struggled to keep up the jollity. The boy and young man she had known, had gone. He had become someone else.

'Raymond is an old head on young shoulders Rob.' Bethany looked at her son with mingled fear and hope. 'He can talk to you much better than I can and everything is confidential. Isn't that right Raymond?'

'That's right. Don't worry mate. Anything you say goes no further than this room. I've been where you are and I know what's it like. I was a heavy drugs user and went through stuff I never want to repeat. Somebody helped me find a way back and I want to do the same for you.'

Rob Carpenter's face was a study in shock and outrage. His reaction was exactly what Bethany had dreaded. For a moment he was paralysed. Then he looked from one to the other, rose to his feet, cursed them both, and strode back down the hallway.

'Mate you can't do it on your own! Let me help you!' Proctor shouted, rising.

Bethany and Proctor looked at each other in dismay and then Bethany rushed after Rob and shouted to his departing back.

'If you won't let me help you, I'll have to go to the police!'

'For hell's sake mum! What've you done!' he shouted in reply.

She looked from the front of the house until his car disappeared, unconcerned about the twitch of a neighbour's curtain opposite. When she returned, she told Raymond Proctor she now had no alternative than to have her son arrested so that treatment could begin.

The police raided at four in the morning on Friday the following week. The crash of the door giving way and the shouts of the police pouring in did not, though, disturb the occupants one bit for by then it was the former residence of Rob Callendar and his house mates and the police rampaged and shouted their way through an empty house.

Bethany Callendar heard the news from Rowley Rowlands with a hollow heart. Instead of her son being in custody he was at large, charged with nothing, but not receiving the treatment he needed. Her hatred for those who supplied drugs to the town spiralled to new heights. She knew, in her heart of hearts, her son was not only a user, but a dealer.

◆ ◆ ◆

When Felicity Spratt asked Raymond Proctor for an interview, he realised it would be wise to cover his arse by running the media request past his boss. His boss realised it would be wise to cover his own arse by running the request past his boss, the co-ordinator of social services, and she realised it would be wise to cover her arse by running the request past her boss, the mayor. To the co-ordinator's surprise, the mayor requested she tell Felicity Spratt that the mayor would also like to have a chat with Felicity.

So it was that Felicity Spratt turned up at the mayor's office fresh from seeing Raymond Proctor, with a notepad already crammed with information and an inquiring look on her face.

'Felicity, I understand you're writing a story about illegal drugs use in the town.'

Bethany could see disquiet on Felicity's face. Was Felicity afraid the mayor was about to discourage her story? Did she think the mayor would not want to besmirch the town's name, to see Tumanako portrayed as a haven for drugs users, a festering, crime-ridden pit ruled by the worst of humanity? Bethany saw another emotion on the face before her as well. Anxiety. What motive was driving the reporter? What did Felicity know?

'Felicity, I want you to know that I support what you are doing one hundred percent. It's no good shoving the problem of drugs under the carpet and pretending we are not so bad as other places. You can quote me as saying illegal drugs have no place in Tumanako and we will do everything possible to rid ourselves of them.'

Felicity started to ask a question but Bethany continued. 'I am, though, worried about you if you proceed with this. You must not get too specific. That is the province of Rowley Rowlands and the police.'

'I'll be careful,' Felicity said. She paused and then completed the question she had started. 'You talk of doing everything possible. What will you do?

'We will raid their drugs houses until we close the last one down. We will prosecute offenders to the letter of the law. If we find gangs are involved, we will make life in Tumanako intolerable for them. We want the supply of drugs to this town shut down.'

'Your crusade appears to be personal.'

They looked at each other for a long moment.

'I hate the drugs...You know my son Rob. You were friends.'

'Yes, I know Rob.'

'I'm very worried Felicity. Rob's not well and I've lost touch with him.' She brushed hair away from her face. 'I phoned his workplace and found he's tossed in his job and gone. Left the house he was in. Vanished. No word to Paul and me.' She touched Felicity's arm. 'This is between us, isn't it?' Felicity nodded. 'If you hear of him, could you let me know. Please.'

'Have you considered posting a missing person's report?'

Bethany turned away for a moment. She recalled the faces on the police website. Some of the cases had given her a jolt. Young women whose disappearance had wrenched the nation years before. She remembered them as if yesterday. Some eight thousand reports a year related to missing persons and ninety five percent of these people, it said, were found within two weeks. Officially, there were some three hundred and fifty long-term missing persons in New Zealand. But as she looked closer at the website, she saw a distinction between missing persons and persons who could not be contacted. The Police Missing Persons Unit did not deal with lost-contact cases. There was though an ancillary comment which she believed applied to her son – if there was an indication of vulnerability or concern for safety, it was a tracing matter.

Felicity's question still hung in the air.

'Yes. I have. I've decided to report him missing and take it from there.'

Felicity promised to let her know if she heard anything of Rob and they parted, allies in the fight against illegal drugs but with little idea what they were getting into.

◆ ◆ ◆

In her monthly meeting with Rowley Rowlands, Bethany learnt of the recent suspected sabotage at the factory. As much as he had wanted to keep the matter under wraps, Steve Polson had felt obliged to report it.

Immediately Rowlands departed, Bethany phoned Steve Polson to give her support and ask if there was anything she could do as mayor to help. She reminded him of the availability of social services' counselling service for any staff who might be traumatised by the sabotage incidents. She wanted to add, 'including you', but stopped short of that. He thanked her but pointed out they had their own Human Resources Department.

'Steve, could it be a disgruntled staff member? Somebody with a grudge against the factory or somebody in it. Is it payback, or perhaps threat? Could drugs come into it?'

He said there was no one obvious. He had not considered payback and dismissed any drugs connection.

When she hung up, she realised that drugs were permeating her every waking moment. Felicity had been right in saying she was on a crusade. Then, she remembered another thing she had to do – phone home to get Paul to turn the oven on and transfer the casserole dish from the refrigerator. She had an early evening meeting but should be home by seven and she knew she would be craving that delicious lamb casserole she had prepared the night before. And a glass of Pinot Noir. She got no response from the home phone so she tried his cell phone. No response there either. Very unlike Paul as that was also his business phone. She was about to hang up when he answered. No problem. The casserole would be steaming away in the oven when she got home.

Except it wasn't. Amid his copious apologies for having forgotten, she had to rustle up another dish from leftovers by way of the microwave. Her family was coming apart.

12

A PULSATING
WONDERLAND

Simon and Patricia Hurley acknowledged they were bitter about Rosemary's spina bifida. Besides the one other child with neural tube defects they were aware of in the district, there were three children with abnormalities that might also have been caused by contamination from the factory. But nothing could be proved. Experts cited genetic background and diet as other possible causes and there might have been another source of pollution besides the factory. Many toxic substances including arsenic, cadmium, chlorine, lead, and mercury could cause birth defects. Industrial solvents and pesticides were particularly hazardous during the mother's pregnancy, as were high levels of carbon monoxide and nitrogen dioxide. Nitrate in drinking water could cause health issues. Simon and Patricia knew women were vulnerable even to air pollution when pregnant because of the changes that occur to carry and develop the fetus. Nothing could be proved against Polson's.

It was when Simon and Patricia were not with her, and alone with their thoughts, that the bitterness sometimes welled up. They would wake in the night and torment themselves over buying the property adjoining the factory, putting in a garden, renovating the house. They had known nothing of the health risks. The property had passed all the required red tape before being sold. It had been such an appealing patch of ground with lush pasture and the river at the bottom and close to town. How pleased they had been with its purchase when Daniel and Charlotte had been little. Soon after Rosemary's birth, they moved several kilometres away to their present property, also by the river.

When they were with Rosemary, as now at the town's swimming pool complex, they were caught up in her sheer joy of life. The Hurley family and Polly loved their visits to the pool, mostly because of Rosemary. Now Daniel and Charlotte were in the water with her while Polly, Simon and Patricia observed from the side. Rosemary lived each moment intensely, putting to shame the apathy and listlessness of many other children, deriving all the pleasure she could from a visit to the swimming pool, the fast-food shop, the downtown mall, the classroom, the forest. Polly, too, was entranced by Rosemary's zest for life.

'Come on Rosie, you can do it!' Polly checked a stopwatch as Rosemary surged to the finish. Rosemary could not kick with her feet but she could pull herself through the water surprisingly well.

'A new record!' Polly shouted as Rosemary touched the end of the pool.

The others clustered around as Rosemary pulled herself out of the pool and Polly helped her into the wheelchair.

'Best by 0.4 seconds.'

Congratulations showered upon her.

◆ ◆ ◆

That afternoon, Simon finalised the latest monthly edition of *Help the Planet, Aotearoa*. The amount of advertising was pleasing. Many new businesses were coming on board with the green cause. Well, it made economic sense, he pondered. They wanted to align with the changing public opinion, capitalise on goodwill towards all things green. There was the tox-free cleaner that could be worked into a sponge, the counter compost bin for plant-based kitchen scraps, and the eco-friendly, washable bamboo-fibre cloths. What change Simon had seen through the years. He recalled how nervous he had been at the environmental group's first demonstration. How self-conscious and anxious. The almost embarrassed unfurling of the banners. The vicious heckling. 'Green weirdos', 'freak show' and offers of free coal had been the least nasty of it.

With monies from the magazine, the sale of produce from their acre of vegetable garden and their orchard, and Patricia's income from her work as a data collection agent for Statistics New Zealand, they could pay their bills but with little left over. They should be doing better. He realised again with a grimace it was always his money paying the bills. Patricia was earning good money but it was vanishing into a deep, dark hole. Then, as he sat and brooded, something snapped. He grabbed his coat and the key to the work van. Patricia had taken the Tesla. He knew it was going to be unpleasant but it was time to bring it to a head.

It was only 4pm and the pub was almost deserted. Just two drinkers, chatting in a corner. But when Simon carried on a few steps he was in the pulsating wonderland of a pokies parlour with a dozen patrons. He saw Patricia at once, at the Sultan's Palace machine at the end of a row. Lights were flashing and strobing all over its front and she was already sunk into a kind of robotic concentration. As he watched, she fed the machine with coins. Simon stood still, taking it all in. It had been a shock coming from the stark, dark, silent pub into the bright, light, noisy pokies parlour. All manner of sounds bombarded him – upbeat jingles always ending on a high note, whistles, bells, a sort of clarion call that he could see signified free spins, and the rattle of winnings sliding down a chute and hitting a tray, giving small, instant returns. Others were winning, why not me, said the rattle. The noise was all from the animations; no one was speaking. Each patron was in a world of their own, cocooned, clutching to the hope that one more spin would bring the riches advertised.

Looking at the nearest screen, Simon could feel himself being drawn into the action, anticipating as the reels spun. He looked across at Patricia. She was clearly oblivious to everything around her. Did she realise the machines were designed to keep more money than they paid out, that losses were sometimes disguised as wins? His heart sank as more money went into the machine. Was life with him so unbearable, were her problems so dire, that she had to lose herself in the pokies parlour? He took a last look and trudged back through the pub and out the door. He was not going to confront her here.

When Patricia arrived home an hour after him, she had

groceries in hand. Now, they were alone as Rosemary was in her room. Simon braced himself.

'I saw you in the pokies parlour today.'

It was five to two on Saturday afternoon and Todd McNab, the local member of Parliament, was enjoying a moment's peace in his office in the main street in town, next door to Lionel Spratt's real estate business. The office opened at two in the afternoon and any constituent was welcome to drop in between two and four and have a word. A tall, fleshy man with a ready smile (opponents might say an unctuous flatterer), he tolerated the face-to-face meetings but they always finished promptly at four. Never a minute over even if it meant a truncated sentence. Many a concerned constituent had been surprised to find themselves suddenly in the street with a hand in the small of the back and a question still trembling on the lip.

This day he dunked his biscuit one last time in his coffee, took two last bites, drained the cup, put it on the bench, unlocked the door exactly at two, and gaped in astonishment. Simon Hurley and others of the Tumanako branch of the Forest and Bird Society were right in his face, choking the pavement and now brandishing their banners in his face and beginning a chant: 'No mining on conservation land! No mining on conservation land! No mining on conservation land!' There was no mistaking the trigger for the protest – on television that week, McNab's Party leader had appeared to support mining for copper on land which the greens treasured for its conservation values.

McNab reeled back a step and Simon Hurley feared he might fall and crack his head. No violence, however strongly they felt, was always the mantra of their demonstrations. To Simon's relief, McNab recovered his equilibrium and flashed his characteristic cheesy smile.

'Perhaps one or two of you might like to come in.'

Simon was suddenly aware of the presence of Rowley Rowlands at his elbow. He had seen Rowlands earlier, watching the demonstrators gather with misgivings. Simon sensed the police were more vigilant of his group since the recent incident of Toni Dalzell and the totara tree. Simon was aware the demonstrators had to tread carefully as the footpath was blocked and Rowlands was entitled to order them to disperse.

'Be quick about it,' Rowlands said.

But with the chanting and the press of bodies and the fury at the prospect of the mining, the blood of the demonstrators was up and they surged forward. Simon and Rowley went to step into the office ahead of them but suddenly found themselves jammed together in the doorway. The situation of hip to hip was acutely embarrassing for both but mercifully it was brief as the pressure from behind spat them inside. Todd McNab's office, virtually empty a minute before, was now too crammed for arms to be raised and banners waved. There was, though, sufficient space outside for Toni Dalzell to raise a loudspeaker to her lips and tell Tumanako what the protest was about.

Rowley Rowlands told Simon Hurley in a few words of one

syllable the protest was to end right then and with a scowl, carved a passage for himself back to the footpath. McNab assured Hurley that the group's opposition to the mining would be relayed back to party headquarters, and Simon announced they had made their point and could leave. As the protesters departed, Lionel Spratt entered to commiserate with Todd McNab. Simon looked back to see them shaking their heads in wonder at how quiet, conservative Tumanako and district had become a hotbed of radicalism. He heard Spratt shout.

'Total bunch of losers! Couldn't open a gate between the lot of you! Wouldn't know what side your bread was buttered on!'

Patricia had not been at the demonstration. Neither had Rosemary. As he made his way home, Simon reflected on his confrontation with Patricia. It had been ugly and upsetting. Amid tears, she had accused him of not trusting her and spying on her. As he had left the house, he had seen Rosemary emerge to comfort her mother.

He could not understand how such an intelligent, responsible person as Patricia could be so in thrall to the pokies machines. The waste of the precious money was excruciating for him and now as he turned the last bend for home, he felt, for the first time, their marriage was shaky.

13

BETHANY
HARDENS UP

T he annual dinner of the Rotary Club was a social highlight of the year for Tumanako and many of the movers and shakers of the district were there. Amongst the honoured guests at the top table were the mayor and her partner and as Bethany Callendar looked around, she took a quiet pride that she was their civic leader. The daughter of mowing contractor Chester Burridge and his incapacitated wife Mary had come a long way. If only they could see her now but both were long dead. She could still, though, feel their love for her.

She began to relax. At one stage she had thought they would never make it as Paul had forgotten they were going out and when he wasn't home by five, she had had to call and remind him. He had arrived home in a flurry, gushing apologies, citing a frantic time at work, and had got ready in record time.

But now, rather than his absence, it was his presence that concerned her. What had happened to the restrained, well-mannered Paul she knew? He was knocking back drinks much too quickly. It was clear to her that the Rotary Club wished to impress for the tables groaned under the food and drink. No sooner were bottles of wine emptied than others appeared. Perhaps a contributing factor was the Rotary President also being President of the Licensed Victuallers' Association. Paul Callendar was taking full advantage, not only repeatedly filling his own glass but attempting to fill the glasses of those around him as well. His judgment had gone. Once he rudely interrupted a conversation and another time, he appeared to be talking to himself.

'Paul, what was that?' she said quietly, putting a hand on his arm.

He looked startled, a little dazed. 'Nothing. I was just thinking.'

She whispered to him to go easy on the drink. He still, though, had a hand on a bottle and when she put a hand over her glass, he turned instead to the glass of the Rotary member opposite and poured until the wine sploshed on the table around it. The rest of the evening, she distanced herself as much as she could from him, circulating after dinner, catching up with those she knew and being introduced to some partners along the way. All the while, she kept an anxious eye on Paul and was grateful when he holed up in a corner with two friends from golf. She hoped that might be a form of damage control, absorbing him and keeping him confined there until it was time to leave.

She had never had to worry about Paul's drinking before. Was it a reaction to Rob's disappearance? Paul had been close to Rob, playing golf and tennis with him throughout his boyhood and encouraging him throughout school. Bethany couldn't wait to make her farewells, pluck Paul from his golfing friends, and get out of there.

The next day Bethany was still smarting about the embarrassments of the night before. Paul had gone straight to bed and they had barely seen each other at breakfast. She sensed he was regretful. At work she put herself on automatic, working steadily through correspondence and then chairing a committee meeting at ten.

The phone call from Felicity Spratt brought relief, and then worry.

'Did he say where he's living?' Bethany asked. 'How did he sound?...Will you be seeing him again?...Was that The Railway around eight?'

Bethany also inquired about the rest of Felicity's research but if Felicity knew more, she was keeping it to herself.

There was relief in knowing Rob was alive but worry in knowing he was still dealing drugs. Should she tell Rowley Rowlands that if he went to The Railway around eight he could likely arrest a drugs user and dealer. The result would be her son an arrested felon, imprisoned for years. He would, though, be getting the treatment he needed.

◆ ◆ ◆

Bethany reversed into a shadowy corner of The Railway carpark at half past seven and waited. She reasoned that most other vehicles would park where there was light and if anyone did park nearby, she would sink out of sight. She had told no-one of her plan.

Rob Callendar arrived in a Range Rover, alone, just before eight. Bethany had not seen Felicity. She had even wondered if she should offer Felicity money to buy drugs from Rob to keep a link with him. But when it came down to it, she couldn't bring herself to do that. She watched the slight figure of her son until he disappeared into the pub. He emerged some twenty minutes later, walking briskly, glancing back and around before he got into the Range Rover. Then, with a quick reverse, he was away.

She followed, staying well back as it was dark and the headlights were like a locater beacon. She hoped she could stay close enough to see him pull into a driveway or park outside a house. But he kept driving and driving until they were in the country and she was on an unfamiliar road. There was a car in the distance but with all the twists and turns, she could not even be sure it was his. To continue was hopeless. He could be just up ahead, or he could have turned off the road anywhere along there.

As she drove slowly back to town with a heavy heart, Bethany became aware of a vehicle closing rapidly on her from behind. The lights were on full beam, dazzling her. She looked away as much as she could and swung the interior rear-view mirror away. But now it was not the lights concerning her but the vehicle itself. It kept coming and coming until It was sitting almost hard against her back bumper. She tensed for its impact.

As best she could, she focused on the road ahead, aware the slightest decrease in her speed could bring that vehicle on top of her or spin her wildly out of control. The vehicle was much bigger than hers. She and her car would become a blend of metal and flesh. She clung to the wheel, terrified, her heart jumping around her chest. Who, she wondered, and why? Was it someone ignorant of the danger? Someone reluctant to pass at night on a narrow road? Or was it a natural-born bully intimidating her on a lonely road at night? And then another thought struck – was it Rob, aware she had been following and now trying to frighten her off? She couldn't believe he would do that to her. He had always been a loving boy. Perhaps it was a gang member? Still the vehicle remained hard behind. As they came into the lights of the suburbs, she became aware she was going much faster than the speed limit. Then suddenly it was just her in the street. Blessedly, the vehicle had gone. She was alone. She braked, pulled over, and sat sobbing and shaking until she had control of herself and could drive slowly home.

When they put Bethany Callendar in office, the electors of Tumanako had recognised the grit behind the charm, but alone at night on the rural road she had been weak and vulnerable. Inwardly, she raged at the cowardly persecution. Over the next week, with the agony of knowing her son was both drugs perpetrator and victim, the rage began to fuel a burning mission. With the help of anyone she could rally, she would clean up the whole festering mess of it. Rob could be with her or against her. Whichever way he wanted to go.

'No pussy-footing around the issue Rowley,' she said when they met at the end of the week. 'We know there's an issue and that it's behind half the crime in the town. The robberies, the bashings of partners, the kids going off the rails. It's got to stop.'

She could see uncertainty in his face. He was a good man and had been doing his best but the tide of drugs coming into the town had become an irresistible flood and he had been powerless to stop it. She remembered what he had said on an earlier occasion – that when crime was attacked in one area, it just seemed to bulge out in another. Would they simply be bringing temporary relief to their neck of the woods while the drugs trade boomed elsewhere?

'We'll need more resources.'

'What resources?'

'Undercover people to provide the information. More bodies to do the raids.'

From her time in social services, Bethany knew it had to go deeper than that as well – more help for families so that parents and children would be less likely to be attracted into the drugs world. Good housing, full bellies, healthy activities, sound role models, encouraging prospects for the children.

Bethany summoned Felicity Spratt and announced the clean-up-drugs campaign. When *The Tararua Mirror* splashed it on the front page and promised follow-up stories, Bethany dropped in to thank them for the publicity. As they chatted, Colin Trainor congratulated Felicity on her foresight in already researching the drugs scene in the town. Felicity said she wished the mayor had waited a bit as she had barely started her research and did not yet have much to write about.

'Can you keep us in the picture Bethany?' Colin said.

'I'll do my best,' she promised. 'There will be some things the police will obviously want to keep under wraps but I'll encourage full and frank disclosure. We want people talking about this. We want people to know what the drugs are doing to our town.'

The staff of *The Tararua Mirror* knew better than most what the drugs were doing. They were the ones who attended the Court, listened to the evidence, heard the sentences read out, and saw the reactions of the relatives. And now they were the ones who wrote the stories as the campaign started. Paul Trainor and his bosses were delighted with the increase in circulation. The newspaper now had a consistent hard edge that had been lacking. Each edition had the latest news from the 'drugs war' front and Trainor took care not to step on the toes of the police. When Rowley Rowlands declared, 'We are all in this together,' Trainor agreed.

But when a bottle smashed through the window of the newspaper office early one Monday morning, the war came too close to home. It was too early for any dog walkers and joggers and the CCTV got no number plate. Just a figure of average build wearing a balaclava and disappearing into the night as fast as he had come. Of more concern than the broken window was the partly burnt rag soaked in petroleum stuffed into the bottle. The rag had harmlessly burnt itself out. The office was lucky to survive.

Colin Trainor had to question how far they were going to take the campaign. Was it worth risking the lives of his staff? There was no doubt in the minds of his bosses in Auckland. The newspaper was prospering under its current direction and, anyway, there was a principle involved. They would not be cowed into silence. Security around the office would be tightened by means of a mobile patrol and *The Tararua Mirror* would continue its campaign.

14

SIMON PONDERS

Saturday morning and Simon Hurley was revelling in the beauty of the first rays of sunlight striking the trees at the back of the property. The gentle mist floating over the land was infused with a pink and golden glow. Utterly enchanting. A knocking at the door broke the spell. It was loud and persistent, the sort of knocking that warned of approaching danger. He opened the door to the disgruntled face of Lionel Spratt.

'Your shit is polluting the river.'

'I beg your pardon.'

Simon's heart skipped a beat. It took him a moment or two to get Spratt's drift. Spratt was dressed in fishing attire.

'A problem with your septic tank. Haven't you checked it lately? It was the pong got me first and then I saw the sludge. I'll have to report it, I'm afraid.'

Simon followed Spratt down towards the river. When they came to the septic tank, Simon saw with anguish the tell-tale lush grass below the tank; it was clearly benefitting from the released nitrogen. He also saw the soggy ground around the tank and smelt the rank odour. They carried on down to the river where Simon saw the seepage from his faulty tank. The waste water had filtered down through the soil into the ground water. He could only mumble shock and regret. He had no idea how long there had been a problem. There might have been bacterial pollution for weeks along the whole course of the river to the sea. His lack of care had indisputably harmed aquatic life and possibly human life as well. It was more than embarrassing – it was a disgrace.

And for Lionel Spratt of all people to discover it. Was it Simon's imagination or did he detect an air of triumph in Spratt? There seemed to be more satisfaction in telling Hurley the bad news than annoyance at the interruption to his fishing. Indeed, it was appalling that the president of the local branch of the Forest and Bird Society and the owner and editor of *Help the Planet, Aotearoa* was responsible for polluting the river. No doubt Spratt would be on the phone to Felicity so that she could tell the world about it. He could only hope that with Felicity's sympathy for the cause, it would be a brief buried deep inside the paper.

'Thanks for drawing it to my attention,' Simon managed to croak as they gazed at the odious discharge.

'One thing's for sure,' said Spratt. 'I won't be fishing for a while in this part of the river. God knows what bloody awful diseases it might have caused already.'

Simon could have told him salmonella and campylobacter for two. He himself would not fancy taking fish from it for now, let alone drink water from it or swim in it.

'I expect you'll have to replace the septic tank. Any repair is only temporary at best.'

Simon could only nod. He knew Spratt was right. As Spratt made his way upstream, Simon trudged back up to the house. Promptly at nine, he phoned Premier Environment to get a new tank installed. That would be thousands of dollars more than they could afford. At least action would be underway before Robin Trethewan, the regional council's compliance officer, visited.

Simon Hurley called on Hector Dunwoodie at the first opportunity. There was a Range Rover parked outside when he arrived and Rob Callendar was on the point of leaving. Hurley knew him from school activities involving Daniel and Charlotte and they exchanged greetings. Callendar was thinner and jumpier than Simon remembered and there was no leisurely chat – Rob Callendar looked as though he couldn't get away fast enough.

As the Range Rover jerked out the gate and shot up Shambles Line, Simon Hurley began to unburden himself to Hector Dunwoodie.

'Hector, there has to be a better way. All that money to dispose of a natural product that surely could be recycled to benefit the environment. The problem was immediate and I had to get the new tank, but it's got me thinking. How can I turn this short-term negative into a long-term positive? You're more likely than anyone else I know to have ideas on the subject. I'm going to front up and feature it in the magazine.'

Hector had looked at the Range Rover until it vanished and Simon Hurley could see he did not have his full attention. He wondered if a wandering mind was characteristic of bipolar disorder. Hector's distraction was so at odds with his intense focus at other times, especially when he was working on a project. Simon wondered, too, if the bipolar disorder, debilitating as it could be with its highs and lows, played a part in Hector's brilliance – he had seen Hector, in episodes of mania, utterly absorbed in his subject. Along with the mania were phases of depression and Simon understood Hector was on drug treatment to stabilise his mood.

But he had misread Hector – Hector had taken in what he had said.

'You probably know I've made a start,' Hector said. 'I'm using my urine to charge my mobile phone and I'm intending to power the lighting with it too.'

Simon soon began to suspect he had triggered a manic phase in Hector. The words began to spill out of him and Simon had to concentrate to keep up.

'I'm looking at whole body waste as well. When I go, I've arranged for my body to be laid in a chamber with bark, soil, straw, and other compounds that promote natural decomposition.'

Hector talked then of biogas which could be harvested from human faeces to generate power for household and industrial needs, including transport, and of using human faecal compost in the growing of vegetables.

Simon nodded. He had read in *Frontiers in Environmental Science* of experiments showing human waste could be used as fertiliser and be as productive as conventional organic fertiliser, with no risk of transmitting disease. The valuable nitrogen, phosphorus and potassium in human waste could be put back into the soil, boosting the soil carbon, helping maintain fertility long-term. There would be none of the greenhouse gas emissions that come with synthetic fertilisers.

'Our faecal waste can also be a foundation for perfumes,' Hector said.

Simon recoiled. That claim seemed a stretch too far. But when he thought about it, there was ambergris, formed from a secretion of the bile duct in the intestines of the sperm whale, so prized by the perfume industry. His tramping party had kept an eye out for ambergris on the beaches of Stewart Island, sadly to no avail. As he departed Dunwoodie's property, he determined to look deeper into the disposal of human faecal waste. In the meantime, there was the new septic tank. The expense was a pain.

The arrival of a threatening email the next morning wrecked Simon's day, and then Patricia's. Their power company said they had failed to pay the previous month's invoice – it was an automatic debit from Patricia's account but the coffers must have been empty. When Simon drew it to her attention, her head dropped and she promised to sort it. The unspoken subject of the problem gambling hovered in the air between them.

She said, so quietly he had to strain to hear her, 'If you want me to take that course I will.'

'I do want you to,' he said.

The following week Daniel and Polly were emerging from the cinema late on Saturday afternoon when they saw Patricia disappear into a pub. Daniel followed her in, inquisitive and on edge. Polly lagged a few steps behind. At first, Daniel thought his mother had done a Houdini act. Three seasoned-looking drinkers sat at a table to one side and a small man with a face like a ferret was drinking at a table on his own. But no mother. Then a tall, gaunt woman in a dowdy brown coat emerged grim-faced from a room at the back and shot through the bar and away. Daniel entered the room and found himself in a pokies parlour. Patricia was settling herself down at The Golden Nugget machine, ablaze with flashing lights. Daniel saw her flush of excitement and her bustle to start playing. For a moment he was rivetted to the spot. Polly followed his transfixed gaze and put a hand on his arm.

Patricia was feeding money into the machine when Daniel crossed the floor. She was at the end of a row with two empty machines to her left.

'Mum.'

Patricia turned sharply, shock all over her face.

'Daniel.' Then his mother was looking beyond him, at Polly in the doorway. For a moment, they were all as if frozen.

'Rosie told me of the fight with dad.'

Patricia pushed a button to release the money she had fed into the machine. The coins clattered into the tray. She reached for her bag.

'Not a word to your father. It's something I have to sort.' She looked beseechingly at him.

Patricia led the way out and drove herself home. Daniel returned home on his bike. Later he phoned Polly and told her that money troubles were tearing his family apart and he was going to speak to his mum. He went on-line and researched the subject. He found that since pokies machines had been introduced to New Zealand in 1987, they had raised millions for charities and their operators but had impoverished thousands of New Zealanders and shattered families. That night, when he got his mum on her own, he told her she couldn't win. She might have a short-term windfall but in the long run, the machines would drain her money out of her.

'It's all right for those who can set a modest limit and have fun with it occasionally, but it looks as though that's not you mum.'

He gave her the name and number of a service that provided free, professional, and confidential support. A part of him felt priggish at telling his mother what to do but who else was going to? It was good fortune he had seen her. It was now up to her.

Patricia didn't tell him but it was the same number Simon had already given her.

The air was ringing with strong language at the monthly meeting of the Forest and Bird Society. The branch was debating whether it should formally oppose the manufacture, distribution, and sale of illegal drugs. Simon Hurley was driving the motion and sensed the majority of members present were with him but Hector Dunwoodie and Toni Dalzell were vehemently against.

'There are adverse environmental impacts,' Simon thundered. Patricia and the others of his family knew how deeply he had researched the subject and how frustrated he became when others came to the issue with personal agendas.

'You're just confusing people if you bring illegal drugs into it,' Hector argued. 'You might as well bring in alcohol addiction and all the other addictions as well. We'll become known as the Tumanako Do-Gooders, or rather, Tumanako Spoil Sports.'

Toni Dalzell nodded vigorously in support. 'Let's just stick to the environment please,' she said.

Simon continued. 'To produce cocaine in South America, there is deforestation as ground is cleared for the cultivation of coca. This involves destruction of habitat, use of pesticides, the death of fauna and greenhouse gas emissions. To produce methamphetamine results in hydrogen chloride gas which is an environmental pollutant and, as well, for every pound of P produced, five pounds of toxic waste is generated. Marijuana production requires large amounts of water. A single plant can need eight to ten gallons of water per day. It also involves large amounts of energy. This further causes high amounts of greenhouse gas emissions.'

'We're going to antagonise a lot of people unnecessarily,' Hector protested. 'Let's stick to what we can see around us.'

His voice had become shrill and Simon did not wish to over-agitate him. The sooner the matter was wrapped up the better.

'All right. We'll put it to the vote.'

The vote was passed twenty-five to two. Illegal drugs, for the Tumanako branch of the Forest and Bird Society, were now an environmental menace. Hector, glaring all round, stormed out but Simon was confident he would soon cool down. If necessary, Simon would visit him on a peace mission – Hector was too valuable a member and too close a friend to remain at odds with them. Toni remained, but in simmering discontent.

There were two other motions on the agenda. The first was that the branch would encourage members of the public to plant a tree to help celebrate a birthday. This was inspired by Leah Namugerwa of Uganda who celebrated her fifteenth birthday by planting two hundred trees and went on to found the Birthday Trees Project. The motion was passed unanimously. The second motion was for members to name extreme weather events after local climate-change deniers. This was prompted by the campaign in the United States of America asking the World Meteorological Organisation to replace the names of tropical storms with the names of United States government climate-change deniers. Simon Hurley himself had put the motion, irked beyond endurance by comments of Barry Fitzwilliam and Lionel Spratt. But Betty Rawlinson, chief librarian and long-time member, had spoken powerfully against, arguing it was too personal in such a tiny community as Tumanako and many would consider it in poor taste. The motion was lost.

15

PATRICIA CLEARS DEBTS

'I must drop in on Hector today.' Simon recalled the arm flung wide in disgust and the last baleful look around the room as Hector stormed out of the meeting. 'You know how low he can get when he broods.'

'It would be a chance to see his exoskeleton,' Patricia said. 'Daniel said he's building it for Rosie. To make her more independent.'

'Yes, I do want to see that… I am a bit worried though about his stand on drugs. He and Toni were so adamant we should not be campaigning against illegal drugs.'

'Brilliant Hector. He's a dear man, wanting to help Rosie.'

'I'll visit him after lunch.' He recalled his last visit when Rob Callendar had left in a great hurry. Callendar had been as jumpy as Hector on a bad day. He wondered how Rob Callendar made his crust these days. He had been a friend of Daniel and Charlotte and gone on to university. What was he doing back in Tumanako?

◆ ◆ ◆

The sky was a charming pale blue for the Green Wordathon of the Forest and Bird Society and the sun was bathing faces. Anyone venturing into the main street between ten and eleven that Saturday morning was likely to be bailed up and invited to consider and discuss the environment. Each member of the society had a target of engaging with at least ten members of the public, and with the main street of Tumanako not exactly choked with people, it was highly likely members of the public would be approached more than once, especially if they didn't wear the green lapel sticker offered by a team member. As the morning progressed, some unusual behaviour soon became evident. People were ducking into doorways and emerging soon after, furtively looking around before moving off; others were crossing the road and a minute later crossing back again; some appeared to be in an almighty hurry and others appeared to have a hearing disability.

But all team members engaged with at least one member of the public. One elderly lady using a walker set Melody Gilmour back on her heels with her opening remark.

'Don't tell me anything that will depress me, will you.'

Melody paused, visibly reshuffling her mental cards.

'I want to enjoy this lovely morning you see. I don't want to hear about the sun boiling away the oceans or the forests going up in flames.'

Melody took in the worn, kindly face and the fragile body. 'No, I wouldn't tell you that.'...I'm a school teacher.'

'We need good school teachers. Tell me what you tell the children. You wouldn't want to unduly alarm them.'

'I tell them there are things we can do now to make the world a better place, cleaner and safer. I tell them we can all make a difference.'

The elderly woman smiled. 'Lovely yes. Perhaps in some ways we need to turn back.' She shook her head. 'Such waste these days with food and clothes. With everything really. Thank you for feeling so strongly about it and doing something.'

Melody offered a green sticker saying 'Cloth not plastic' for her lapel. The elderly lady looked around her at the other team members approaching people.

'Yes, thank you, I will have one of those,' she said, and pushed onwards.

Toni Dalzell did not have to approach her first member of the public. The member of the public approached her. Marjorie Flett had seen the flurry of activity and immediately honed in on the woman who had caused so many tongues to wag with her scaling of the totara tree. There had, too, been the incident at the beach clean-up and town gossip had Toni Dalzell as the woman who had had to be rescued.

'Good morning,' Toni Dalzell said brightly as Marjorie Flett approached. 'So pleased you are taking an interest. Would you like to hear some of the things we can all do to help our planet today and in the future.'

Marjorie Flett waved a hand across her face. 'No, I'm not worried about all that.' She came uncomfortably close to Dalzell. 'Tell me about yourself. How are you? And how is your partner?'

Toni Dalzell reared back. She had come to discuss climate change, not details of her private life. 'Excuse me. My partner? What's that got to do with you?'

Marjorie Flett was not known for her sensitivity or empathy but even she could read the furious spark in the eye and the aggressive body language. 'Never mind. I'll let you get on with it.' And Marjorie Flett was away, adeptly dodging the next team member who tried to cross her path.

By the end of it, Simon rated the Green Wordathon a success. The target of ten exchanges per team member had not been achieved – it would have taken a dozen sheep dogs to round up all those who had taken evasive action – but green issues had once again been dragged into the light of day at Tumanako and there was even the possibility of one or two new members.

◆ ◆ ◆

Daniel was alone with his mother.

'So you see mum, with the holiday job at Polson's and my shifts at the café in Christchurch, along with the student loan of course, I can get by. Charlotte, too, is getting there. Another three years, hopefully, I can be pulling in a decent salary. Two years for Charlotte.'

'That's good to hear.'

'How are you doing? Have you contacted that problem gambling service?'

She looked away.

'I'm worried about you mum. Rosie told me how upset you were after the fight with dad.'

Patricia put her hands to her face and spoke with her head down. 'Just let me be Daniel. I can stop by myself.'

He realised it had to be her wish to stop. But he made one final appeal.

'I can do the gambling cessation course with you.'

She looked up and studied his face. 'You don't have a problem... Do you?'

'No.' Then he grimaced. 'I don't have any money to have a problem with.' They sat in silence for a minute reflecting. 'Life's all about numbers in a way, isn't it. Accumulating them.' Then he remembered the demonstration and the glimpse he had had of Rob Callendar flitting through the crowd, covertly distributing drugs and collecting money. 'Do you remember Rob Callendar I used to knock around with in year thirteen at school?'

Patricia stirred, her thoughts momentarily off her own situation. 'Bethany's son?'

'Yes. He's gone completely off the rails. Rob was a good student but he always did have a streak of the rebel in him. First boy at the school with long hair. After the holidays, first with a moustache too but they made him shave that off.'

Patricia remembered Rob Callendar very well. He had been in their house more than once and she had frequently seen him taking part in school activities with Daniel and Charlotte. She recalled Felicity Spratt and him being in the house. 'It's a shame he's gone that way. Dreadful for Bethany and Paul. I suppose they know about it.'

'I suppose so. Lots of others do.'

The next week, just after eleven on a Friday morning, when Simon was in the garden collecting produce for the Saturday market and Rosemary was assisting, Patricia drove into town, did her supermarket shopping, and then slipped into a pokies parlour in a suburban hotel. It was her first time in this one and she stood in the entrance for a moment, getting accustomed to it. Some twenty machines, half of them occupied. She chose the most isolated and quickly got settled, feeding in a fifty-dollar note and sighing with satisfaction as the lights flashed and the symbols began to spin.

'Please let me win,' she murmured to herself.

Within half an hour she was down to two dollars and torturing herself over whether she should put in ten more or call it quits for the day. Another thought swirled as well. She had still not paid that electricity bill and any day now the power would be switched off and there would be an almighty row with Simon. Exercising more willpower than she knew she had, she saved her last two dollars, gathered her things, and left. As she went through the bar, she passed two middle-aged men drinking at a table. There was a younger man in the bar as well, thin, with a moustache, sitting on his own and looking towards the doorway to the street. With a start, she recognised Rob Callendar and was reminded that in Tumanako there was always the possibility of running into people you knew.

On an impulse, she went up to him. 'Rob, isn't it. I remember you from school. You probably don't know me. Patricia Hurley. Daniel and Charlotte were at school with you.'

He was clearly disconcerted. He looked again at the doorway in alarm and then back at Patricia and finally managed to speak. 'Mrs Hurley. Yes. How are things? How are Daniel and Charlotte?'

'They're good. Busy at holiday jobs in town now. Back to university soon...How about you?' She took in the haggard face, the bags under the eyes, the sallow skin.

'I'm good thanks. Just waiting for a friend and then I'm away.' He glanced again at the doorway.

Patricia suddenly saw a way to avoid another terrible row with Simon. They had never had a blow-up like that before. Rosemary so upset and Daniel on and on at her. Why shouldn't she be able to play the pokies? It gave her pleasure like nothing else, took her away from her worries over Rosie, and over the remorseless bills it was her share to pay. Working for Rob Callendar would be an opportunity to clear her debts, save their marriage and keep her family together. Rob Callendar was potential salvation.

She lowered her voice though the only ones who might overhear were the two on the other side of the bar room. 'Rob, if there's anything I can do to help.' He looked at her embarrassed and agitated and she realised he had misunderstood and was thinking she was sorry for him. 'No, I mean help you in your...job.'

She now had his full attention and he began to look at her

differently, appraisingly. She could see the intelligence in his eyes. A sea change was taking place in his attitude towards her. Mrs Hurley was now far removed from the school and her home where she had provided him with home-made ginger beer all those years before. Now it was not the prim and proper, conservative Mrs Hurley, mother of Daniel, Charlotte, and Rosemary, but Mrs Hurley who played the pokies in the morning, talked to him in a hotel bar and had an obvious need of money. She would be quite unlike anyone else in his network. She could be useful. Who would suspect?

'No buying or taking, understand,' she found herself saying. 'I would only act as a messenger.'

Rob Callendar had temporarily lost interest in whoever was meeting him. He stopped glancing at the doorway and invited her to sit down. In recent times, much buying and selling had moved on-line, including to social media platforms, with identities disguised, but however it was arranged, it all came down in the end to product having to be delivered and money having to be collected. Many people had now switched back to buying from people they knew personally. In discussion, Rob Callendar soon determined that Patricia would best work from the pokies parlours and take part in occasional other pick-ups and deliveries.

From that moment, Patricia became more circumspect than ever. She disguised missions into town as shopping or work-related, constantly switched her venues and varied her approaches to them, and took care to put in obvious work hours at home, though much of it was not data collection for Statistics New Zealand but data collection for Rob Callendar. Gratifyingly, payment for her services began to flow, mostly in cash, and within weeks she was able to clear her debts including the relentless electricity bill that had seemed to hover over her life forever, causing such misery.

Simon soon became aware that Patricia was on top of her bills and was delighted when she contributed two thousand dollars towards the cost of the new septic tank. The next month she suggested they have a luxury weekend away, just the two of them, as a family friend was happy to look after Rosemary, and he embraced her and said how good life had become since she had focused on her work and given away pokies.

16

BETHANY FRONTS UP

Bethany Callendar took pride in knowing what was happening in her town. She received minutes of meetings of local bodies and read them. As patron, she took particular interest in the Tumanako branch of the Forest and Bird Society. She read with satisfaction of the society's stand against illegal drugs and phoned Simon Hurley to congratulate him.

'So pleased Simon you've addressed that matter. People don't realise how far the tentacles of the drugs industry reach.' She paused. 'Simon, have you seen Rob in your comings and goings recently?'

'As a matter of fact, I have Bethany. I saw him recently, at Hector Dunwoodie's. Didn't have much chance to have a word with him. Rob shot away just after I turned up.'

With the demonstration that had involved the totara tree still raw, Bethany inquired about the society's future activities. To be forewarned was to be forearmed.

'We've got a bird-watching trip coming up last Sunday of the month at Bushy Park Sanctuary, Whanganui. Vehicles depart at nine from the Cenotaph. A hundred hectares of predator-free native bush Bethany. Good chance to see some birds you might never have seen before and some magnificent native bush as well. And doing it in comfort – Devonshire teas in the Edwardian homestead.'

Unsure if she would be free, she pencilled it in her diary, wished him luck with it, and decided to pay a short surprise visit to Hector Dunwoodie. She had read Felicity Spratt's story in the *Mirror* and he was clearly one of the more interesting of her citizens. She had heard he was before his time and she would rather spend time with a free thinker than with the sycophantic social climbers she often had to tolerate. Besides, It would be good to get out of the office for an hour. Most appealing of all, Dunwoodie had been with Rob. As a courtesy, she phoned first. He sounded surprised but mildly welcoming.

'If you want. I'll be here.'

She half expected him to add, 'Whatever.' Hardly a fulsome welcome, but at least not hostile. When she pulled up in his driveway just twenty minutes later, she was reminded of the priceless advantage of being mayor of a small town.

Hector and Bertie immediately put her at ease. 'How ya going?' they both said and Bertie added, 'You're a genius'. She was relieved Hector was so relaxed. She had seen him in a manic phase at a meeting of the Forest and Bird Society and it had been very disconcerting. She could imagine him in such a phase gluing himself to a wall, throwing tomato sauce on a famous painting, cycling on to a runway to keep a private plane on the ground, changing his name to Less Carbon Now, or tying himself to a tree.

Hector offered to show her round the house – he presumed that was why she was visiting – but to his surprise she waived the offer and asked instead if they could have a cup of tea and a chat. He was happy to oblige and looked flattered now that the mayor should want to talk. She told him she had read Felicity's article and congratulated him on his enterprise. She then came quickly to the point of her visit.

'Hector, I believe you're in touch with Rob, my son.'

'Rob. Yes, I see him from time to time.'

Bethany thought she detected some unease. There was a slight tremor in Hector's right hand.

'I'll be honest with you Hector. I'm a mother out of touch with her son. Rob and I have fallen out and he wants nothing to do with me.'

'I'm sorry to hear that.'

She could see sympathy in his face. Hector lived on his own with no family as far as she aware, and certainly he would know of isolation and possibly estrangement. Bethany suspected Hector was part of Rob's drugs run. She did not know a lot about bipolar disorder but she did know from her time in social services, that those suffering from it could experience feelings of worthlessness and depression and perhaps Hector had been in that dark place and had turned to drugs.

'How did he seem to you?'

'All right. A bit strung out.'

'I'm worried about him.'

They sat in silence for some moments. Bertie softly chattered to himself.

'I don't know where he lives,' Hector said eventually. 'I can give you his phone number though.'

'Thank you.'

He knew it off by heart –significant, she thought – and wrote it down for her. It did not appear to be the one she already had which had drawn no response from him, so she slipped it gratefully into her bag and left.

'This is the very sort of publicity Tumanako does not need!' Alison Peabody was not only a long-time member of the town council but chair of Destination Tumanako. Her eyes narrowed and nostrils flared as she recalled the television programme of the previous night regarding Tumanako's war against illegal drugs. 'All the work we have done promoting Tumanako as a paradise for those who love the outdoors and a haven for those seeking rest and recreation, and now the whole of New Zealand sees us as a cesspit of drugs users where visitors take their lives in their hands as soon as they set foot in the place. This ill-advised campaign must stop immediately!'

'Hear, hear,' piped up Trevor Rudge, deputy chair of Destination Tumanako.

Bethany Callendar observed drolly that but for the shrillness of Alison Peabody's attack, Rudge would probably have remained quietly slumbering and the opposition would have been reduced by one. Now Maia Matenga was on her feet, fighting the good fight.

'Now, more than ever, we need to support the mayor's stand against the invasion of drugs in our community. So many of the problems of the town stem from the drugs. I was horrified to hear recently that there have been instances of our young people being approached by drugs touts in the street. The television programme presented our problems accurately and rather than condemn the programme, I move that we write to the producers and express our thanks to them.'

'Hear, hear,' said Rudge again, not fully awake. Alison Peabody shot him a look of contempt.

Back and forth went the argument until Bethany Callendar herself swung opinion firmly in favour of the anti-drugs campaign by displaying the great sheaf of letters of congratulations from other councils and from local schools and organisations. The coup d'état was a report from Rowley Rowlands detailing the number of arrests and indicating a downward trend in criminal behaviour. The meeting not only passed the motion of thanks to the television producers but passed a motion of thanks to the police.

It was tremendously satisfying for Bethany Calendar to emerge triumphant from having her campaign attacked from within. For all the occasional frustrations of the job, such moments made it worthwhile. Not that it had brought her any closer to Rob, she reflected as she drove home. Darkness had closed in by the time she approached the house and she felt a pang of fear as she activated the garage door. A memory stirred of headlights blazing and a vehicle threatening to ram her. She shivered. If someone were going to attack her, now would be the perfect time.

When she was safely in the house and her nerves had settled, she determined to have security lights and cameras installed right around the house.

◆ ◆ ◆

'I'd be lying if I didn't say the campaign wasn't taking its toll,' said Rowley Rowlands. 'On me.'

Bethany looked at him in surprise and then sympathy.

'It's not the extra activity. It's not even the extra paperwork. It's all these others coming into our patch and putting their spoke in.' He looked at her appealingly. 'How much longer are we going to keep it up?'

She could see his point of view. Not many people like others looking over their shoulder while they go about their work.

'It's gone beyond you and me now Rowley. The district

commander and the politicians are into it boots and all.'

She had to admit she had been taken aback by the tremendous response from the public to crush the drugs problem in Tumanako. The advocates for law and order had come out in force on talkback and in the newspapers and the politicians had leapt onto the bandwagon. Bethany considered herself centrist in her political views but she could see that she had unleashed a right-wing tide.

Rowley Rowlands dropped his head resignedly. 'Yes, I can see that. There are other regions taking it up now. One thing – the spotlight should go off us a bit and hopefully we can get back to normal.'

'A better normal,' Bethany said.

Rowlands nodded. 'We've given things a decent shakeup.'

'I think one of the best things you've done is to get more into the schools and work with the families.'

Rowlands agreed but his face then winced. 'One thing though bugs me to hell. Who is the linchpin in town for the drugs coming in from outside, and for the ingredients of the meth that's being made here?' He flexed his fingers as though he wanted to put them round the throat of the person or persons responsible.

Bethany could only look at him aghast and hope it wasn't her Rob.

On the following Saturday morning, Paul Calendar was at his office and Bethany was alone at home. She read the *Herald*, made herself a cup of percolated coffee, and looked out on her manicured back garden. One indulgence she had never regretted was hiring a part-time gardener. It had been wonderful having the pleasure of the garden without any of the pain. Not many people, she surmised, liked weeding. Having finished the coffee, she sat and meditated. Then, mind made up, she gathered her bag, ensuring she had her cell-phone, and went for a drive to the Railway Hotel and then along the country road where she had followed Rob. If only she could talk to him. She had tried the telephone number Hector had given her but it had been useless. The phone had rung and rung but nobody had picked up.

The first time she had travelled this way had been in the dark and all she had seen was the vegetation at the side of the road and the occasional gate, lamp post and road sign. The journey had been too dark and too fast for her to read any name. She had, as well, been too intent on the vehicle in front. And on the return trip, she had been too dazzled by the lights from behind and too terrified to see anything but the road directly in front. The memory made her sweat slightly and then the sweat turned to a clammy chill. Now, she passed several access roads to properties on both sides. She remembered how suddenly she had lost sight of Rob's vehicle and it wasn't as if she hadn't been looking – she had been glued to his tail light and the road had been fairly straight. He must, then, have turned off sharply and probably on the left-hand side of the road. She reckoned, too, it had been about half an hour's drive from the pub though she had been driving much faster that night.

On this return trip she had already been driving for about half an hour so she gave it another ten minutes. Then, rounding a bend, immediately on her left, was a turn-off obscured by a screed of bushes that would hide tail lights within seconds. She stopped just up the road, turned round with great care on the narrow road, and came back for another look. Not only were there bushes at the entrance, but the side road beyond turned sharp left and any vehicle that entered would vanish moments later. There were five rather ramshackle letter boxes by the roadside.

It was a better chance than most that it was the road Rob took. She quickly turned into it to get away from the bend and the risk of a crash, and drove between the bushes, emerging into open countryside. The landscape changed dramatically to wide, undulating, endless paddocks. The road stretched far out of sight, heading towards the ranges. It was shingle and one lane and she guessed it provided access only to the properties along it, though you never knew with some rural roads; it might link with another road beyond. She drove slowly onwards, on red alert, scrutinising, collecting herself. Then far in the distance, moving towards her, was a small cloud of dust. As it neared, she saw a man on a farm bike. She pulled onto the verge and got out. He stopped and turned off the motor. He was short and thick-set with a great shock of white hair poking out from under his cap and a face as seasoned as old leather.

'G'day,' he said. He looked at her as if he knew her but couldn't quite place who she was.

'Good morning,' she said. He continued to look at her quizzically and she wondered if it was because she was mayor or he was just curious about the presence of a stranger. The silence was filled by the cawing of a magpie and the bleat of a sheep. She realised she was interrupting his working day and came straight to the point. 'I'm looking for Rob Callendar.'

She could see now that he recognised her.

'Rob Callendar...Mrs Callendar isn't it?'

'Yes, that's right.'

For a moment he said nothing. She heart sank but then she remembered that country people often took their time. 'No, I don't know of any Rob Callendar in the valley...Family obviously.'

'My son.'

He looked at her intently, his interest piqued.

She didn't add to the story he would doubtless tell his own family later. Any curiosity the farmer might have had as to why the mayor didn't know her son's whereabouts remained unsatisfied.

He rubbed his chin. 'That's not to say he's not living here. There are some I don't know living in abandoned farm houses. Not all of them have a post box either. Tucked away well back from the road. All sorts living cheaply. You wouldn't know who you're living next to now.'

She thanked him and drove on for a few more kilometres and

then could see no point to it and turned back.

From an old homestead on a distant hilltop, Rob Callendar saw the car turn round for no obvious reason. It was a reminder he had to stay vigilant. He went back inside. There had been that other time a car had followed him from The Railway Hotel. He had ducked out of sight while another of the boys raced after it and sat on its bumper. Was it undercover police or another gang?

17

POLLY UNDER PRESSURE

The factory was as familiar as home to Polly Polson. All her life there had been the factory. In her first years at school, she had been the factory owner's grand-daughter and later the factory owner's daughter. With most of the other children's fathers being factory staff, that could have been a burden, making her the target of jealousy. But there were few sniping comments; her friendly nature and lack of pretence deflected any hostility. She was not mollycoddled at home. She did her share of work around the house and worked conscientiously at her holiday job in the factory office.

She worried about her father much more than about herself. One morning at breakfast she raised her concerns with her mother after Steve left for work.

'He's too quiet and withdrawn mum. He never used to be like that. The other day I saw him sitting in the porch beside Towser and they were both the picture of misery.'

'I've seen that too,' Stephanie Polson said. 'Dogs do pick up on the moods of their owners.'

They had acquired Towser, a labrador retriever, as a pup from a friend. He was even-tempered, friendly, and kind, and they all loved him. The love was reciprocated.

'Is dad getting enough sleep?' Polly asked. 'I know how ragged **I** feel if I'm missing out on sleep.'

'I'm not sure he is. He often tosses and turns in the night. I want him to phone the medical centre and see Tony.'

"Trouble is, even if he does, he might not open up,' Polly said. 'You know what he expects from others – don't complain, just get on with it.'

'I'll have a talk with him tonight and insist he makes an appointment with Tony.'

Polly thought of something else. 'We used to do more stuff together too mum. It's ages since we've been to the house at Mt Maunganui. We always have such a ball there. Dad loves the walk up the hill and then a dip in the hot pool at the bottom and lunch at the café on the corner.' Polly saw a wistful expression on her mother's face. She remembered Stephanie herself saying it was too easy to get caught up in the humdrum grind of everyday life. 'We've got that beautiful house there right on the beach and hardly ever use it.'

The Mt Maunganui section had been in the Polson family for three generations. Polly had seen the building on it evolve from a two-bedroom holiday bach made of fibrolite to a palatial six-bedroom, three-bathroom mansion of finest timber and tiles.

'With everything that's been going on, he deserves a break,' Stephanie said.

Polly knew her mother was referring to the three instances of sabotage. They both had that unnerving feeling that somebody meant them harm, and if they felt it, what must Steve be feeling as the owner/manager? The three cases to date had been comparatively insignificant with only minimal damage, though an addicted fisherman or rabid 'greenie' might disagree, but with the amount of chemicals on site, and the nature of them, there was potential for much more harm.

'The factory's got the increased security now so surely dad can leave the place for a weekend and we can go and enjoy ourselves at the Mount.'

'Good plan Polly. I'll make the doctor's appointment for him myself if I must, and write in that weekend on the calendar right now.'

◆ ◆ ◆

Polly considered inviting Daniel to join them for the weekend at Mt Maunganui but then dismissed the idea. As close as she and Daniel were, she believed that weekend should be just for the Polsons. It would be a time of healing for Steve particularly and she wanted nothing to interfere with that. At Mt Maunganui, the three of them would tap into many happy times through Polly's childhood and they could all properly unwind. Come to think of it, a week would be better than a weekend. With a weekend, they would barely be unwinding than they would be back at the workface. Still, even a weekend would be a start and they could have a proper break later.

One Saturday morning, Polly joined the Hurleys at the swimming pool to share Rosemary's delight. Once Rosemary's small, neat body was in the water, and she was beaming and laughing, she was just like anybody else. Rehabilitation experts had instructed parents and siblings how best to help Rosemary in the pool, and Polly had sat in on one of those sessions. Now Polly lent a hand in the aqua therapy. The expert had assured them the exercises, performed against the resistance of the water and assisted by its buoyancy, would not only increase Rosemary's muscular strength, but help with her balance. Benefits had quickly become apparent. The mental benefits were as important as the physical – Rosemary couldn't participate in most other sports and activities but she loved her sessions in the pool and looked forward to them all week.

One thought occasionally caused Polly a stab of anguish. Though it was never aired and could never be proved, Polly was aware the Hurleys suspected contamination from the factory site for Rosemary's condition and Polly felt a sense of associated guilt. She was sure it had increased her commitment to the green cause. Whatever the cause of Rosemary's spinal bifida, Polly would do whatever she could to ensure a cleaner, greener world. There was something else – her family had taken more than its share of nature's resources to create wealth and she was determined to give back.

In *Toni's – hairdressers of distinction*, Polly caught up with some of the town gossip. The proprietor was Toni Dalzell herself, celebrated rock climber and indomitable environmental warrior. Her effervescent personality suffused the salon and clients usually exited on a 'high'.

Polly loved the free and easy atmosphere of *Toni's,* and the banter. She was soon on the back foot trying to explain her relationship with Daniel Hurley.

'You mean you are simply friends,' Toni was saying. 'Not lovers.'

Polly could feel herself blushing beneath Toni's relentless probing of the relationship. 'We are more than just friends, but we are saving ourselves for long-term.'

'Saving yourselves for long-term? Extraordinary. How do you do that?'

Polly was totally flustered, briefly attempting an explanation but then giving up amidst laughter. Cindy Spratt joined wholeheartedly in the laughter. Toni's salon was such a contrast with the brisk and usually intense atmosphere of the real estate office. Toni recognised few barriers and spoke freely of her past relationships, hugely amusing the clientele with her ribald observations. Polly knew of a marriage break-up with a farmer somewhere up north and various other liaisons. Polly noted, though, that Toni was keeping quiet about her present relationship and she identified a way to take the pressure off herself.

'What about your own current love life Toni? You've not told us anything about that.'

Toni smiled, aware of Polly's ploy and not entirely letting her off the hook yet. 'I'm not altogether a tell-tale Polly. I do have some discretion. But I can assure you I am not saving myself for later, like you.'

Again, Polly found herself blushing to her roots but laughing along with the others. Rumour at Forest and Bird was that Toni was in a relationship with Valerie Tosswillow who had a dental practice in town, but like most stories about Toni Dalzell, it changed with the telling and where one or two of the more conservative might have seen her as a devouring femme fatale, others saw her as a delightful free spirit bringing much-needed liberation to the town. Polly revelled in her company. Toni, at twenty-seven, was only six years older than her in chronological years but half a lifetime in experience. She was also an avid 'greenie' and keen mountain biker. Polly knew there was only goodwill in Toni's banter.

Salvation for Polly from the teasing came from afar, in a phone call. It was not on the salon's telephone but on Toni's cell phone and Polly heard a vaguely familiar male voice before Toni disappeared with the call into the back room.

Polly pinched herself as the Polsons – all three of them – arrived at Mount Maunganui for the first time for months. Despite mild protests from Steve, they followed the family tradition of climbing The Mount itself, the large lava dome officially known by its Maori name *Mauao*. Their ascent, though, had none of the competitiveness of before. Steve and Stephanie puffed their way up from vantage point to vantage point towards the top, while Polly was 'tail-end Charlie'. On reaching the summit at two hundred and thirty-two metres above sea level, they could all see why it had once been the site of a pa and feel it in their spent legs and breath. The ascent always gave Polly a sense of history. She knew battles had been fought between Maori tribes on the Mount itself and at Pilot Bay at its base, and between British troops and Maori at nearby Gate Pa. Land was at the root of the latter conflict, and possibly the two former conflicts as well.

When Polly thought about it, the land and its resources was still at the crux of much conflict today, on a global scale, pitting ruthless developers against conservationists. The amount of plastic they had gathered in the beach clean-up along one tiny strip of coast had shocked her and that day she had reaffirmed her vow to personally do all she could to help her planet. In recent months the planet had been talking to them, saying 'Too much' and sending heat waves, forest fires and flash floods.

Steve Polson broke her train of thought. 'You know, looking out on all this, it seems incredible that the first house at Mt Maunganui was built as recently as 1906. Mr J.C. Adams was the owner and he had the privilege of having the street named after him.'

Polly's thoughts shifted to what was before her and she blinked at the contrast. From battles, fires, and floods she gazed out on an idyllic holiday scene. Tiny dots of people were riding the Pacific breakers to the shore while other dots were picnicking on the golden beach and under nearby trees.

Splendid buildings looked out over the beach and the sea and on the balcony of one of them, a woman scanned the scene with binoculars. Crowds thronged outside the cafés. Polly knew that at the base of Mauao, others would be luxuriating in the salt-water pools that were heated by hot bore water to a warmly caressing 39.9 degrees centigrade and she savoured the thought that soon the Polsons would be wallowing in them too. If she wished, she could use the hydrotherapy pool or have a massage.

As they descended, Polly considered the best thing about the excursion was the three of them being together at ease. And, as well, away from the factory. As much as she appreciated the living it gave them, she was pleased they were away from its chemicals, fumes, noise, and dust.

18

A SANCTUARY
BECKONS

Simon Hurley came off the phone after yet another vigorous debate with Hector Dunwoodie over Extinction Rebellion (XR).

'No, Tumanako's too small for that Hector. We would antagonise the whole town,' were his parting words.

The tactic of XR, formed in the United Kingdom in 2018, was to use non-violent civil disobedience to achieve lasting change. The symbol of the movement was a stylised, circled hourglass, known as the extinction symbol, to serve as a warning that time is rapidly running out for many species. Twice, XR had brought central London to a standstill for days.

'Can you imagine our group attempting to bring central Tumanako to a standstill for days?' he said to the others over breakfast.

'Would anyone notice?' Daniel asked.

'There is one other who would vote with Hector to support it,' Patricia said.

They all knew who she was talking about. Simon had seen signs though that Toni Dalzell was becoming more circumspect since her scare at the beach clean-up. She had been more subdued at the last Forest and Bird meeting. Besides, arrest for civil disobedience would be distinctly unhelpful for her hairdressing salon.

Discussion soon turned to the One Plastic-free Day campaign which the Tumanako branch of Forest and Bird was launching that day. They would each take a picture of an object they wished to avoid using plastic for, post it on social media, and encourage others to do the same.

'Straws,' said Charlotte.

'Disposable wipes.' Rosemary.

'Chip and snack bags.' Daniel.

Simon needed a moment but then his eye fell on his recently purchased biodegradable natural adhesive bandage strips alongside an old packet of the traditional ones in the cupboard.

'Bandages.'

Mention of disposable bandages had clearly impressed but Patricia drew most accolades.

'Receipts.'

Yes, so many receipts, containing plastic, were testimony forever in landfills to people's profligacy.

'And speaking of receipts,' she continued. 'Here's the receipt for an early Christmas present I've bought us.'

She gave the receipt to Simon with the widest smile.

Again, he was momentarily lost for words before gathering himself. The receipt was for a new music system and on the accompanying brochure Simon read of satellite speakers, four-hundred-watt peak power, multi-device capable with tuneable EQ – whatever that was – and THX-certified sound quality.

'A sound system?'

'We've never had a proper one and I thought why not?' Patricia said.

The brochure quickly found its way into Daniel's hand and then the sound system itself was out of its package and, at Patricia's choice, filling the house with the luscious, resonant sound of *Unchained Melody* by the Righteous Brothers.

They all gave Patricia a hug and thanked her. The whole family loved music and Patricia's gift would enrich their lives. Simon was delighted she had stopped gambling on the pokies and had turned her finances around. Daniel and Charlotte, too, were proud of her and later Daniel murmured to Charlotte, 'Thank goodness we saw her in the pokies parlour and made her face reality.'

Patricia still occasionally disappeared. Sometimes she said she was doing fieldwork for her data collection and at other times she said she was entitled to some 'Me' time too.

It was the first visit of the Tumanako branch of Forest and Bird to the Tarapuruhi Bushy Park Sanctuary, twenty-five kilometres from Whanganui City, and members rejoiced at the fine weather as they travelled through forest and farmland down State Highway One and then State Highway Three. The pale glass of the sky turned to blue and the sun raised small clouds of steam from ground damp from showers the previous day.

Members brought with them a trip sheet compiled as usual by president Simon Hurley. It explained that Tarapuruhi Bushy Park was a hundred-hectare, predator-free native bird sanctuary set amongst virgin, lowland forest. In 1962 the sanctuary had been bequeathed by the landowner, Mr G.F. Moore, to the Royal New Zealand Forest and Bird Protection Society and hence to the public of New Zealand. There was accommodation available and some members were staying overnight. The sanctuary had three- point- four kilometres of well-formed walking tracks suitable for Rosemary's wheelchair. From the tracks, members could expect to see korimako/bellbirds, kereru, North Island robins, tieke/saddlebacks, hihi, piwakawaka/fantails, grey warblers, pukeko, tauhou/silvereyes, sacred kingfishers, and white-faced herons, amongst many other species. The sanctuary was home to kiwi but members had almost no chance of that sighting unless they were staying overnight. Patricia was not with the group, citing work pressure, and neither were Polly (holidaying with her parents at Mt Maunganui) and Daniel and Charlotte (boosting their earnings at their holiday jobs).

After the long drive, everyone headed into the heritage homestead for its bathrooms and Devonshire teas. Then, refreshed and replenished and eager to explore, club members vanished into the bush in twos, threes, and fours so that in moments Simon discovered that he was not only club president, organiser of the outing, and producer of the trip sheet, but also custodian of lost property (one member had dropped her cardigan) and care person of Rosemary, a role usually shared with Patricia, Polly, Daniel, or Charlotte. Simon did not mind that role in the least. It would be a lovely memory for the two of them to share and he knew that Rosemary would be bubbling to tell the others all about it on return.

As Simon looked around and listened, it was as if the forest had swallowed up the others for all he and Rosemary heard was the occasional call of a bird. Simon reminded himself that nature lovers did tend to move with the silence and stealth of jungle guerrilla fighters. He and Rosemary shared an interest in the flora as well as the fauna and, using their map, headed towards a large northern rata named Rätänui which was estimated to be between five hundred and a thousand years old. It was forty-three metres high with a girth of over eleven metres. Simon mused that it might even have been growing here when the land was empty of people.

Rosemary could propel herself on the flat, firm track and Simon could see she was entranced to be amidst the forest. Her head turned constantly as she identified tree species and peered for birds. Mahoe and rimu reached for the sky and high to his left he heard a korimako/bellbird, loud and clear. The path led to a swampy, open area and Rosemary was thrilled to see a white-faced heron. She knew that two or more had flown over from Australia in the 1940s, liked the look of the place, and stayed here. Simon and Rosemary stopped and admired it and then Rosemary pushed herself onto the boardwalk that crossed the swamp to forest on the other side. The boardwalk was damp and slippery and the water each side looked deep. Simon quickly took hold of the handles of her wheelchair and carefully steered a middle course. Rosemary pointed excitedly overhead at the Australasian swamp harrier that was circling. Then they were off the boardwalk and in the shadows of the forest. They were sharing the forest with tens of other nature lovers but to all intents father and daughter were alone, creating a treasured memory. A harsh screech high in the forest canopy to their right got their attention.

'Long-tailed cuckoo.' Rosemary knew the sound well from the recording of bird sounds she had played so often it was in danger of wearing out.

'Extraordinary bird,' said Simon. 'Back now from the Pacific islands.'

The long-tailed cuckoo was one of the long-distance flyers and navigators. In winter, it migrated north. The bird they had heard could recently have been anywhere from Micronesia in the west to the Pitcairn Islands in the east. In flight, its tail was as long as its body. The species lays a single egg in the nest of much smaller birds so that the chicks have host parents. Simon was aware that twitchers were sometimes regarded as oddities, like train spotters, but as he often said to the others, who could not marvel at the birds on knowing of their amazing ways?

Simon stepped off the path to get a glimpse of the bird. It fed on cicadas, lizards and other invertebrates that could be anywhere from ground level up, but it preferred to be deep in the forest canopy. He would be lucky to sight it but nothing ventured, nothing gained. He pressed on to the next tree and then the next, peering for the bird brown on top, with long beak and long tail feathers. But nothing. Then another faint sound, a cry, more human than avian. He turned back, with a shudder.

In moments he was back on the path but Rosemary wasn't there. Simon began shouting 'Rosie!' Behind was the swamp they had come from; ahead was the path winding deeper into the forest. She would surely not have turned back without him; the boardwalk would be too hazardous on her own. But he ran back to check, calling her name. Silence. Then he turned and took the path ahead that wound out of sight. Panic began to clutch at his heart.

Please God let me see her. What was that cry about? Rosie where are you?

'Rosie! Rosie! Rosie!'

But only the forest looked back at him and his last call hung on the air.

It was Melody Gilmour who found her. Melody had been nearby with two others and had hurried to Simon's shouts. She had seen crushed vegetation at the side of the track and then Rosemary's wheelchair at a crazy angle down the bank. She shouted to the others and clambered down after it. Rosemary had been tossed out and was sprawled at the base of a tree, motionless. Blood trickled from her nose and she was deathly pale. Melody shouted again and Simon hurtled down the bank in giant strides and knelt by Rosemary. He checked for vital signs, praying she had not cracked her head against the tree. Then he felt the faintest of breaths and felt a pulse. He prayed she had landed on the bank itself with its cushioning ferns and mosses.

If she'd hit her head on the tree...

He put her with great care into the recovery position and covered her with his coat. As he watched her coming around, beginning to shiver from the dampness of the ground, he felt faint and nauseous himself. He could see how it had happened. Being full of curiosity and an explorer at heart, Rosemary had pushed on a little further and hadn't seen how the ground fell away on the last bend. One wrong push followed by another and she was over the bank and out of control.

Melody, assisted by two others, dragged the wheelchair back up the bank onto the path. It appeared to be undamaged. Simon was not sure he could say the same about Rosemary. She would have to be checked at Whanganui Hospital. She was at least talking now and could move her arms freely. She said she felt only shaken and sore. When her head cleared and she was breathing better, she asked to be carried back to the path and the wheelchair. Simon and others raised her carefully and carried her cradle-style in their arms up a gentle rise a little further along. Then, with a good recovery seemingly achieved, no sooner was Rosemary back in the wheelchair than she lost control of her bowels. She was mortified; the trip into nature's paradise had become a nightmare.

Rosemary remained in Whanganui Hospital overnight for observation. Simon believed she had been unconscious for a time and the medical staff were concerned about possible after-effects of the shock. Simon stayed in a nearby motel. When he called home to explain the situation, Daniel took the call. Simon calmed his and Charlotte's fears. They would tell Patricia when she returned from town. When Patricia phoned in the early evening, Simon assured her Rosemary was in good hands and was resting. He said the incident had happened so quickly. Her comment was so faint he had to ask her to repeat it.

'I should have been there.'

'You had your work to do. You've been doing so well lately.'

'No. I should have been there.'

They had an unspoken agreement that Rosemary would never be left alone in an unfamiliar setting.

Simon and Rosemary arrived home to hugs and kisses of relief. Rosemary appeared to have bounced back well from the trauma. Later, when the others had gone to bed, Daniel made a tentative approach to say something to Simon. Then he seemed to think better of it and trailed off into silence. Simon encouraged him to say what was on his mind. Daniel said he and Charlotte had seen Patricia in a pokies parlour.

'We talked about that,' Simon said. 'That was before. She's stopped that now. You've seen how she's turned things around.'

Daniel looked at him as though he wasn't convinced.

Over the next week, the son's uncertainties transferred to the father. When Patricia left for town the following Saturday, leaving Simon and Charlotte at home with Rosemary, Simon followed her. He was careful to stay just close enough to keep her in sight. He saw her park on a side street in town and get out and walk. It was no saunter – she walked with purpose and Simon had a good idea where she was going. Nearby was a small bar – *The Thirsty Fish* – and at the back of it was a pokies parlour. She disappeared up a lane leading to the bar.

When Simon entered the bar, only a bar man was there. Simon carried on, feeling sick at heart, bracing himself for the ugly confrontation to come. There were seven people there. But Patricia was not one of them. She wasn't there. He had been wrong. As the truth of that sunk in, he felt profoundly relieved and, at the same time, disappointed in himself for suspecting her. And when he stepped out onto the street, there she was, approaching from the other direction, expressing surprise that he was in town as well.

It was now Patricia's turn to sigh with relief. She had seen him following her, ducked into the lane beyond *The Thirsty Fish* and crossed to the other side of the street after Simon entered the pub.

19

BOMBSHELL FOR BETHANY

V itriol was flying at the Tumanako council meeting. The monthly police report from Rowley Rowlands had been received and three councillors had commented favourably on the fifteen drugs-related convictions. That was more than usual but fewer than the previous month and Rowlands expected the downward trend to continue. He wrote that other police districts appeared to be following Tumanako's lead.

'That's all very well,' said Alison Peabody, 'but the damage has been done. A visitor to town was overheard to urge her daughter to get her shopping done quickly and get the hell out of town as it was full of druggies. This list of drugs convictions can only confirm that visitor's fears. Anyone would think Tumanako is the drugs capital of New Zealand and that senior sergeant Rowlands is Eliot Ness at war against the Chicago mob. Destination Tumanako now has a tremendously difficult job to ensure visitors that the town is safe for the whole family.'

Trevor Rudge rose laboriously to his feet.

'Councillor Peabody is quite correct. We want visitors to feel safe, to know that they can stop in Tumanako, stay a night or two, visit the town's attractions and get a good feed. Not have to worry about drugs, assaults, and thefts. The sooner the over-the-top anti-drugs campaign finishes here, the better. Anyone would think we were Soddem and Gomorrah.'

Maia Matenga ignored the comments of Peabody and Rudge. She complimented Rowley Rowlands on his report, and moved that the police be congratulated on their work. Bethany Callendar seconded the motion and it was carried by ten votes to two.

An incident at the northern entrance of town the following day became the talk of the town. At a roundabout, a driver made a wrong judgment and collided hard with a logging truck. His mistake cost him his life. When comments emerged from family that the driver had been harassed by police over drugs, Peabody and Rudge had a field day.

'That poor man,' said Alison Peabody, 'badgered by the police beyond distraction. He was probably so worried that he didn't pay due attention and drove straight into the path of the logging truck.'

'Drugs, drugs, drugs,' said Trevor Rudge. 'That's all people talk about. There never used to be any of that. Let's get back to normal and give people space to do their thing without harassment.'

Bethany Callendar, while passing her condolences on to the family of the deceased, drew people's attention to the coroner's report that found the driver of the car had been profoundly under the influence of methamphetamine. One thing all parties agreed on was sympathy for the driver of the logging truck.

Bethany Callendar discussed the incident face-to-face with Rowley Rowlands. 'Have you any idea who supplied him with the drugs?'

'There are people of interest.'

She steeled herself. 'Is Rob one of them?'

He looked her in the eye and grimaced. 'He could be. I can't be sure.'

They sat in silence.

'You'd tell me, wouldn't you?...I'd rather have him in prison being treated than killing himself with drugs somewhere out there.'

'I know.'

She had to wonder though, when they parted, whether Rowley Rowlands knew more than he was letting on.

◆ ◆ ◆

Bethany Callendar had begun to be troubled by insomnia. It had started on the night she had felt troubled in the car as she approached her garage. She lay on her back, her mind whirling.

Is it fear for me or fear for Rob? Where is he? What's become of him? He's so thin, so jittery. That vehicle harassing me. The bottle through the window of the newspaper office. Perhaps it's nothing to do with that. My broken home life. So many meetings. Trying to squeeze in time to see Paul. Our lives so out of sync. Sometimes I don't even know where Paul is.

Sometimes she would get up, make herself a cup of tea, read for twenty minutes or so and then go back to bed. Usually, she would eventually fall asleep. The security lights and cameras at their home had helped ease her mind. She had mentioned the lights and cameras to Rowley Rowlands and received his nod of approval. Paul had considered them an over-reaction but she put that down to his wanting to minimise alarm. Either that or being reluctant to spend the money.

One Saturday afternoon when she was in the house alone and in idle mood – Paul was playing golf – she re-ran the camera over the door to test its effectiveness. She set the time to seven in the evening, two nights before, when she was attending the council's finance committee meeting. The sharpness of the picture was impressive and its range was wide enough to show the flowering cherry near the front door to advantage. A neighbour's cat briefly appeared. Then a shower of rain was captured. The clarity was amazing – individual raindrops, clear as you like. Half-asleep, she let the film run. Until something wrenched her wide awake with her heart thumping. It was Paul. He glanced for a moment directly into the camera. There was someone behind him but so shielded Bethany could not make out who it was. They disappeared into the house. Bethany re-ran that section of film, once, twice, three times, and then so many times she couldn't say, each time stopping it at the first sight of Paul when the other person was most discernible. The glimpse of a breast made it obvious it was a woman. Bethany felt sick in the pit of her stomach. She realised she was breathless; her heart was going too fast. He had never strayed before, at least as far as she knew. For minutes stretching to more than an hour, she sat and mulled over her discovery. She knew she must confront him and face whatever uncertainties the future held.

When she heard his car late in the afternoon, her heart started thumping again and she felt faint. He entered the house with triumph. She heard him before she saw him.

'Hello dear. Get ready to look at the winner of the stableford! I don't think I've ever putted better. Just twenty-four putts.'

Normally her face would have been alight at his success and they would have celebrated with a glass of wine. Now his smile froze.

'What is it?'

'I ran the film from the security camera. From when I was at the finance committee on Thursday night.'

Paul glanced away and then turned back, sombre. 'Thursday night.' He paused. 'Tanya was here, helping me with a swag of tax returns that had come in…You didn't think…'

Tanya Spring, his assistant at the office. Totally professional. Regular attender of the Presbyterian church and on the Parent Teacher Association. Lovely Tanya, a pillar of the community.

Bethany gasped. She hadn't realised she'd been holding her breath. She felt foolish and unfair. She had immediately jumped to the worst conclusion and only on the evidence of an obscure picture. *What's happening to me? My distress over Rob is colouring my whole world?*

'I'm sorry. I thought…'

He turned and disappeared into the kitchen. Moments later she heard the kettle boiling. Then he was back, sprawled in his favourite chair, with a cup of coffee. Bethany went to the sideboard and poured them each a generous glass of Pinot Noir.

'Let's celebrate your success.'

◆ ◆ ◆

That night, though, in the small hours, Bethany mulled over the peculiar manner of Tanya Spring's entry into the house. She had been standing too close to Paul and he had appeared to be concealing her as best he could.

On the following Monday, Bethany dropped into Paul's work. Paul was out of sight in his office overlooking the street, possibly with a client. Tanya Spring occupied the immediate work place. She and Bethany had been friends for years.

'Bethany. So good to see you.' A woman of medium height, immaculately presented, she rose from her chair and approached with arms wide. They hugged, Tanya more wholeheartedly than Bethany.

'Tanya. It's been a while.'

'We all get caught up in our busy lives, don't we. We need to take a break more often and have a coffee to get things in perspective. It's been rush, rush, rush around here, that's for sure. And I bet the work of a mayor is never done.'

They chatted about family and then Bethany, heart in mouth, switched the subject back to work.

'Thank you, by the way, for taking the trouble to help Paul on Thursday night at our house.'

Tanya appeared momentarily taken aback but quickly regathered her composure. 'Oh, that was no trouble at all. This is a crazy time of year for us and Paul needed a hand. I was happy to help.'

There is a God in heaven. I trust this woman absolutely. Should Tanya be unfaithful with my husband, the entire moral compass of the world is askew and there is no hope for any of us.

Bethany took her leave with a light heart and a light step.

But Bethany was not to know that when Tanya Spring had paused, she had been taken aback by Bethany's use of the word 'night'. When she had helped Paul out at home, it had simply been to deliver work papers and it had been late on the Thursday afternoon, not at night. After delivering the papers, Tanya had gone straight home to prepare dinner for her family.

20

FINGERS POINTED UNFAIRLY

A CCTV camera at the factory showed that the fire began with wisps of smoke and flashes of flame. Investigators endlessly replayed the film but no one was seen until the brigade arrived when men wielding hoses thick as anacondas filled the picture. The cause remained a mystery. At first an electrical fault was suspected but that was ruled out. Nothing suspicious like petrol cans, lighters, or matches was found.

It was the night watchman, Gordon Frame, who phoned it in. Despite a penchant for having *Best Bets* always handy, he was conscientious at his job and regularly checked the premises. He confided later that when he saw the flames, he was shocked to his bootlaces, but he was straight through to the fire brigade and they were there within minutes. Steve Polson was told that the sprinkler system was on the point of being activated but still, without Frame's prompt action, the damage to the factory would have been much worse. There was only a charred wall and Steve Polson personally thanked Frame. It had been a better appointment than the previous one.

The deluge of water used to fight the fire caused more damage than the fire itself. The water inevitably went further than the immediate site into storage areas and became contaminated with a cocktail of hazardous substances used in timber treatment. These included toxic wood preservation chemicals such as pentachlorophenol, pesticides, polynuclear aromatic hydrocarbons and compounds of chrome, copper, and arsenic. There could as well have been toxic chemicals such as tannins, phenols, resins, and fatty acids leached from the timber and soil. The factory had strengthened its defences against a spill since the last incident but, when there is an abundance of it, water has a habit of penetrating the strongest barriers. Despite the best efforts of the fire service, the noxious stream flowed the short distance from the factory to the river and the next day a warning went out to all the property owners downstream and to the public.

There was uproar from all the tiny communities down to the coast. As Bethany Callendar said to Steve Polson, it was fuelled by fear of the unknown more than fear of the immediate pollution. In Tumanako, people began to look at others sideways. The offender or offenders could be hidden in plain sight right in their midst. Did anyone really know his neighbour?

It was now the investigation had an unfortunate side-effect. Suspicious eyes turned on the eccentrics of the district. They were harried and hustled by self-appointed vigilantes and questioned at length by the police who were duty-bound to follow-up the denunciations. The self-righteous turned on the most vulnerable of all – the harmless souls who had withdrawn into themselves to find their peace. In the cities, these casualties of life could drift anonymously from day to day but in towns they were too readily apparent. Old Gymshoe Jim, stalking the streets and lanes at all hours, mind whirling with who knew what, was reported to the police and visited and questioned by Rowley Rowlands. Mad Tom was another who writhed at the end of a finger of suspicion.

Hector Dunwoodie became a person of interest. Not only was he an eccentric living on the outskirts of town with a parrot, carrying out bizarre experiments, he was a 'greenie' and a known extremist. One especially rabid denunciator said it would be better for Hector's own sake if he were taken into care before he harmed himself or someone else. In truth, the town would have been better if the denunciator himself had been incarcerated, but some began to nod in agreement with him as Hector had been seen near the factory at dusk on the day of the fire.

The next time Hector was in town, he came back to his electric van to find a flat tire. It was years since he had had a 'flattie' but he set to and changed the wheel. When it happened again, two days later, he looked around to see if anyone was lurking and sensed one or two looking at him.

Rowley Rowlands picked up on the rumours and thought he better pay Hector a visit. It might rule the man out as a suspect and help squash talk that Rowlands was spending too much time on drugs and not enough time on the sabotage. He had always regarded Hector as a harmless eccentric and occasional public nuisance. He understood he had a medical condition but that did not give licence to tie himself to trees in the main street or otherwise run amuck.

Bertie welcomed him in with, 'Who's a pretty boy then?'

Rowlands had to smile. Hector had given Bertie an hour out of the enclosure shortly before and Bertie looked content now to be back enclosed, nibbling on his fruit and nuts. When he lowered his head, Rowlands obliged and gave it a rub.

'Somebody let my tyres down in town the other day. It's happened twice.'

Rowlands turned away from Bertie, frowning. 'I'm sorry to hear that.' He sat at Hector's invitation and accepted the offer of a cup of tea. 'People are worried about the factory. You know, the incidents up there.'

'Nothing to do with me. I can't say I like some of the things that go on up there with the chemicals but that's a battle someone else can fight.'

'You were seen near the factory in the early evening of the fire.'

Hector looked away. 'Yes, I was up there. Just before closing. Picking up some shingle for a pathway.'

Rowlands took up Hector's invitation to have a look around. He looked inside and out with a policeman's eye, toured the workshop, was rivetted by the sight of the exoskeleton, had his attention drawn to the new shingle pathway and by the time he exited through the vegetable garden, was not sure he was ready for the brave new world that was coming.

'An auber, you say. With hearty texture inside that is a substitute for meat.'

He was still shaking his head when he drove away. At the end of a tough day, he was sure an auber would not do it as much as a lamb chop with mint sauce. He didn't know much about Hector's stuff, but he did consider himself a good judge of people, and he would have been surprised if Hector was the saboteur.

◆ ◆ ◆

One glance at her father at an unguarded moment, and Polly could see that the benefits of the weekend away at Mount Maunganui were dissipated. He sat with head down and face drawn, and even Towser, their adored Labrador, had picked up on his mood and moped at his feet. Despite no injuries and minimal damage, the fire had knocked the stuffing out of Steve Polson. It hadn't helped that the ramifications were ongoing.

'Endless bloody explanations to be given and forms to fill out,' Polly heard him lamenting to Stephanie, 'and most of the damage caused by the water from the fire brigade.'

'Thank heavens for the brigade though,' Stephanie said. 'We have to be grateful. A lot of them volunteers, dashing away from whatever they were doing.'

Steve conceded that was true and said he would donate to their Christmas fund.

The following night Polly heard him say to Stephanie, 'I

sometimes feel as though I'm not here, that I'm outside my body looking down at myself. Other times I've driven somewhere and can't remember how I got there. It's like that period of my life was blank.'

In the silence that followed, Polly could picture them, in the adjoining room, sunk in gloom. Her mother's face would be creased in concern and her father's sombre as a tombstone, so unlike their usual selves.

'Steve, you need to go back to Tony,' Polly heard Stephanie say. 'Whatever he said to you and whatever he gave you last time, helped.'

Polly knew that Tony Hartshorn, their GP, was one of the 'good guys'. He had looked under the weather himself the last time Polly had seen him. A case of physician needing to heal himself.

'Something to help me sleep would be a good start,' Steve said. 'At three in the morning I'm sometimes just lying there worrying, waiting for the danger round the corner.'

'I know you are dear.'

Polly could wait no longer. She entered the room and gave him a hug she didn't want to end.

What a difference a day and a pernicious rumour can make, for the very next evening Polly and her father were at daggers drawn.

Steve Polson remained at the kitchen table after dinner, frowning. 'There's talk at the factory of that dingbat Hector Dunwoodie being the saboteur.'

It was the first time Polly had heard him speak so overtly of a saboteur, let alone accuse someone.

'It would never be Hector. No way. And he's not a dingbat.'

'They say he was hanging around the factory late that afternoon and nobody saw where he went afterwards.'

'Hector would never do anything that would harm the environment. He cares too much about people to do that.'

'Can you be sure what he'd do? Isn't he the one who tied himself to the totara tree? He sounds like a loose cannon who needs to be locked up.'

'Hector's bipolar but he's a lovely man. He's always thinking of things that can help people.' Polly looked at her father who was so gloomy, so sad. 'Dad, this isn't like you. You always see the best in people.'

He shrugged and went to bed.

The next day Daniel Hurley visited Polly at home. Steve Polson was at the factory and Stephanie was in town. Polly, still raw from her clash with her father, explained what had happened.

'It's not like dad at all. It's like he's become someone else.'

Polly could see that Daniel was dismayed. Daniel had known her father all his life and had always looked up to him. Steve Polson too, through Daniel's job, was helping to pay his way through university.

'He probably feels he's carrying the whole town on his back.'

'That's why we got away to the Mount, to give him a break. Now, with this latest thing, we're back where we started.'

Daniel sat in silence. Polly could see a mirror of her own disbelief that Hector Dunwoodie was the saboteur. Next moment there was an arm round Polly's shoulder and Daniel was hugging her. She turned and kissed him and he kissed her back.

When Stephanie came through the door, they hastily disentangled. Stephanie discreetly left the room and shortly afterwards, Daniel left.

It had not been difficult to find a theme for the next demonstration of the Tumanako branch of the Forest and Bird Society. Simon Hurley, in the course of ongoing research, had discovered that some eight hundred million people in the world did not have enough to eat and, at the same time, that one third of the food produced in the world was never consumed. He also discovered that eight percent of greenhouse gas emissions worldwide were due to food waste partly because when food ends up in landfill, it produces methane. Simon was so appalled, he was momentarily paralysed.

Soon, the Hurley family and other club members were busy making banners and the campaign began. Melody Gilmour made the importance of not wasting food a theme at the school and was staggered by the good feedback from parents, grandparents, and the children themselves.

'My grannie said she had to eat what was put in front of her or she went to bed hungry,' one boy reported.

A grandfather sent a note congratulating her, saying he had always eaten everything but had drawn the line at tripe and onions, sheep's brains, and black pudding.

Some parents remarked to Melody that their children had got quite cranky about it and were telling off siblings who left food on their plates, and that the parents themselves had been inspired to recycle any left-overs into other meals.

The club's display on a Saturday morning in town was arguably the best received of all their presentations. There was widespread admiration of the 'Forget best before and just eat it' and 'Don't dispose, donate' banners, and the pile of papers with recipes to transform wasted ingredients into delicious meals was gone within an hour. The astute observer would have noticed that all the food packaging on display was biodegradable.

21

TURNING POINT

The petrol bomb through the window of The Tararua Mirror had lingering effects for Felicity Spratt. All very well for the head newspaper honchos in Auckland to gloat over the rise in circulation and the increase in advertising revenue, but Felicity woke several times from nightmares of such a bottle smashing through the window of her flat. And was it a coincidence, that vehicles blinked an indicator at her from a distance and then drove away as she neared?

Was the satisfaction of being an investigative reporter worth it? There had been much laudatory feedback but also grumblings that she was fostering a negative image of Tumanako. She had found an unexpected ally in her father. Unexpected because they were usually on opposite sides of public issues, she to the left, he to the right, but as an avowed 'law and order' man, he had texted his congratulations at every article. Thinking of her father led to thinking of her mother, standing in the shadows behind him. Felicity sensed a free spirit there waiting to break out. There might have been comfort for her mother in never having to decide for herself, but to Felicity's mind, it came at a heavy cost.

'You have started something you know,' Colin Trainor said to her one day in the office. 'Rowley Rowlands told me that people on the fringes are coming forward with useful information. They've had enough of family members getting caught up in drugs.'

'Not surprising,' Felicity said. 'The violence and intimidation that goes along with it.' Another thought struck her. 'It's so duplicitous. There are people in collar and tie and sitting on committees who help keep it all going by doing a bit of drug-taking on the side. And not just weed.'

Drugs counsellor Raymond Proctor had opened her eyes to the extent of illegal drug use as well as impact on the family. He had introduced her to Henry Taylor, a former gang member who had an epiphany one day after the death of a nephew from a drugs overdose. Her interview with Taylor had been the basis of an article. He had spoken to her on condition of anonymity.

'There's probably not a lot further you can take it, is there? You've covered all the angles.'

She could see in the slightly anxious expression what Colin Trainor was getting at. He and Pru Hardacre had been the ones to pick up the pieces of broken glass and clean the carpet after the police had finished their investigation. She could see concern for her personally.

'No, there probably isn't. Unless I can identify the contact in Tumanako for most of the drugs coming in from outside. It's too well organised to be random.'

'When you get as specific as that, you're moving into Rowley Rowlands' territory.' He looked out the window at Tumanako commencing another day and then back at her. 'I think it's time to wrap up the series Felicity. You can always write a news report if there's a development.'

She nodded. She was ready to move on. She thought of Bethany Callendar and Rob. A part of her would have loved to write about the mayor and the son who had turned bad. It would have gone far beyond the town itself. But it was too personal and there were issues of confidentiality.

'There's plenty else,' Trainor said. 'The on-going saga of the sabotage at Polson's needs looking into.'

Felicity's reporter's instinct perked up at that. Yes, there was a story there. Right under her nose. Even better, she knew all the key players at the factory personally and there were no issues of confidentiality.

Her father expressed regret that Felicity's series on illegal drugs was coming to an end but her mother was relieved

Felicity returned to her series on local personalities. Next, Bac Nam Nguyen.

I came to New Zealand with my parents,' he told her. 'They are dead now.' He briefly brought his hands together in a prayer gesture. 'I was only four, but I remember some of it.' He looked far away and then through the window at his children playing

in the backyard. 'We ran away in the night with nothing. All my parents' money was for the ticket on the boat.' He winced and looked sad. 'Terrible. Hardly any food or water. There were pirates. A storm might have saved us for the pirates left in a hurry. Our boat began to leak. At last, a ship came and towed us. We were in Indonesia. There was a camp.'

He paused and Felicity wondered if she should stop there for old wounds were reopening.

'Bac Nam, if it is too much.'

He waved away her concern. 'In Indonesia my parents applied for asylum. The camp was very overcrowded and there was much sickness. Some died. We were lucky – we were there just three years. Some more than ten years. New Zealand accepted us and we arrived in Auckland in 1979. Most Vietnamese refugees were in Auckland, Wellington, and Christchurch but we came with four other refugee families to Tumanako. We were friends with them in the camp. Our families were sponsored in Tumanako by the Rotary club. We are very grateful.'

'What did you think of Tumanako?

'It was a safe place. My father got a job in a fish shop and later in the factory. We had food. Our life was good.' Then he remembered something else and smiled. 'But it was so cold at first. Like living in a refrigerator. Our clothes were hard as a board on the washing line in the morning. And one night our chickens froze.'

'What about you? How was it for you? Such a big change.'

'Better for me I think than my parents. They had lost their family in Vietnam. Some killed, some left behind. And I learnt English quicker than them and got used to New Zealand ways much faster. At home we spoke Vietnamese but otherwise for me it was mostly all English. I translated for my parents and answered many of the people who came to the door, and the letters.'

'They must have felt powerless.'

'Yes, very difficult for them.'

'Where did you meet Linh?'

'We met in Auckland. Introduced by friends. We married the next year. We have the three children, James, Ben, and Helen.'

'Typical Kiwi family.'

Bac Nam Nguyen laughed. 'Not completely.'

Felicity delved into other adjustments migrants to New Zealand had to make. When she asked if people ever took advantage of the migrants, his answer set her pulse racing.

'There are bad people who try to use us to carry their drugs.'

Felicity's pen momentarily stopped its shorthand. 'Which bad people? In New Zealand?'

'Sometimes. But mainly over there. When our people go back to visit family, the criminals sometimes ask them to help them. We would never do that. Our families are too precious to us.'

She was aware from her research that most illegal traffic to New Zealand was from Asia though there were significant drugs from Mexico too. The drugs originated in the 'Golden Triangle' of Myanmar, Thailand, and Laos where the borders met at the junction of the Mekong and Ruak Rivers. The region had been known for a long time for its opium and heroin trade, but Felicity had learnt that it was now also one of the biggest producers and distributors in the world of synthetic drugs. Clandestine laboratories pumped out crystal and tablet methamphetamines by the tonne for militia groups and organised crime syndicates. The thick bush and rugged terrain made it difficult for Thai police to patrol but they still confiscated huge amounts of methamphetamine pills, ice, heroin, ketamine, and chemicals used to make illegal drugs. The drugs that got through were trafficked on by sea, air and even parcel post to other countries, including Australia and New Zealand. Once they arrived in New Zealand, a distribution network moved them throughout city, town, and hamlet. From clan lab in the hills of Myanmar, they arrived at pubs and elsewhere in Tumanako.

As Felicity shared a traditional meal of pho (beef noodle broth) with the family, steaming hot and delicious, she pondered the information Bac Nam Nguyen had given her.

The next day an incident convinced Felicity it was time to wind up her probe into drugs. A night-shift worker biking home came across a badly beaten body in the gutter outside *The Tararua Mirror*. It was Henry Taylor, the former gang member who had spoken to her on condition of anonymity. The doctor at the hospital in Palmerston North said another hour or two lying in the street and it would have been homicide. Taylor had two broken ribs, a fractured pelvis, three missing teeth, severe bruising, and severe blood loss. Later that week, when Felicity visited him in hospital, she saw the shudder of fear as she approached and she turned on her heel and left.

◆ ◆ ◆

Felicity arrived home late that afternoon, at the same time as a police car. She knew both police officers, a man and a woman, and briefly exchanged greetings. She assumed it concerned her interview with the former gang member and with a heavy heart and heavy guilt, invited them inside. It was soon apparent it was not Felicity they wanted to see but Melody Gilmour.

'You are the owner of the red sedan, registration GKR478, parked in the driveway?'

'Yes.' Melody understandably looked anxious and edgy.

Felicity flinched. *Oh no. She's been drinking.*

'Can you confirm that you were driving it at 4.45pm in Wattle Street and that you abruptly turned and drove the other way when you saw the police drink/driving checkpoint?'

'I suddenly remembered somewhere I had to go. An appointment.'

Felicity shrunk within herself.

That's very lame. She won't get away with that.

'Who with? ...I caution you to be careful as there could be consequences if you perjure yourself.'

'A friend.'

The officers asked Melody to accompany them outside and open her car. Felicity trailed them out, hanging back. The officers searched the car but came up empty-handed.

Thank God they found nothing incriminating.

'You'll need to accompany us in the police car to the police station.'

Melody looked at them beseechingly. 'Can my friend drive me?'

They nodded and Felicity returned to the car she had parked just moments before.

'Thank you so much Lise,' Melody murmured. It would have taken some explaining if principal, teachers, students, or parents saw her in a police car.

There was little Felicity could say as she followed the police car to the station. She recalled Melody saying her father and brother couldn't control their drinking: 'Judgment gone and dangerous behind the wheel'. She also recalled Melody saying she would finish that drink and not drink any more.

Melody's blood alcohol level considerably exceeded the limit. She was also charged with evading the police check point. She would now have to brace herself for a substantial fine and her name in the newspaper. She hoped she would keep her driver's licence. And her job.

'How can a good day turn to bloody custard so fast,' she lamented to Felicity.

22

A TRYING INTERVIEW

Walking one day in the main street of Tumanako, Bethany Callendar felt oddly isolated. It was the feeling she had had one night in her twenties when she had travelled solo to London and taken a room in an inner-city boarding house. That night she was aware of the millions of people around her but had no one to talk to. Now, walking to her office, she was unsure if the feeling of isolation stemmed from her public or personal life or from both. In the restless night that had followed her viewing of the security camera – before her meeting with Tanya Spring had quelled her suspicions – she had felt like an unwanted party in a ménage à trois. Perhaps some of that feeling still lingered. There had, too, been the bullying motorist in the night who could have caused her to crash and die. And the disappearance of Rob. Where was he? Now, another thought caused her brow to crease – a meeting looming, then another and another. She entered her office with the frown and a faltering step. Why ever had she aspired to be mayor?

A telephone conversation later that day helped provide the answer.

'Rowley, you've shocked me.'

'The proof was in the packet Bethany. He was primary school, ten years old, and a drugs runner. They were paying him with lollies and bottles of fizzy drink. Worse case we've seen.'

She put the telephone down with renewed purpose.

The following Saturday, in small Kowhai Park near the centre of town, a celebration of Tumanako's sport and culture helped raise Bethany's spirits. Throughout the afternoon prominent local sports people provided photo opportunities, and gymnasts, trampolinists and horse riders demonstrated, musical and kapa haka groups performed, and there was food, glorious food, with esoteric ethnic offerings besides sausage rolls and hot dogs. The air was filled with delicious aromas from Maori hangi, Pacific Islands umu and Asian, Middle Eastern, Indian, Italian, Greek and Eastern European dishes, and some expressed surprise at how cosmopolitan Tumanako had become.

After weeks of depressing headlines about drugs, the afternoon was an explosion of colour and joy. Townspeople of all ages poured into the park. As Bethany looked over the gathering, she smiled to see Simon Hurley and other 'Forest and Birdies' had taken the opportunity to push positive messages towards a cleaner planet. She agreed this was no place for dire warnings about deforestation, the burning of fossil fuels, methane emissions, shrinking ice caps, extreme heat, fires, and floods. Rather, the promotion of tree planting, protection of wetlands, the use of solar, wind and wave power, recycling, soil conservation and restoration, biodegradable products. She could see people were looking at the displays and not turning away with drooping shoulders.

Paul was by Bethany's side. He had been more his steady, amiable self since her questions about the security-camera film, though he did appear to be drinking more. She made a mental note to draw that to his attention at the right time. How ludicrous it seemed now that she had suspected her golf-playing, conservative, accountant of a husband was frolicking on the wild side. She had been getting paranoic. She looked at him now, in polo shirt, old-fashioned walk shorts and floppy hat, the very model of a man more ready to sit down, read the paper and do the cryptic crossword than cavort with a slut behind her back. She followed his eye. He was looking at a group who had just entered the park. The Polsons – Steve, Stephanie, and Polly. They were carrying foldable chairs. Bethany was thrilled to see Steve there, away from the factory. She hoped he realised how much good he had done for the town and how many of the mouths here he fed. There were others she recognised also coming through the gate: Melody Gilmour, Felicity Spratt and Cindy Spratt, several council staff. She spotted Hector Dunwoodie and, with him, that woman who had scaled the totara tree. The hairdresser. There were so many though she didn't know. They were all her people. It was a reminder that Tumanako was growing. There were new sub-divisions going in and the population would soon exceed eight thousand.

Then she stiffened and found herself clutching Paul's arm. There was a memory of a futile knock on a door, a ferocious dog and a man arriving after her, knocking and having the door opened for him.

She drew Paul's attention to the man.

'There. Going round the back of the bouncy castle. The tall one, with the beard, in the jacket and jeans. I saw him at Rob's house. The house Rob had before. He knows Rob. Rob let him in.'

Bethany was already moving, hurrying after the man. Paul followed, having difficulty keeping up in the crush of people. Bethany reached the bouncy castle and pushed on in the direction the man had taken.

As she pressed through group after group, Bethany knew she should not have been surprised. With such a crowd, it was a prime opportunity for drugs pushers to make surreptitious contact with buyers. How easy it would be to slip a packet to someone with a handshake or a hug. She came to the Forest and Bird display. Patricia Hurley was hovering nearby and caught her eye.

'Patricia, did you see a tall man with a beard pass this way?'

Patricia looked at her startled and swung her bag behind her back.

'No. When?'

She joined Bethany in peering every which way. Paul had caught up by now and three pairs of eyes swivelled. Their task appeared hopeless. There were at least two thousand people there and they must have included many tall men with beards in jacket and jeans.

'Can you be sure dear? Both times it was at a distance and there are so many tall, bearded men here.'

She was sure it had been the man but she had to concede Paul had a point. And anyway, what would she do with him when she found him? Make a citizen's arrest? Report him to Rowley Rowlands? He would deny everything.

◆ ◆ ◆

Slade Branagh was a familiar face to viewers of TV1. He had weathered the grind and tumult of news reporting and in-depth interviews exceedingly well. At forty-six, he was clear-eyed, lean-bodied and had a full head of dark hair which he kept playfully tousled. His reporting style was distinctive – he had a dash of the poet and tragedian in his make-up and rather than rattling out the bald facts, he tended to linger on people and events to draw out emotion. A recent report on flood damage had plunged people into reflection and misery all over the country and the business-minded had wished they had shares in a tissue company.

This day he was interviewing Bethany Callendar for the *Sunday* current events programme. Bethany initially had been more excited than nervous about the interview. It was, after all, national exposure of the pernicious trade in drugs but as the time of the interview neared, she worried over what direction Branagh might take and became more nervous than excited. It was one thing to talk to a local reporter and friend who would respect personal boundaries, another to talk to a national reporter who might like nothing better than to expose raw emotion.

Bethany Callendar would have been even more nervous if she had known someone had been talking to the reporter. Indeed, that the information from that person was the only reason he was in Tumanako.

Slade Branagh and his camera crew spent the morning filming around Tumanako, capturing its rustic, 'blue collar' feel as well as its endeavours to gentrify itself – the colourful plantings in the main street, the sculptures of its arts community, the posters promoting the next production of the repertory society. Branagh then interviewed a clearly reluctant and laconic Rowley Rowlands. Back issues of *The Tararua Mirror* had provided Branagh both with the feature articles of Felicity Spratt and the reports from the court room and he began with a summary of recent convictions. His first comment had Rowlands reeling.

'By all accounts, Tumanako is sinking under a tide of illegal drugs.'

Rowlands shuddered and glared at him. 'Nothing of the sort.

The police have got a handle on it and the courts are carrying out their side of it.'

The interview proceeded with Rowlands on the back foot throughout. It left the viewer in no doubt that vast amounts of illegal drugs were being distributed and consumed in Tumanako and that the children of Tumanako were already heavily embroiled in the drugs scene. Alison Peabody and Trevor Rudge would be apoplectic at the damage to 'the salt of the earth' image fostered at Destination Tumanako.

As Slade Branagh and his crew left the police station, Rowlands called Bethany Callendar and gave her a heads-up.

'We're a cesspit of drugs.'

It was too late to pull out of the interview. She could only hope to steer it in the direction she wanted – that the town was aware of the drugs problem and was doing something about it. From her talks with other mayors and with heads of social services, Bethany was sure the problem in Tumanako was no worse than in many other districts. Indeed, she was sure it was much less than in some. She went into the interview determined that the problem would be aired but that Tumanako would not be unfairly pilloried.

And Bethany Callendar was carrying the day with her forceful, relevant answers until Slade Branagh dropped a bombshell on her.

'I understand you have a personal interest in the current crisis.'

She looked at him in confusion.

'The disappearance of your son Rob.'

The camera caught Bethany's shock and distress. Viewers from North Cape to the Bluff could see a mother aghast at her greatest fear laid bare. Rob was highlighted in a class photograph at school. There was a photograph with Bethany, Paul and Rob highlighted. The interview ended soon after.

Paul, too, was mortified by the interview. Branagh had emphasised that Rob Callendar was missing but had also strongly implied he was mixed up in the drugs world. The manner of it was gut-wrenching. The mother-son angle was the story which a part of Felicity Spratt would have loved to reveal but did not. Bethany and Paul Callendar now had something else to worry about. Had the disclosure about Rob Callendar and drugs endangered Rob yet further? Both knew from book and film that gangsters prefer to go about their business in the shadows. Witnesses tend to forget or change their minds or vanish. What would Rob Callendar think if he saw the programme? More alarming yet – what would others in the drugs world think?

Bethany's anger at the blindsiding interview did have one fortunate side effect – it drove away the depression that might otherwise have brought her low. She was determined not to be a victim herself. Like her father had been. Like Steve Polson was becoming. She decided it was time to recognise the contribution Polson's had made to Tumanako. As a client on behalf of the town council, she would nominate Polson's for the biennial business awards.

The television interview prompted both sympathy and animosity. There were those nauseated at the intrusion on Bethany's private grief and a few who revelled in it. On a whim, she went to the controls of the house's security system and re-ran the film from the camera that monitored the front door. Thankfully, nothing.

23

CHANGES FOR POLLY

Polly and Stephanie Polson were thrilled Steve was being recognised for his contribution to Tumanako. Twelve years before, when the Tumanako Business Chamber founded the awards, Polson's won not only the large business award but the supreme award, but since then, it had been overlooked for more flashy enterprises with dazzling websites. It didn't help that Its chimney had become as familiar as the hat on the wash-house wall.

Polly and Stephanie were on their feet applauding at the Gala Awards Friday night of bubbles and five courses when Polson's name was announced as supreme winner and Steve rose and went forward for the second time that evening. He got a double hug on return and a 'Well done darling' and a 'Proud of you dad'. Steve didn't say a lot but Polly could see the award had been a tremendous fillip.

The next morning Polly and Daniel rode out together on their mountain bikes. Charlotte was working. For more than an hour they powered along the bush tracks, up, down, over tree roots, ducking and diving, leaping and sliding, and when at last they came off the track into the picnic area, they were spent and collapsed onto the grass. As they drank deep from their water bottles, Polly told him about the awards night and the accolades for Polson's.

'It's a great company,' Daniel said. 'And your dad's a great boss.'

Polly nodded. She had never taken her father for granted. 'It's given him a big lift. He had been really down, you know. I was worried about him. Mum was too.'

Two tuis gambolling in a tree got their attention. Back and forth the birds went, seemingly oblivious of the two humans. Was it play or courting? Their song was clear as a bell but then surprised with rasps and creaks. The air was still and the late-morning sun beat down as Polly shuffled over to Daniel and they lay side by side looking up at the clear blue sky. A thought occurred to Polly: how Toni Dalzell would tease her if she could see her now.

'You never know about people do you,' Daniel said. 'You'd think the boss in his big house wouldn't have much to worry about.' They were each lost in their own thoughts. Eventually he spoke again. 'I think he knows the factory could be a lot better but he's wary about having a big upheaval.'

'What do you mean?'

'The factory could be made a lot cleaner. Less toxic.'

Polly was as familiar as just about anyone with the factory's processes. The sights and smells had always been part of her life.

'Making cement for one thing. It's the third largest source of industrial air pollution in the world. We could use less cement by using supplementary materials in concrete mixes. We could make the cement kiln more efficient too. And there's advanced technology like carbon capture to help zero out emissions.'

Polly could see the passionate 'greenie' in him but also the clear-sighted engineer. He never said much about it but she knew he was doing brilliantly at university, winning scholarships and awards. That was no surprise. He had shown an insatiable curiosity about the world ever since she had known him and topped the class right through school. Dux in his final year.

'And then there are the toxic chemicals used as timber preservatives and in the adhesives as well. Even the completely cured adhesives can produce hazardous materials for humans and the environment. They can harm the skin and eyes, lungs, and liver.'

'Are there alternatives?'

'Yes, there are. There are adhesives which are biochemical and much more benign than the petrochemical. Many countries have introduced policies which prevent the use of toxic chemicals. The gap is being filled with copper-organic preservatives, organic fungicides and insecticides, and water-based preservatives. They are more expensive though.'

It was all rather dismal and they sat for a while in silence, gazing over the bush, listening to the occasional song of a bird.

'So, there's a money factor.'

'A big money factor, especially initially, upgrading equipment and procedures.'

'Have you talked to him about it?'

'We've discussed new equipment and procedures. Your dad's very forward-thinking. He knows there is a better way of doing things and I think it's been getting him down.'

That was something else for Polly to consider – that when Steve Polson received the award the previous night, a part of him might have felt like a pretender.

'Dad's very aware of pollution and worker safety. He insists on workers wearing gloves when handling CCA-treated wood and masks where there could be air pollution. Staff are instructed to wash hands and face before eating or drinking.'

'I know. But it goes a bit deeper than that.'

Daniel spoke about the new technology available, such as the Transverse High Grader. After the raw log is put on a conveyor belt and the bark stripped to be used as garden mulch, the Transverse High Grader machine decides what size boards are to be cut from each log. The scanning software 'sees' the log with cameras, assesses the log's weight, density, and size, identifies any knots, twists, or bark pockets in the wood, and analyses the best boards to cut from each log. The log is then sent to the right saw.

'So one or more people lose a job.'

'No. A worker is still needed to oversee the scanner. The machine just makes everything more efficient. It means greater value from each log and saves time. Where the worker at present spends an average of forty-two seconds per log, the scanner makes decisions in a fraction of the time.'

Polly could see that Daniel was in seventh heaven talking about the latest technology. Any tiredness from the mountain biking seemed to have fled as he went on to speak about the Continuous Drying Kiln that could take trucks off the road and save emissions, and above all, about the state-of-the-art Polytechnik energy centre. Instead of burning waste oil to power the kiln, the sawmill could burn its own wet sawdust and use the steam to power the drying kiln.

'We're burning about half-a-million dollars in waste oil a year so it would be a huge reduction in our carbon footprint.'

By now the magic of the afternoon had gone for both Polly and Daniel and they rode back to town, not talking much.

That evening, reflecting on her day, Polly realised she now looked at the factory differently. The factory had always been the epitome of everything solid and good. It was at the heart of the town. And her dad was at the head of it. It disturbed her that in recent months too many things had gone amiss at the factory to be accidental, suggesting somebody out there, or more than one, hated the factory and wanted to harm it. Daniel had in the past occasionally cursed the chemicals but there had been nothing like his damning of the factory that afternoon. Polly realised his condemnation had shaken her deeply. The factory was no longer the embodiment of everything good. There were questions about it. Serious questions. Daniel had helped explain her father's low moments.

Within the month Polly was back in Christchurch, immersed in assignments towards her business management degree. She had little time to dwell on the challenges facing her father and the factory. Throughout secondary school and her first two years at university, she had always achieved her academic targets with grit and hard work, but as March turned into April, she found herself struggling in this third year. She felt a persistent fatigue and weakness and even attending lectures became an ordeal. Instead of biking she began to go by bus and some days she didn't attend at all. Her grades began to drop. Finally, at the urging of Daniel and Charlotte, she accepted she needed help and turned to the university's medical services.

Soon there were other indications besides the fatigue and weakness that all was not well. Skin lesions began appearing on her body. Poisoning of some sort was suspected. At first the doctors hesitated in blaming dioxins due to their omnipresence – everyone has background exposure and a certain level of dioxins in the body, especially in the central North Island where background levels of arsenic are naturally high in the volcanic soil. But Polly's levels were found to be much higher than average. Inevitably, eyes were pointed at the factory where she had spent so much of her time since childhood. Could the poisoning have come from contaminated ground there or from the preservatives used in the radiata timber? No one could be sure. Risk estimates for cancer related to direct contact with CCA-treated wood ranged from one additional case in a million people to one in ten thousand. Stephanie was horrified when she learnt of the latter end of the scale, especially when she also learnt that the United States, Canada, and Europe had banned the use of CCA-treated wood in residential and recreational settings as long ago as 2004.

Polly had a chronically upset stomach and lack of appetite and began to lose weight. When she developed a lingering fever and drenching sweats, she was admitted to Christchurch Hospital. Very quickly her face swelled, a swelling developed on her neck and she was diagnosed with B cell non-Hodgkin's lymphoma. She had tumours of the lymph nodes of the neck, armpits, and groin area. The medical staff were unsure of the cause but poisoning of some sort was considered possible. The initial treatment was chemotherapy followed by radiation therapy. There were distressing side effects of nausea and hair loss, and reduction of her normal white blood cells, leading to increased risk of infection. She was given injections to stimulate the white blood cells to recover sooner so that risk of infection would be reduced.

Stephanie took long-term accommodation in a nearby motel and Steve visited at weekends. The hospital became as familiar to Daniel as his flat and Charlotte was a frequent visitor. One weekend Simon, Patricia and Rosemary flew down to see Polly. Previously, it had always been Polly solicitous to Rosemary; now, the comforter had become the comforted. Looking at Polly and Rosemary together, Stephanie could not help but wonder if the estimate of one in ten thousand disorders due to chemicals was correct.

Steve was fearful and wracked by guilt. Had Polly been afflicted by the factory? Stephanie wanted her family out of the factory and out of Tumanako. With a daughter grievously ill and a husband tormented, the toll had become too great. For Steve Polson, the situation was more complex – he had to consider his workforce and his clients and the protection of family assets. There was also family heritage but that now slipped away to nothing – he was past caring whether the name 'Polson's' remained emblazoned above the front gates.

Deeply wrought from a visit to Polly's bedside, Steve and Stephanie had a heart-to-heart discussion and began to look at a life beyond Tumanako.

24

TOXIC PHONE CALLS

Simon Hurley was busy finalising a 'green' raffle with proceeds towards the public displays of the Forest and Bird Society. The first prize was solar panels, the second a mountain bike and the third a one-hour presentation on how to 'green' a household. He heard that Barry Fitzwilliam was mischievously suggesting there should be a fourth prize of a two-hour presentation on how to 'green' a household.

A knock on the door alerted Simon to the arrival of visitors from out of town, keen to get a sighting in nearby forest of the yellow-crowned kakariki or parakeet which had been thriving since intensive trapping of mustelids, rats, and cats. Simon was a part of the trapping team and knew that a stoat could take out whole nests, including the female when she was sitting on a nest. He would personally accompany the visitors as the yellow-crowned kakariki was difficult to spot being shy and favouring the canopy in tall, unbroken forest.

'Patricia, they're here!'

They had both set aside the morning to venture into the forest which they loved so much.

Patricia appeared from the small room in the front of the house which she used as a study. 'I'll give it a miss, Simon. I've just got too much to do.'

They greeted the visitors and chatted with them over a cup of tea.

'I'm sorry I won't be with you,' Patricia said. 'I'm up to my ears with data collection. I need to get a report away this week.'

Simon was appreciating the money she was bringing in and the huge turn-around in her financial situation, but he would miss her company in the forest.

'Can't you squeeze in one morning of Me time?'

She grimaced. 'Not really. It would make me late in delivery.'

As Simon and the visitors departed, he suddenly remembered he had forgotten his cell phone and turned back. A phone in the familiar shade of purple was tucked at the back of a lampshade by the door. He didn't remember putting it there but that meant nothing – he sometimes had to get Patricia to phone his phone to locate where it was. He grabbed it with relief and was halfway out the door when stopped by a shout.

'Wait! Hang on a minute!'

The shout was shrill and panicky. Simon and the visitors all stopped in alarm, peering back to identify the problem. Something crucial left behind? Accident? Medical event? Fire?

'You've got my phone!'

Simon took in Patricia's tense and anxious face and the hand grasping for the cell phone.

He examined the phone more closely. 'Sorry, I thought it was mine.'

As he went back inside to find his own cell phone, Patricia regained her composure.

'Apologies all'. She was smiling now. 'When I saw him disappearing out the door with it, I could see all my contacts going out the door with him.'

'One of us needs to get a cell phone case with a different colour,' Simon said.

'I will tomorrow,' said Patricia. 'My mistake.'

As Simon drove away, he pondered the importance to people of their cell phone and wondered how they had ever got by without one. It was such a mixed blessing – a godsend as a handy record of contacts, provider of useful information and instant means of summoning help in an emergency, but a menace as a time waster, spreader of misinformation and instant means of harassment. He could understand Patricia's distress. To be without your phone nowadays, for both personal and business reasons, was like being without your right arm. When you worked from home and were out and about, it was indispensable.

Mid-morning, Patricia emerged from her study with a phone conversation on hold. She was alone at home with Rosemary but looked furtively around even when she went out into the garden with no one within earshot. Her face was pale and the knuckles of the hand holding the cell phone were white. She held the cell phone slightly away from her ear, as if distancing herself from what was coming down the line. Then slowly, she began to walk, up one row of vegetables and down the next, listening more than speaking, her face screwed tight and her body tense. She stopped walking at one point, held the phone even further away, and looked at it in disgust, as though half-inclined to toss it. But then she seemed to change her mind and resumed walking up and down. Did her thoughts go to Simon and the others in the forest, winding through the ancient trees, breathing deep of the rich, oxygenated air, at ease amidst the lichens and mosses and luxuriant vegetation, listening to the chatter of the yellow-crowned parakeet and peering for it in the canopy, not listening to demands and thinly veiled threats?

When she eventually returned to the house, she found Rosemary soiled and tearful.

'I felt it coming on and called out mum but you weren't here.'

'Sorry darling. I was outside on an important phone call and didn't hear you. I'll make sure it doesn't happen again.'

Rosemary had done her best to clean herself but was still soiled. Patricia lowered her head and avoided Rosemary's eye as she busied herself undressing her, helping her to sit in the shower, and fetching fresh clothes.

When Simon returned home, invigorated from his walk and the sighting of a small flock of yellow-crowned kakariki, Patricia did not mention Rosemary's incident and Rosemary herself never said a word, perhaps fearful of a repetition of that other clash over Patricia's gambling on the pokies. Rather, Patricia was unusually quiet and Simon was prompted to comment.

'Now you're on top of the money, you must learn how to enjoy it. Not stay at home on a beautiful day like today when you could have been with us in the bush. Rosemary could have come too. She would have loved it.' He thought of something else. 'Isn't that why you chose the job of data collection for Statistics New Zealand – so you would have time to fit it in around our lives, not the other way around?'

In the background he heard a door slam and realised it was Rosemary's.

'Is Rosemary all right?'

With Daniel and Charlotte now back at university, Patricia decided it was best that she and Simon sleep in separate rooms. There was the downside they would be unlikely to have the comfort and release of sex so often, but she generally felt too fatigued for sex anyway. In separate rooms, not only would they each be in blessed silence, away from the other's coughs, snorts, and snuffles, but she would have privacy for the phone calls in the dead of the night. If she was lucky, she would get four or five hours sleep each night between the phone calls and the rest of the time she would fitfully doze.

One night, when Simon was having trouble sleeping, he got up to make himself a drink. To his surprise, he heard a faint noise from the side of the house and thought he had left his cell phone on. He followed the sound to Patricia's bedroom. She was talking to someone. Simon realised it must be on the telephone since they had no visitors. Pressing an ear to the door, he could pick up the occasional word from her side of the conversation. She was speaking quietly but intensely.

'You are never to visit me at home,' she said. 'That would be the end of it.'

Simon thought he heard a male voice from the other end of the line and earthy words. The call soon ended and, in the silence, he became aware his heart was hammering. He crept away from the door and continued through to the kitchen.

So Patricia's found herself a lover. The separate bedroom was to get away from me and save herself for him. The trips into town for data collection are a cover for her meetings with him. All this money she has now could be coming from him. Is that why so much of it is in cash? It's like she's prostituting herself. Who does she know who would gift her that sort of money?

Sick to the pit of his stomach, he made himself a drink and took it back to his room. He felt too distraught to confront her then. That could wait till the morning.

How had it come to this? Patricia having an affair with person unknown. What other lies has she been hiding? All that money that went on the pokies. Is she still playing the pokies? Is he giving her the money for that as well? What to believe?

Simon must eventually have fallen asleep exhausted for when he woke and drew the curtains, the bedroom flooded with light. When he went into the kitchen, Patricia was there with Rosemary. They had finished breakfast and Patricia was already getting ready to go into town. She had her coat on and handbag in hand.

'Not like you to be sleeping in so late,' she said brightly. 'I was just about to wake you.'

He gazed at her with empty eyes.

'You still look half asleep... I need to pop into town for a few bits and pieces. A new case for my cell phone for one thing.'

Surely to God she's not at it already. This hour in the morning.

'I won't be long.' And after a kiss of Rosemary's cheek, she was out the door.

He couldn't have followed her even if he'd wished. There was Rosemary to care for and he was still half-groggy from the night.

When Patricia returned, she brought in a letter from the gate and disappeared with it into her study. When she emerged, she was frowning. Later, when she was busy with Rosemary in another part of the house, Simon did something hitherto undreamt of – entered the study and rifled through the papers on her desk. There, dated the week before, was a letter from

Statistics New Zealand. It must have been the one she had brought in that morning. He scanned the contents.

'This is a second, formal warning that unless there is immediate improvement in job performance, your position as data collection officer will be terminated.'

It is proof Patricia is lying. Her money is not coming from her exceptional work for the government but from some other source. What source will she claim when I confront her? She can't claim a big win at the pokies. What other explanation can her devious mind concoct?

He waited until Rosemary was immersed in research in her room and told Patricia he had read the letter from Statistics New Zealand.

Patricia began to protest. 'You had no right...' But his look made her trail off into silence and the full depth of her misery and fears was exposed when she broke into sobs. She admitted she was as addicted as ever to the pokies and shocked him by saying she had been so desperate to get out of debt she had been running errands for drugs dealers. It was his turn to be shocked into silence.

The money towards the new septic tank, the money for the new sound system, other payments she had made – all from drugs money. And that other thing.

'What about your affair?'

She looked at him wide-eyed, stunned.

'An affair? There is no affair.'

'The separate bedrooms. I heard you talking to a man in the middle of the night.'

'That was Ross, my handler.'

Handler! My God! What's she got into?

'There's no affair. I would never have an affair. How could you think that?'

Between sobs, she confessed all – how she had used some of the drugs money for the pokies and was now facing demands to pay it back immediately. As her body heaved, it was apparent she was too unhinged to talk further and Simon took himself into the garden to work out his distress and agitation.

Later that afternoon Patricia told her manager at Statistics New Zealand by email that unfortunate personal circumstances had affected her performance but now they were behind her and she was committed to doing her best possible work for them. That night she enrolled in the gambling prevention programme and wordlessly showed Simon the confirmation of her acceptance. When Rosemary was in bed, they formulated a plan to pay back the money owed to the drugs syndicate to get them off her back.

That night Simon Hurley fell into an exhausted sleep, cursing the use of substances that damaged the planet and substances that destroyed a person's own life and the lives of those dearest to them.

25

A PLEA TO STOP

'Earth Day' on 22 April was more a day of quiet reflection for the Tumanako branch of Forest and Bird than an expression of concern about the planet. That was to do with Polly Polson, so grievously sick in hospital in Christchurch and constantly at the back of members' minds. The 'Earth Day' call to action gave them a joint purpose and a temporary distraction. It helped that the day was brilliantly fine and they were out amidst nature. After performances in Kowhai Park, they moved in groups of three or four throughout the town, guerrilla gardening – planting seeds in neglected public spaces. Patricia Hurley then led them on a guided wildflower walk.

Felicity Spratt followed with interest. She was not only obtaining a story for *The Tararua Mirror* but sloughing off stress. She was intrigued that Patricia was leading the group. Felicity was struggling to remember where Patricia's name had surfaced recently. Amongst all her comings and goings, she had heard Patricia's name and been startled by the mention. Now, as Patricia led them by the orange-red crocosmia, arum lilies, ox-eye daisies, wild carrot, and others, that reference was nagging away at her. Simon was there, always by Patricia's side. This outing was impractical for Rosemary and she was in the library with a family friend, researching.

Melody Gilmour clung to Patricia and Simon, making notes. This would be an ideal trip for her students as end-of-term neared. Get them out of the classroom and show them something natural and beautiful close to hand, worth preserving. It had surprised her when someone said Patricia was an acknowledged authority on wild flowers in this central part of New Zealand and indeed, an authority on the entire botany of the region. It had been a hobby that had blossomed into deep and impassioned study.

With Earth Day satisfyingly celebrated, the group dispersed. Felicity was driving Melody as Melody was still disqualified. They had no sooner got in the car than Felicity's cell phone pinged with a message. She checked it.

'Stop investigating Felicity. Please.'

The message had flashed like a meteor across the screen and then was gone. It was impossible to tell who had sent it. She knew it would not be family though the 'please' did make it sound personal. Unlikely to be Rowley Rowlands. His name would be with it. She doubted it would be Bethany. Bethany had never wanted her to stop. Rob Callendar? Felicity shrugged. She had virtually stopped investigating anyway. She was only following up news stories now.

They drove on into town and went their separate ways. Felicity dropped into Bac Nam Nguyen's fish shop to check a couple of points from their interview. Melody got back to the car first. She was standing on the pavement, her back to the road, wearing a wide-brimmed hat against the sun, absorbed in her cell phone, when a black SUV pulled up behind. A door opened.

A man stepped quickly out on the far side. There was a pause. Then a flaming Molotov cocktail sailed through the air.

Melody heard the whoosh of the flame and the tremendous crash of the bottle striking Felicity's car. She instinctively reeled away and tumbled to the ground. The attack was over in seconds. The bottle had just missed a window, rebounding onto the road. With a screech of tyres, the SUV vanished, leaving just the smell and sound of burning petrol. Melody found herself on hands and knees listening to the sizzle, too shocked to move. Soon people came running and Melody was helped to her feet and led away. Concerned citizens directed traffic away from the scene until police took over. The fire brigade was there in minutes and doused the last of the flames.

When Felicity returned, she was horrified to find Melody pale and shaken and her car at the centre of a police and fire brigade investigation. Later, police attempted to quell public fears by saying the attack had been targeted and the public at large had nothing to worry about. Melody was unimpressed as she considered herself a member of the public at large. It was thanks only to fortune and the ineptitude of the perpetrators that the car had not been blown up and Melody killed.

The police believed it was a case of mistaken identity, that Melody, having her back to the road and wearing the wide-brimmed hat over her blonde hair, had been mistaken for Felicity. They believed the perpetrators were probably the same incompetents who had attempted to burn the office of *The Tararua Mirror*.

Felicity pondered the situation ruefully. Did the drugs barons not know or accept that she had wound down her investigation? She could see that this latest action would have the opposite effect to that intended and the authorities would crack down even harder. She was still embroiled up to her ears. Another thought struck – had her connection with Bac Nam Nguyen been a factor in the attack? Was he somehow involved in the drugs world? Her mind was spinning.

Is my ambition as a journalist at the heart of it? The attack could easily have killed or seriously maimed Melody. Am I more like dad than I thought? Selfish. Needing to have my way, carrying on regardless of the effect on others. But doesn't relentless drive for a scoop make a good reporter? While mum is pleading with me to pull back, dad is still urging me on, so proud his daughter is helping lead the fight against drugs. But is it more about me than drugs anyway? The desire for attention. The desire for control. Do I browbeat people, like dad browbeat mum? Is absorption with myself the reason I don't have a partner? So full of myself there's no room in my life for anyone else? But I did have a boyfriend in my last year at school – Rob Callendar – and there have been two men friends since. Of sorts.

That evening her mother phoned and invited Felicity to visit and have a chat. Felicity did not want to leave Melody on her own, despite the armed police guard parked in the street outside, and invited Cindy there. They hugged for an age and then Cindy held her at arm's length and Felicity could see the love and fear in her eyes.

'I couldn't stop shaking when I heard.'

'Don't worry mum. It's over now. There'll be no more stories.'

'Thank the Lord for that.'

Felicity clarified the situation. 'Nothing prompted by me, that is. Just statements by Rowley Rowlands and reports from the court room.'

'Do you have to do those?'

'Part of the day-to-day job. They can't blame me for that.'

Felicity busied herself making a cup of tea for them.

'Poor Melody. How is she?'

'She's in her room. Went to bed with two Panadol. She'll be sleeping now. She'll be all right; she knows it was nothing to do with her.'

They drank their tea, reflective.

Felicity broke the silence. 'It hasn't been a great time. Polly so sick, Melody drinking, and now this.'

They talked about Melody's problem with alcohol. Cindy had seen alcohol addiction in her own family and her advice was succinct.

'She must stop completely.'

Felicity could see the determination and toughness in her mother and raised the matter frequently on her mind. 'Mum, wouldn't it be better if you took a job in another office and got some time away from dad?'

Cindy looked intently at her daughter. 'He likes having me there.'

'Dominating you, keeping you under control, having you cater to his every whim.'

'It's not like that, Felicity. We do look after each other.'

Felicity looked away, unconvinced.

Felicity's phone rang. It was Bethany Callendar. Cindy took the opportunity to end their conversation, excused herself, and left.

Bethany was worried about both Felicity and Melody. Felicity assured her they were both fine. Bethany congratulated her again on her series of articles but said it was time to stop, adding that Rowley Rowlands agreed. Felicity knew that Rowley Rowlands had never wanted her to start. Bethany assured Felicity she would have the protection of the police twenty-four hours a day for as long as necessary. Felicity confirmed she had finished her drugs probe.

'Molotov cocktails are not us, Felicity.'

When the call ended, Felicity went to the front window and drew the curtain aside. She could see the driver at the wheel of the police car. She had once quite fancied being a policewoman but now was sure she had made the right career choice, despite the recent alarms. A life of stake-outs and surveillance was not for her. She would prefer to be a reporter in the thick of it than a sentry on the battlements, a fire warden in a national park, a quality checker on a production line, a video surveillance operator, or a police officer on a protection assignment.

She turned on the television and was watching it desultorily, half asleep, when the phone rang again. It was her father.

'Felicity, is your mum there?'

Those drums were beating again.

'No, she left half an hour ago.'

'She hasn't arrived home.'

Felicity hurried out the front door. She immediately had the attention of the policeman. She explained the situation and he phoned it in.

Cindy Spratt's car was found minutes later midway between the two houses. There was no sign of Cindy. A ripped piece of dress indicated there had been a struggle.

26

CLARITY FOR BETHANY

The search for Cindy Spratt was intense and relentless. There had never been anything like it in Tumanako. Besides the massive response from the police, there was the private search driven by Lionel Spratt and involving Felicity. She was so stricken with anxiety and guilt she could barely think straight and Colin Trainor suggested she take the week off.

'That's the last thing I want,' she said. 'I'd go mad with worry. The police will tell me when there's any news.'

She did get news that morning but it was not from the police but Hector Dunwoodie. He had heard about the kidnapping and phoned Felicity.

'It's a message to you and the police to lay off.'

Felicity felt sick.

Hector continued. 'They know Rob Callendar's a friend of

yours. They've got him off deliveries now. They found someone else for that. Rob's working in a P lab. Not getting out a lot.'

That last was a typical Hector understatement.

Felicity could get nothing else from him. She knew Hector was not one for long telephone conversations and he hung up soon after. She could tell he was upset and was sure he would have told her if he had known where her mother was.

◆ ◆ ◆

'It's time somebody told you.'

Bethany Callendar was alone in her office at work when she took the call. She didn't recognise the woman's voice.

'I beg your pardon. Told me what?'

Bethany wondered if the caller was about to dump a festering heap of abuse on her and braced for it. Pot hole in the caller's street? Dog running wild? Rubbish not picked up? Lack of disability parks? Increase in rates? But it was nothing of the sort.

'Your husband.'

Her heart stopped. 'What about him?'

'He's cheating on you.'

For a long moment, only silence connected them.

'Who is this?'

'Valerie Tosswillow. I have a dental practice in town. Toni Dalzell was my partner for three years. My personal partner, that is, not my professional partner.'

Bethany was finding it difficult to breathe and she could feel a pounding in her head. She had to lower her head to clear it.

The voice continued. 'Toni Dalzell has left me. She is having an affair with your husband.' The voice paused. 'Are you there?'

Bethany at last found her voice. 'Yes, I'm here.' But she found she had nothing to say. She knew the woman was telling the truth and that her marriage of twenty-nine years was over. Her mind flicked back to the security camera footage and to Paul sneaking the woman into the house. Their house. Hers and Paul's. And she could envisage the rest. Making love to the woman in their bed. Hers and Paul's.

'Well, anyway, I thought you had a right to know. Why should they get away with it?'

Valerie Tosswillow hung up.

Bethany felt empty. A few words from someone she had never met and the world had rolled over. When Maia Matenga knocked and entered, she found Bethany slumped at her desk, pale and hollow-eyed.

'What's wrong?'

They were friends as well as work colleagues and Bethany was ready to talk. The deputy chair of the council had now become Bethany's closest confidant. Bethany considered if she herself was partly to blame for the situation. Taking on a job that involved meetings at night, taking work home, meeting Paul on the run, never getting away together. And on top of that the torment over Rob. Where was he? Was he all right? Assaults and Molotov cocktails. Cindy Spratt missing. For the next half hour, personal matters had precedence and the agenda of the drainage board could wait.

◆ ◆ ◆

Bethany was not one to wallow interminably in grief. That afternoon she sat in *Toni's – hairdresser of distinction*, having her hair done by an assistant. She thought it was just as well the appointment had been at short notice and she was not with Toni herself. To have the hands which were caressing Paul, running through her hair, would have been too much. Bethany suspected she might have seized the scissors herself and hacked off great swathes of Toni's glorious chestnut hair. As it was, she quietly seethed as she observed her treacherous husband's lover from an adjoining seat. Toni Dalzell was at least twenty years younger than him and, Bethany grudgingly conceded, in the prime of her life. The woman at the top of the totara tree, so athletic, so lithe. And so apparently insouciant about the havoc she was causing, carrying on with jokes, constant banter, and anecdotes with another client. The tinkling laughter made her wince.

'He couldn't find them anywhere. Looking high and low. Getting everyone else to look as well. And would you believe it, they were on the top of his head!'

Was she talking about Paul? She surely wouldn't have the effrontery to parade her affair here.

Toni Dalzell had earlier acknowledged the presence of the mayor in her salon and Bethany wondered if her position had helped her get the late-notice appointment. Bethany sat mainly in silence thinking, as the assistant went about her work.

Is Toni Dalzell observing me as much as I am observing Toni Dalzell? I want to interrogate Dalzell about her intentions towards Paul. Is it a wild adventure to have a fling with the mayor's husband, or does she have longer-term intentions? Valerie Tosswillow seemed to suggest it was the latter. And, for that matter, what is Paul's intention? Will he carry on with Toni Dalzell and eventually announce his departure or is it a brief, midlife fling that would have remained hidden if Tosswillow hadn't phoned? There will be everything else to sort out: the selling of the house and the dividing of the assets.

As Bethany departed for home, she realised she was replanning her life on a stranger's phone call. She needed confirmation from Paul and she was determined that it would not be like last time when he was able to fudge the situation and involve Tanya Spring. No more distortions and lies. The disclosure of his treachery needed to be on Bethany's terms and ideally involve the public humiliation of Paul and Toni Dalzell if he had indeed betrayed her.

That night she said nothing to Paul and avoided him as much as possible. But when he was showering, she went to his cell phone.

◆ ◆ ◆

La Vie en rose was the restaurant of Mount Paradiso, a prestigious hotel resort complex in the central North Island, far removed from anyone in Tumanako who might have a sudden craving for high-end dining followed by massage and viewing of the stars and milky way in that 'dark sky' haven.

When Bethany Callendar had gone to her husband Paul's cell phone, she had discovered that rather than attending an accountancy conference in Wellington as he had declared, he would be at Mount Paradiso. And not only did she have the dates of his occupancy, but the name of his companion and the very booking time of their dinner at *La vie en rose*. The information had removed the last of any maudlin sadness at the imminent dissolution of their marriage for Mount Paradiso and *La vie en rose* had once been in the thoughts of Bethany and Paul themselves. They had contemplated Mount Paradiso years before for her birthday but had finally decided against because of the cost. Now Paul was going there with another. As Paul continued to shower (removing, Bethany suspected, any suspicious residue of close contact with Dalzell), Bethany checked her diary. To her intense chagrin, she had a meeting that night. But then with a stab of resolve, she decided it was not a crucial one and she could make a rare apology.

In Maia Matenga, she had a confidant, co-conspirator, and

witness all in one. They themselves could do with an evening away at Mount Paradiso and it was in a spirit of both anticipation and retribution that they set out on their journey.

A forkful of medium-rare fillet mignon steak dipped in tartare sauce was halfway to Paul Callendar's mouth when he became aware that the mayor and deputy mayor were standing by the table and not looking at him fondly. Rather, with the stony faces of inquisitors before a hanging, drawing, and quartering. For a long moment it was a tableau, frozen in time. A waitress fluttered briefly and vanished, perhaps sensing Armageddon was nigh. Toni Dalzell gazed intrigued, as if she were a disinterested spectator, or was this déjà vu for her?

Toni Dalzell broke the silence. 'Mrs Callendar.'

Bethany looked at her silently, with contempt.

Without a word, Paul Callendar lowered his fork, nodded his head to Toni Dalzell in the direction of the door, and left the dining room, Dalzell a step behind him.

The waitress was instantly back and ushering Bethany and Maia to another table. It would be bitter-sweet dining for Bethany and a bitter-sweet evening, knowing that nearby, Toni Dalzell was cosseted in the arms of her husband. Still, there was the memory of his shocked face to relish. And the public unveiling of his treachery. And the certainty that any love-making, at least for him, would be sullied by the confrontation. There was also the message she had left for him in an envelope at reception.

Bethany steeled herself to deal with the misery of her crumbled marriage, as she had every other setback in her life. There were other things to consider: Cindy Spratt missing, Rob's whereabouts unknown, Polly Polson battling for her life in hospital in Christchurch, Stephanie and Steve Polson beside themselves with worry, Molotov cocktails in the street. Tumanako required a firm hand at the helm.

The district was in turmoil as the homes of known drugs offenders were raided. Lionel Spratt was adding to the ferment. He had become like a one-man band of vigilantes, spurring the police on, suggesting likely targets and prowling the town streets and the country roads himself, his office temporarily closed. He knew the district just about as well as anybody, and had contacts all over the place. It was time to call them and his phone rang continually from informants. Twice he was able to steer the police to where a wanted felon was hiding out. Rowley Rowlands became concerned that Lionel was making himself the most hated Spratt of all and offered him protection which he refused.

Felicity Spratt had never seen her father so driven. Neither had she seen him so distraught. He was missing his wife profoundly and was terrified at what might be happening to her. As she shared the agony of living in limbo with him, she realised his intensity and drive was motivated by love. It had been a long time since Felicity had felt so close to her father.

Amidst the ructions of the search, daily life in Tumanako rolled on. Children continued to go to school, the wheels of commerce kept turning, sport and recreation carried on. And the members of the Tumanako branch of Forest and Bird maintained their mission to save the planet. So it was that

Bethany Callendar arrived back from Mount Paradiso to find a request to launch a mobile workshop that would take the protect-the-environment message to workplaces and schools.

She agreed totally with the workshop's simple but significant urgings. They showed the individual could make a difference: switch off lights and power when not in use, boil only as much hot water as needed, recycle, plant trees, use public transport, cycle, keep vehicle tyres properly inflated, avoid throwaway plastic, live in a house with low energy consumption, try to use natural sources of light, use light bulbs such as LED, run dishwashers and washing machines on eco-friendly settings, do only full loads of laundry and use the bright colours cycle whenever possible, take short showers with a low-flow showerhead, turn off the tap when brushing the teeth. Yes, yes, yes – she ticked them all off.

Bethany was impressed that the display showed people by 'hands-on' as well as by video how they could make a difference. It showed people using a power strip to easily unplug electronics, powering the computer down when away, using stairs instead of lift, ensuring good home insulation, changing air filters, hanging clothes to dry, avoiding petroleum-based fibres such as polyester, using mulch on soil, having a plant-rich diet, reducing food waste, building a rain barrel for garden irrigation, meeting on-line, using sensors to dim lights or switch off.

There was a 'plug' for Forest and Bird itself and for other organisations doing good environmental work. Yes, the mobile workshop said, it is up to each of us.

27

MORE CHOPPY BOBS

Bethany wondered what thoughts were running through Paul's head when she moved back into the house on Sunday morning. He had moved his last things out of the house late the day before, spurred no doubt by the message in the envelope: 'Out by Sunday.' It was an abrupt end to what had been twenty-nine years of mostly happy marriage.

She hoped that emotionally he was in tatters over his transgression but she suspected he would be more concerned about the financial ramifications of the split. He had muttered about a rental house in their brief conversation since the fateful meeting at Mount Paradiso which had confirmed all. She wondered how long the liaison of the svelte hairdressing rock climber with her ageing former husband would last. Life in the rented house with the affair splattered in public would not be the delicious adventure of before. He might be struggling to understand what her 'ME' generation friends were saying while she might be baffled by his talk of dogleg, quadruple bogey, and flop shot as she washed his smalls.

The thought of sleeping in her bed again was repugnant. She wondered if she should have it fumigated or sold. Indeed, the more she thought about it, the more she considered a total 'make-over' was in order. Sell the house and its large section and move into one of those smart new town houses on the rise overlooking Tumanako. There she would be above worry level, with no more room than she needed for herself and visitors. And Rob, if he wanted to return.

And how was she emotionally? She had to concede she had not come through the break-up unscathed. She had been eviscerated by the phone call from Valerie Tosswillow and the first sight of Paul and Toni Dalzell together in *La vie en rose* had momentarily shrivelled her to nothing. But rage had done much to drive away despair and now she could feel the rational side of her brain clicking in. Thank God she would not have to put up with him any longer as a consort at official functions. If it was a mid-life crisis, there was nothing glamorous about it. Lately, his drinking had become much heavier and his standards had slipped hugely with embarrassing rants and repetitions, sloshings of wine, and interruptions of others with inane comments. She shuddered when she recalled Paul subsiding, drunk, on to the shoulder of Dame Francesca Potter at the top table and beginning to drool. She had had to summon help and get him out a side door.

The following week she took the opportunity to support the Polsons in Christchurch, visiting Polly in hospital and having a long tête à tête with Stephanie. In Maia and Stephanie, Bethany had two faithful friends she could unload to. When she saw Polly in hospital battling B cell non-Hodgkin's lymphoma, it put her own troubles in perspective. They were grim enough – a drug-taking, drug-dealing son and a treacherous husband – but she could at least pick up her life and carry on. Besides, her son and husband's issues were self-imposed, not like Polly's. She heard that Polly had started radiation therapy and was pale and fatigued but Bethany was tremendously encouraged to learn that for those in the fifteen to thirty-nine age group, there was an 85.9 percent chance of cure of B cell non-

Hodgkin's lymphoma. She knew, too, that Polly was a fighter. It was serendipitous that Daniel and Charlotte Hurley were close at hand to provide support.

It was a relief for Bethany to have time away from the goldfish bowl of Tumanako. It had been clear within days that the grapevine of Tumanako grew in fertile soil and had tendrils everywhere. News of the marriage break-up had filtered back to her by way of sideways looks and pointed fingers. In Christchurch she felt the relief of anonymity and it was refreshing to chat freely and without baggage. She had a stimulating conversation with Frank Hamilton, the mayor of Waitaki District Council, a widower as it happened, and they promised to keep in touch.

On return home, another task awaited which would take her mind off her own travails – a public appeal for information about Cindy Spratt. Bethany fronted the television appeal with Rowley Rowlands, Lionel Spratt, and Felicity Spratt. Rowlands assured the public that the police had 'rolled back the clock' and that Tumanako was now largely in a sound state of law and order and the campaign against drugs would be eased. Felicity Spratt, likewise, said she had finished her series of articles about the scourge of drugs and was now focused on other local issues. There was no point, they were saying as loud and clear as they could, in keeping Cindy Spratt hostage. Lionel Spratt beseeched viewers for any information on the whereabouts of his wife. He said she was a totally innocent bystander and he appealed from the depths of his heart to those who had taken her.

While Rowley Rowlands delivered a veiled threat – 'We will never stop looking for her until we find her' – Lionel Spratt appealed to the captors' humanity – 'Please relieve her suffering and our suffering and return her to us.' For any viewer with an ounce of empathy, it was a profoundly moving appeal. But Spratt accepted that the appeal was probably not to the captors' milk of human kindness but to whatever vestige of good there might be in their curdled view of the world.

Viewers could see the toll Cindy's disappearance had taken on him. He appeared to have shrunk; his eyes were gleaming as from a skull and his clothes were hanging loose. His face now was more pale than florid and the observant viewer would have noticed a vein throbbing on his forehead. From being a loud, obnoxious, elephantine bully, he had become a bereaved victim. The strain, too, could be seen on Felicity. She repeated her father's message.

Bethany rallied the town behind the appeal and told New Zealand by newspaper, radio, and television: 'Tumanako is suffering. We are a caring community, a trusting community. Please, everybody, help return Cindy to her family.'

Some locals grumbled that the police were kowtowing to the drugs monsters but the appeal had a galvanising effect on Tumanako and places beyond. The police received a flurry of sightings, some unfortunately from well-known busy bodies and conspiracy theorists. Marjorie Flett had heard something she felt obliged to pass on. All the leads would have to be checked out.

As word spread about the husband of the mayor having an affair with a hairdresser and national-class rock climber, business was brisk at *Toni's – hairdresser of distinction*. People flocked to see one half of the liaison at close quarters and to thrill at their proximity to such goings-on. Clients included regular customers of a rival, long-established salon, *Hair*

Boutique. Many of its clients entered *Toni's* with a Victorian Vintage hairstyle but emerged with a more avant-garde feathered long fringe or choppy bob and, for some weeks, there was much discombobulation in Tumanako, with people standing in front of mirrors coming to terms with the new look and looking at others with surprise as well. The traffic was not all one-way. Bethany Callendar was well-liked and admired in the town and some clients deserted *Toni's* in dudgeon and took their custom to *Hair Boutique* and elsewhere, causing yet more need to come to terms.

Some of the more conservative elements in town muttered that the shop rent of the upstart minx should be raised to drive her out but, when people probed further, they found to their dismay she not only owned the property but the fashion shop beside it. She may have been outrageous but she was no mere rock or social climber – she had a sharp business brain.

Word came back to Bethany that there had also been repercussions for Paul's accountancy practice. Tanya Spring, bastion of conservatism, had left his employ in outrage. Reflecting, she had put two and two together, smartly made four and apologised to Bethany for having been an innocent participant in Paul Callendar's cover-up. Paul Callendar also lost three clients – two church groups and a service club. As well, he soon lost Toni Dalzell. Bethany learned from one of those who always seem to know such things that Toni Dalzell's 'high' from the liaison had quickly turned to a 'low' in the full light of day and she had returned to her previous partner, Valerie Tosswillow.

With so much tittle tattle going the rounds, so many knowing looks, nodding heads, and sly remarks, Bethany Callendar felt obliged to make a public statement. Better to live in the full blast of publicity and have done with it, she reasoned, than to live amidst half-baked truth, innuendo, and snide remarks. Already she had heard one particularly nasty twist of the truth – that Paul Callendar had discovered Bethany in a compromising position in the garden shed with a visiting tree trimmer.

At a full council meeting, with Felicity Spratt present on behalf of *The Tararua Mirror* and the public gallery packed (some had had to be turned away and were craning their necks outside), she announced the end of her marriage and asked for privacy.

'I would be grateful now if Paul and I can get on with the rest of our lives without the current ferment of ill-advised conjecture. It is a sad time for us both after twenty-nine years together.'

She sat down with relief. The elephant in the room had been addressed. She sensed sympathy and support from her council colleagues.

Councillor Alison Peabody rose and broke the silence.

'I am sure you have the commiserations of us all. I do sincerely hope that the pressures of the job have not affected your private life.'

Bethany frowned – was Peabody implying the break-up was Bethany's fault?

'Thank you, councillor Peabody,' Bethany said. 'Can we now consider the matter closed.'

A part of her would have liked to disembowel her double-dealing husband and his self-serving moll in public but she was pleased she had handled the matter with dignity. Her restraint had put her above the rabble. Later, though, in a heart-to-heart with Maia Matenga, she admitted she felt at times empty and lost.

'It's hard Maia. Really hard. I'm angry, I'm sad, I'm lonely, I'm hurting...I've lost Rob. I've lost Paul. Is Alison Peabody right? Have I driven them away?'

'Nothing of the sort. You're the most considerate person I know. Men and the mid-life crisis. My Henry might have been heading that way until I kicked his butt. Bloody fool.'

Bethany looked at her in surprise. She knew how close Maia and Henry were. She couldn't imagine those two apart. She pondered life's mysteries.

◆ ◆ ◆

The role of Toni Dalzell in the break-up of the Callendars' marriage presented a problem for the Forest and Bird Society. Both Bethany Callendar and Toni Dalzell were committed members and both had firm friends there. Bethany was patron and Toni a vigorous participant in displays and demonstrations. Toni had wisely been absent at Bethany's launching of the mobile workshop and Bethany wisely steered clear when Toni helped staff the display. Members could but hope that time would be the great healer.

Simon Hurley had been as agog as anyone at news of Paul

Callendar's affair and the break-up of the marriage but now displayed a studied indifference. The great wave of the branch's work must continue, submerging any rips and whirlpools of human frailty and transgression along the way. He and Patricia had their own challenges that threatened to tear them apart.

With so much turmoil in the lives of some of the movers and shakers of Tumanako, no one noticed that week after week, month after month, Polson's carried on as it should with no unexplained breakages of equipment, no leakages of chemicals, no mysterious fires. The night watchman had become superfluous. It was something to be grateful for. Steve Polson did, though, confide in Stephanie that the factory was not as important to him as before. When he returned to it from Polly's bedside, he had to wonder if the factory had caused her illness and would have happily given it away to have Polly well again. There was no longer a burden of heritage.

28

A CHANGED MAN

T he 'get tough' policy on drugs and the raids in search of Rob Callendar and Cindy Spratt had unnerved the criminal element in Tumanako and crime in general was down. Some clan labs had vanished and word was that others were jittery. Clearly, it was not comfortable to manufacture when police might rampage through the door at any moment. One informant told Rowlands that drugs were being used more for their tranquillising effect than as a 'high'. As Bethany walked the town conversing with shop keepers, several remarked on the decline in shoplifting and expressed their satisfaction that odorous receivers of stolen property had been arrested and were awaiting trial. How happy were the pursuers of Mammon when law and order reigned!

There was, though, always that one almighty blight hanging over the town – the disappearance of Cindy Spratt in distressing circumstances. And for Bethany and Paul Callendar as well, the disappearance of their son Rob.

Bethany was liaising regularly with Rowley Rowlands. He invited her right inside his investigation, along with Lionel and Felicity Spratt. It was unprecedented for the media to have such access to information but Rowlands knew Felicity would respect boundaries. It was paramount that the eyes and ears of the community were on red alert and the media had a crucial role to play.

One afternoon Bethany and Felicity had a heart-to-heart at a downtown coffee shop. Bethany sensed that Felicity was more likely than anyone to hear of Rob's whereabouts. They both, too, were as one with Lionel Spratt. Bethany was profoundly affected by his endeavours to recover his wife. He was devoting every waking moment to the search with another realtor minding the business of Tumanako Realty in the meantime.

'I was worried she was so much under his thumb,' Felicity said. 'In fact, I told her she should get another job so she was out from under at least some of the day.'

'We all need time to ourselves,' Bethany said.

'I think I misread their relationship to some extent,' Felicity said. 'She means more to him than I thought.'

'Lionel can be overbearing,' Bethany said. 'Bull at a gate. Pushy.'

'Yes.'

'He had to be pushy in his job,' Bethany said.

Felicity's brow creased. 'There is that other thing.'

'What?'

'Mum might just have walked out. Faked an attack.'

They looked at each other in dismay. They had both been fully briefed on the missing person situation by Rowley Rowlands. They knew that every year in New Zealand more than eleven thousand missing persons' reports were submitted to police. Most people were found within seventy-two hours. Others simply vanished. Some had dementia. Some did not want to be found, perhaps because they owed money. Some – a few – were kidnapped.

'But I think it's me Bethany. She disappeared after she had spoken to me, and there was the torn coat and I was probably the target of the Molotov cocktail. It's me they're getting at.'

'You can't beat yourself up Felicity. You were doing your job.'

Felicity drank the last of her coffee. 'Mum's missing but not on purpose, and not lost. She was taken.'

Bethany put a comforting hand on Felicity's. 'There's no point them holding her now. But if she's not released soon, it'll be over to Rowley Rowlands to turn the whole district inside out.'

'Dad's wanting to bust into every dodgy house now himself.'

'It's horrible not knowing and fearing the worst. You know there's Victim Support, don't you.'

Felicity did know but she wouldn't use it – yet.

In the next week twice her heart skipped, first in the street and then in the supermarket, when she thought she saw her mother but no – mistaken identity. As for her father, he was soon running on empty. His loss of weight was striking enough, but more striking even than that, for Felicity, was his change of personality. Where before he had been bombastic and overbearing, always knowing what was best, he was now humble, even deferential, listening to people with intent, anxious to co-operate. She could see, and Bethany could see, that Lionel Spratt had changed because of his devotion to his wife. He would do whatever it took to get her back.

Felicity realised she had to return to work for her mental health. Colin Trainor could see that and was relieved. They were busy enough with just the three of them, let alone down to merely him and Pru Hardcastle. Felicity went back to the weekly round of annual meetings, awards, traffic accidents and sports events with thoughts of her mother ever swirling at the back of her mind. She pondered a subject for her next article in the personalities of Tumanako series. Toni Dalzell would make a riveting read but Felicity quickly dismissed the idea. Too raw. What about the mayor herself? No, again too raw.

It was Felicity's attendance at a symposium for farmers that provided her next choice of subject. Barry Fitzwilliam, farmer and regional councillor, was a well-known climate-change denier and his views would be sure to stimulate a response for and against. He was surprised to hear Felicity's proposal for an article but after an initial show of reluctance, accepted with pleasure.

A bosom buddy of her father, he had clearly been shaken by events.

'Sorry to hear about your mum,' he said. 'Dreadful business. And poor Lionel, what a state he's in.'

Fitzwilliam was accustomed to seeing someone as physically imposing as himself, not the hollow-eyed, shell of a man who had stood on his doorstep appealing for help in looking for his wife.

Felicity struck gold through her attendance at the symposium. Fitzwilliam provoked outrage at question time, and was at the centre of a fracas that threatened to spill over into fisticuffs in the foyer. She was used to his putting the world to rights with her father, a fellow true-blue conservative, but when Felicity spoke to him afterwards, he was shaky and wobbly, far removed from the coolly poised dogmatist she had always known.

For an hour a government representative had explained how farmers might minimise the effects of climate change by reducing greenhouse gases. The agriculture and energy sectors, he said, were the two largest contributors to the country's gross emissions, at fifty percent and forty percent respectively. He said to make animals emit less gas, their feed must be changed. He cited researchers at the University of California, Davis, who had found that adding one percent of red seaweed to cows' diets resulted in sixty percent reduction in methane emissions, and Dutch researchers who had developed a chemical that limits methane production. Researchers in New Zealand had identified a bacteria in the stomachs of cattle that specialises in methane production. Now, if that bacteria could be attacked with a vaccine...

The speaker impressed Felicity with the good sense of his suggestions. He spoke of achieving zero emissions for farm machinery and equipment and advocated low and no-tillage practices, reduction of the nitrous oxide in fertilisers, and the use of nitrification inhibitors on pasture.

At question time, Fitzwilliam could contain himself no longer. As he rose, his simmering discontent exploded into rage.

'Absolute bloody rubbish!' he thundered. 'I've never heard such alarmist and irresponsible tripe in all my days! Do you think I'm going to go down to the bloody coast and get bloody seaweed to feed to my cows? Have you not heard of natural climatic cycles...'

The speaker stood shocked and open-mouthed. But he had no need to defend himself. As Fitzwilliam continued to protest, opposition flooded in from all sides until Fitzwilliam found himself drowned out by the furore and rocked by the fists being waved in his face and the insults being showered on his head. He sat for a while in foul mood and then withdrew into himself as question and answer continued.

'It wasn't just the pointy-headed boffin. They all turned on me,' he complained later to Felicity.

Felicity was quietly delighted. The incident had provided an arresting intro to her article.

That evening, when she responded to the ping of her cell phone, her heart nearly leapt from her body. It gave the address of a property north of Tumanako. Nothing else. No name attached. There was only one thing it could be – the location of her mother. The message had to be from Rob Callendar. Nobody else would tip her off. He must have obtained access to a phone.

Felicity knew the general area as broken country, all dips and hollows, much of it covered in scrub and forest. Most of the roads in the area were unsealed, leading to small farms or plantations. She phoned Rowley Rowlands and got very little sleep that night. He had ordered her to stay away.

Felicity went to work as usual the next morning and told Colin Trainor and Pru Hardcastle of the development. She called Rowley Rowlands but he was unavailable. She struggled to focus on her work. When her phone rang mid-morning, she nearly dropped it in her haste to grab it. It was Rowlands. He said the police armed offenders squad had visited the property and arrested two people who were being interrogated. Cindy Spratt had not been found but the police believed she may have been held there. Forensic examinations were continuing. Rowlands said he had already phoned Lionel Spratt and he would phone Bethany Callendar next. He assured Felicity he would let her know of any developments.

'She may have been held there.' The words reverberated in Felicity's mind. The police statements were always understatements. 'Visited the property and arrested two people'. She could imagine the mayhem of it: the shattering of the door, the furious barking of dogs, the shouts to drop any weapons, the guns trained on the occupants, the hands grasping and handcuffing, hustling them into the police van. Felicity was sure her mother had been held there. Victimised because of her. And why had her mother been moved? The kidnappers must have found that someone had informed the police. Only a small, tight circle of people would have known where her mother was being held. The kidnappers would likely work out who had informed.

She feared now for Rob Callendar as well as her mother.

When Bethany Callendar put down the phone, she decided to visit the police station. The call from Rowley Rowlands had been her only connection for some time with the world her son now inhabited.

'You've arrested two people?'

'Yes.'

She could see that she was only there on sufferance. She determined to stay no longer than needed.

'Can I see them?'

She realised that would be irregular but she had to try.

'No...But I can show you their photographs.'

A glance and Bethany could identify the tall, bearded man who had knocked on her son's door while she watched from her car.

''That's him. He knows Rob. And he might know where Rob is.'

Rowlands would only say the man had a history. He thanked Bethany for her information and said it could be useful in their interrogation. She left the station with a flicker of hope. She was still, though, full of fear for both Rob and Cindy. Where were they and what was happening to them?

Her roller coaster of emotions continued Saturday morning when she officially opened a greatly expanded town council native plant nursery. Thanks to a climate-controlled facility, she was able to announce there were even kauri seedlings besides those of forty-eight other species. The nursery would not only supply the needs of the town council but the needs of commercial growers, farmers, those involved in major reforestation, and hobby gardeners. The nursery would fill a market gap with high-quality New Zealand native plants. As she gazed around the plants, she became aware they were serving another useful purpose – helping her tortured brain focus on something positive, chasing away demons. It was a reminder she needed to get out again into the bush with Forest and Bird. If only she could avoid Toni Dalzell. She would have a word with Simon Hurley.

29

A CHILLING MESSAGE

When the hen house blew up in the dark of the night, Patricia and Simon Hurley knew matters had come to a head. For weeks Patricia had received threatening messages from the drugs gang to pay back the $5,435 owed. But the money was long gone into pokies machines. In town that day, with the terrible boom of the explosion and the nauseating smell of over-cooked chicken still in his ears and nose, Simon scrabbled together the money and left it in their mail box. Within the hour, there was the roar of a motor bike and the money was collected.

'I hope that's the end of it,' Simon said.

Patricia looked at him in misery. The boom had been so loud and the fire so bright they had both first thought it was from Rosemary's bedroom in the front of the house. And it was from her windows they had drawn the curtains aside to see the leaping flames. The explosion had hurt Rosemary more than anyone for it was she who had named each hen and for her it was Beatrice, Emily, Agatha, Sarah, Roseanne, Katherine, and Amelia who had been fried, not just a bunch of chickens. Patricia voiced the fear of them both – what if the next one was thrown at the house itself? The gang seemed to be getting better at throwing Molotov cocktails.

Though his bank account was drained, Simon felt a measure of closure. There was only one way now to go and he would do everything in his power to help Patricia. First, the gambling cessation course. Addiction to the pokies and involvement in the drugs trade had brought her to the brink. She was only a police probe away from being in a jail cell.

'I'll do the course if you want me too,' she had said months before.

'Yes, I do want you to,' he had said.

But that had not been good enough. The wish to stop had to come from her and now it did, in awareness her marriage might crumble under the debt and the subsequent events. She had face-to-face counselling, attended a clinic, read the literature, and joined a group of survivors. Simon and Rosemary themselves had roles to play in providing love and support. Simon was told he must protect his finances and not lend money. Patricia withdrew from pokies machines a day at a time. She was now ready to accept facts about the toll of it, such as the more than one billion dollars lost on pokies machines in New Zealand annually. She had such a desire to help others she began to think she might eventually become a counsellor herself.

Then there was Patricia's job with Statistics New Zealand. She had excelled at the work before her subsidence into the gambling, interested in the diverse subject matter and with an aptitude for figures. Indeed, it was only her superior work record in the past that had given her a second chance. Now, spurred on by her contrition and by Simon's financial sacrifices, she threw herself into her work and soon regained the confidence of her employer.

Daniel and Charlotte, in Christchurch at university, heard by phone of the razing of the hen house. The incident plagued their thoughts for days and broke their sleep at night. They asked many questions which Simon answered as discreetly as he could. There was no need for the children to know their mother had been a drugs runner.

His mother's pokies machine addiction had always puzzled Daniel.

'How can anybody not see that the machines are programmed to win?' he said to Charlotte. 'What's the great attraction besides the fluke of an occasional small win followed by more losses?'

The sense of curiosity in him had to be satisfied. One day, after seeing Polly in hospital, he visited a pokies parlour inside a bar near the university. That night he reported to Charlotte.

'It was good fun, until I realised I'd gone through twenty dollars in fifteen minutes.'

Charlotte shuddered. Twenty dollars for a university student was a lot of money, nearly an hour's work under the Student Job Scheme.

He had had to wrench himself away and could understand how his mother had been sucked in.

'I'm never going to play the pokies in any place I'm living in,' he vowed to Charlotte. 'Only when I'm away somewhere on holiday and then with a limit.'

◆ ◆ ◆

For Simon, responsibilities as president of Forest and Bird in Tumanako were a welcome relief from the challenges of home. A 'turn-off lights' campaign was his next initiative. Unnecessary lights not only wasted people's money, the group's posters declared, but wasted precious power needed elsewhere. There was a plug as well for LED lights. The LED lights were energy efficient, produced zero toxic elements and were a hundred percent recyclable. The house needed fewer lights and the lights had a longer life-span. Solar-powered lighting also got a mention.

Rowley Rowlands was not impressed.

"We've just been waging a campaign against crime. Break-ins

and burglaries are down. Why the hell would you want to turn off the lights? Why not have a turn-off-water campaign instead?'

Simon Hurley knew Rowlands was being facetious but assured him he was not referring to street lights and made a mental note to have a 'turn-off water' campaign later.

Bethany Callendar was initially as concerned as Rowlands but agreed with lights-off in principle, except for security purposes. She was still living at home with her security cameras and lights and had no intention of removing them.

Simon had one more use for the cell phone which Patricia had used to communicate with the drugs gang. A farewell message. The wording preoccupied him. The message had to have the ring of finality and it also had to carry a hint of danger for the gang if they persisted in harassment. Monies owing had been paid but Simon suspected the gang did not give up its own so easily – Patricia had been a valued distributor and collector and they would want her to continue. There was, too, the complicating factor that both sides could dob the other into the police.

Simon got up in the early hours and began scribbling a signing-off message which Patricia could later phone through. He rose from the table, satisfied it was the best he could do. It was not as if he had had much practice in writing messages severing connection with a drugs gang with a penchant for throwing Molotov cocktails. Patricia appeared soon after. She, too, wanted to get it done. With furrowed brow and grimace, she read Simon's words: 'I have paid back your money and owe you nothing. Do not contact me again. I would be nothing but trouble for you. The phone is now destroyed.'

Being the courteous person she was, Patricia nearly added a 'Thank you' on the end. The threat in it sounded as weak as a slap in the face with a strand of soggy pasta, but it was the best they could do. Simon then sent the message, smashed the phone with a hammer, and dropped it in a receptacle containing other rubbish made of metal for recycling. Then he and Patricia embraced. That part of their lives, they hoped, was over.

A gambling cessation counsellor warned Patricia and Simon that the road ahead would be long and torturous, with the likelihood of glitches and backslidings, but they set out to build a new life together. It would require readiness to adapt, discipline, and intelligence. The same attributes as their global battle.

In the hope they had pulled Patricia from the brink, Simon took to the garden and orchard with new enthusiasm, and threw himself into making *Help the Planet, Aotearoa* the most vibrant and relevant magazine of its kind. Patricia had nowhere to go but up. She also worked with a passion.

For Simon, the greatest challenge was not to follow Patricia when she went out in the car. She was aware that Simon did at first mount surveillance, by their mutual agreement. She said she welcomed his vigilance as protection against her potential weakness. But it became tiresome for both when Patricia parted items on a library shelf to find Simon peering at her from the other side, or reached the end of the supermarket bread aisle to see Simon hovering near the buns and sponges tracking her every move. She became aware what mighty efforts it took to repair trust once it was broken. But day by day they kept strictly to the plan they had formulated together and the day came when Simon did not follow Patricia out the gate.

Simon, Patricia, and Rosemary all relished the occasional visit to Hector Dunwoodie. He had been nearly as shocked as them on hearing of the bombing of the hen house and offered to start them up again with three hens of his own. Simon knocked up a temporary hen house and they called on Hector to pick up the hens.

'Come in come in come in,' said Hector.

Bertie was pleased to see them too.

'Rise and shine. Time to play,' he said, to Rosemary's delight. Bertie perched where Rosemary could reach him and she rubbed the top of his head. He fluffed his feathers to show his appreciation and softly chattered to himself. Soon Rosemary followed Simon to examine the latest developments in Hector's workshop while Patricia lingered to have a word with Hector.

'I've finished Hector. No more deliveries from me.'

He could see she meant it and shrugged.

'I've cut down a bit,' he said. Then he smiled. 'I'm probably drinking more of my elderberry wine though.'

She noticed a tremor in his hand. He saw her frown.

'That's not the drugs or wine. That's the lithium carbonate I take.'

Patricia knew the lithium carbonate controlled the symptoms of bipolar disorder and prevented future episodes. The fine-hand tremor was a complication.

'Thank goodness for modern medications,' she said.

Pity there wasn't one for gambling addiction, she thought. She and Hector joined the others in the workshop and then proceeded outside to pick up the hens. Rosemary was already considering names. As they were leaving, Hector drew their attention to his swampy section of land and Simon was thrilled when Hector confirmed he would be turning it into proper wetland.

Patricia looked down towards the swampy pasture and remembered they were in Shambles Line.

'My mum and I picked up my father there sometimes when he worked at the old abattoir.'

Simon looked at her in surprise. 'I didn't know that.'

'Oh yes. A long time ago now. About thirty-five years. She wouldn't allow him in the car until he'd had a shower.' Then she remembered another thing. 'I used to play down there with someone else you know. Stephanie Polson, or Stephanie Curtis has she was then. Stephanie would be there with
her grandma picking up her grandpa.'

The next promotion of the Forest and Bird Society took place in the Hurleys' own backyard with Simon urging the revival of home vegetable gardens. There were so many benefits of growing your own food, he told some fifty people.

'It's fresh, it's handy, it's had no chemicals on it and best of all, you know you've done it all yourself. With a little bit of help from nature of course.'

Home vegetable gardens were the featured subject in the latest edition of *Help the Planet, Aotearoa* and Simon had copies of the magazine on hand. At the end of the two-hour session, he had the satisfaction of signing up five new subscribers. But later, a scrawl he discovered on the new hen house spoilt the morning: 'No one walks out on us.'

30

BIRD RESCUE

Felicity and Lionel Spratt did, in the end, accept the help of Victim Support. A missing person's case could sear a community and even a nation, let alone the family involved. One thing that helped console was awareness of Cindy Spratt's inner strength. A quiet exterior concealed a gritty core. In her youth she had been a champion gymnast and Felicity knew the courage that took from her own confronting experience with the wooden horse in gym class. And in recent years she and her father had seen how indefatigably Cindy had helped nurse her mother in her last days.

◆ ◆ ◆

Patricia Hurley found she was looking at Rosemary differently since the recent visit to Hector Dunwoodie. The information from Hector about the abattoir had made her question Simon's and her long-held suspicion that Rosemary's spina bifida had been caused by contamination at the site adjoining the factory where they had lived when Patricia was pregnant with Rosemary. Her father, her mother and she herself had been exposed for years to the chemicals at the abattoir site. Could they have been the source of the spina bifida? And Stephanie's grandfather, mother and Stephanie herself had been exposed for years to the chemicals and her grandfather had succumbed to cancer and now Polly was being treated in Christchurch Hospital for cancer. Was there a link, or were other factors more significant, or was it simply bad luck?

Patricia returned to Hector's to find out more.

'The abattoir closed just before I bought the property,' he said. 'They demolished the buildings, took the heartwood native timber out and dumped the rest. The only part left was some of the concrete floor. It's still there.'

He grimaced as he considered events since. 'Barry Fitzwilliam was looking to buy the land there for grazing for his dairy cows but he couldn't have done that anyway, as it was.'

'Why not?'

'For hygiene reasons, abattoirs use large amounts of water and there are large amounts of wastewater that must be treated before release. The wastewater contains blood, fats, proteins, and pathogens and these must be dealt with by chemical, biological or aerobic treatment. The abattoir had tanks full of chemicals like aluminium sulphate, ferric chloride, ferric sulphate, and poly-aluminium chloride.'

Hector looked down from his deck towards the site of the abattoir and sniffed the air.

'There was still a stink from down there when I moved in. Iron in the air.'

'So there would be potential for water and land contamination?'

'No doubt about that. The underground tanks, especially, could leak into the soil for a long time undetected. The chemical storage had to be on concrete floors but there could always be spillage. There probably wasn't much of a clean-up back then, if any at all.'

'Unsafe then even for dairy cows.'

'Would you want to drink their milk?'

Patricia could only purse her lips and mumble. Hector had given her much to think about. She made a mental note to talk to Stephanie too. She had seen the look of concern Steve Polson sometimes directed at Rosemary and since Polly's affliction, she had seen him look the same way at her.

'Really,' Hector continued, 'I should get people in to clean that area properly, even if it's for a wetland.'

Patricia had another reason besides the abattoir to visit Hector – the message scrawled on the hen house wall: 'No one walks out on us'. She needed closure of that part of her life and could think of no one else to talk to but Hector. His advice was succinct.

'Do nothing. You've paid them back. You've told them you're out. That's the end of it.'

Except it wasn't. At that moment an ear-splitting shriek from Bertie drew their eyes to him and then to what he was looking at. Two bulky, heavily tattooed Scum Dogs gang members had entered the room and closed the door behind them. Patricia recognised them as two of those who had given her drugs for distribution and received monies she collected.

'What the hell!' said Hector. 'You can't just walk in when you please.'

'We just have,' the older of the two said. He had the battered face of a prize fighter with more losses than wins on his record and the large, bulbous eyes of a dead fish. Those eyes panned from Hector to Patricia and back again. He and his companion had adopted a 'power stance' – legs wide and feet firmly planted.

Bertie by now was highly agitated, squawking the house down and fanning out his wings. Patricia was astonished at the wing span.

'Too bloody noisy here with the bloody bird. Go in there,' the man said, indicating the kitchen.

Hector led the way, followed by Patricia and the two home invaders.

'What d' you want?' asked Hector.

'This is handy, having you both together,' the man said.

'What d' you mean?'

'You owe us money,' he said, pointing to Hector, 'and you are still working for us,' he said to Patricia.

Patricia did not know a lot about bipolar disorder but she had experienced one of Hector's agitated moods and the disturbing change in his appearance and behaviour. He was in his sixties and spare in build but in his manic phase she had seen him unpredictably ferocious. Now, she could see the rage building.

'I owe you almost nothing,' he said. 'A hundred bucks.' Hector went to a tin on a shelf and took out the money. 'There's your damn money... You didn't come here for that. You came for her.'

The gang member didn't deny it. He pocketed the money and turned to Patricia.

Bertie had by now flown to the kitchen side of his enclosure and was shrieking from there as if warning the whole flock of predators at hand.

'If that bloody bird doesn't shut up, I'll bash its bloody head in!'

Patricia now realised they had tracked her to Hector's. It was she who was putting Hector and Bertie at risk.

'I'm no use to you any more,' she said. 'The police are on to me and I would only lead them to you.'

'You're talking crap. We haven't seen any police on to you.' The gang members looked at each other as if to confirm. 'Anyway, the boss says you're too valuable to let go.' He looked at Patricia, wracking his brain, searching for the words his boss had used. "Irreplaceable," he said. "Our own Matter Harry".'

Patricia could see that Hector was now at boiling point. His face was flushed and his body taut.

The older gang member was no student of body language. Ignoring Hector, he reached into a pocket of his jacket and brought out packets of drugs which he handed towards Patricia.

'No,' she said. 'No more of that. I told you, I'm out.'

The man's face curdled. 'I can't go back and tell him that.'

He took a step towards Patricia.

For Hector, it was a step too far. In a flash Hector was beside Bertie's enclosure, opening the catch. Bertie shot out of it like the winged avenger straight for the two gang members who were conveniently near him. His beak was snapping at them and came away with flesh and fabric. They flailed their arms at him, swearing and cursing. The younger one grabbed a rug off the floor and went into a foetal position in a corner, pulling the rug over himself. This allowed Bertie to concentrate his attack on the leader.

But when the older gang member grabbed a poker and began to

direct blows at the whirling, shrieking Bertie, Hector changed tactics. He reached into a drawer, grabbed a can and shouted at Bertie to go back into the enclosure.

Events had taken an unexpected turn and the older gang member was scratched, torn, and deeply shaken. But when the avian aerial attack had finished and the wings were out of his face, he still had the poker in his hand and posed a threat. He unleashed a stream of abuse at Hector and then at his companion, who was now sheepishly rising from his corner refuge.

'Out!' said Hector. 'Go! Or you'll get this.' He brandished the can in front of him. 'Pepper spray! Right between the eyes!'

The gang member stood there, still clutching the poker, but indecisive. Patricia could see the wheels of his mind turning. To turn tail and go would be a humiliation, a complete debacle. What lie could he make up on return? On the other hand, he had a weapon and with a few blows could kill the bird, pummel the two of them into submission and get back control.

He glanced nervously towards Bertie back in his enclosure awaiting instruction, tightened his grip on the poker and took a step towards Hector.

'You bloody weasel Dunwoodie!'

A jet of Hector's own concoction of pepper spray hit the home invader in the eyes. It was directed well away from anyone else and Bertie. The man's mouth was agape in pain and his hands clutched at his throat. There was fear, pain, and panic in his face. He was blinded and incapacitated and Hector knew he would not be a danger to them for at least seven minutes when he would recover his vision. Hector felt quite within his rights to take the offensive. He now brandished the can in front of the other home invader.

'Get him out or it's the same for you.'

The man hastened to comply, grasping the stricken man by his shoulder and leading him to the door. The normal, caring side of Hector now came to the fore and he turned from assailant to healer, offering medical advice all the way outside.

'Breathe normally,' he urged. 'Breathe normally. And blink.'

The breathing would help control panic and the blinking would encourage tears which would help flush the irritant from the eyes.

Hector did not mind the lack of thanks for his advice. He was just happy and relieved to see them stumbling away towards their car parked up Shambles Line. When they were well gone, Patricia followed and Hector turned to Bertie and rewarded him with a fresh bowl of fruit, nuts, and seeds.

'Yummy food for Bertie! Bring it on!'

When Patricia told Simon what had happened, he immediately told Felicity Spratt, reasoning that the more publicity the better. It would send a message to the drugs gang that the eyes of the police and community were on Hector Dunwoodie and help ensure his safety. Hector did not invite the publicity – he preferred to have no public association of himself with criminals – but he saw Felicity's point. The purists amongst the journalists would baulk on learning that Felicity had promised Simon to omit any mention of Patricia but she argued to herself that she was not so much distorting the truth as not revealing all of it. Anyway, the essence of the story was Bertie flying to the defence of Hector and driving the home invaders off.

Simon also felt an obligation to refer Hector to social services for drugs counselling. Simon understood that Hector was not a heavy user of illegal drugs, but he was concerned that even occasional use made him vulnerable to the demands and violence of the drugs suppliers. He shivered to think what might have happened to Hector and Patricia if they had not been armed with Bertie and pepper spray. Hector had protected Patricia and when Simon heard her story, he vowed to protect Hector.

'You can't go cold turkey,' he told Hector, speaking from personal experience of working with the addicted. 'You need a plan and an expert overseeing you.'

It was then out of Hector's hands. He was visited within the week by Raymond Proctor and a withdrawal programme was drawn up. Hector was put on appropriate medication that would be gradually reduced. His vital signs would be regularly monitored. Proctor's last instruction would prove the most challenging: no elderberry wine in the meantime. There followed weeks of watery eyes, runny nose, chills or sweating, joint pain, nausea, and trouble sleeping, but Hector persisted. Whenever he thought of quitting the programme, he remembered two unwanted visitors and an iron bar being raised to kill Bertie and maim Patricia and him. Never again.

Felicity phoned Patricia to get her side of the story, and Patricia was able to oblige – anything to throw the spotlight on the home invaders and discourage a repetition. Felicity also visited the scene to interview Hector and get a photograph of Bertie fanning his wings. She recoiled herself in alarm when Bertie spread himself wide. Hector said he had a wingspan of a hundred-and-ten centimetres.

'When that's coming at you at speed, as well as a beak that can crack hard-shelled nuts with ease, you'd rather be somewhere else, believe me.'

Hector's initial reticence to speak soon dissolved under Felicity's enthusiasm and encouragement. He went on to explain that parrots could be aggressively protective of their owners and that drugs gangs in Colombia were said to train thousands of birds to alert them of police raids.

The story was of huge interest locally. Paul Trainor took care to say in a box at the top that this was a news report, not part of Felicity Spratt's series on the drugs scene in Tumanako which had finished. The story soon went national and then international. Animal lovers everywhere were captivated. A *National Geographic* team from overseas visited and did an in-depth piece on animals as sentries. Guard geese, their article said, had been used throughout history and had even been used on 'Scotch watch' at a distillery in Dumbarton. Guard llama were used in farming, often running towards an intruder emitting a startling alarm call that sounded like a rusty hinge. Donkeys, dolphins, ostriches, and emus also got a mention.

Councillors Alison Peabody and Trevor Rudge writhed at the international blaze of publicity associating Tumanako with a drugs-related home invasion. But most citizens were still revelling in the story of Bertie coming to the rescue of Hector and welcomed the attention. As far as Hector was concerned, the more mention of Bertie and the less mention of pepper spray, the better.

31

ANGST ALL AROUND

Bethany Callendar was acutely aware that today's sensational story can be wrapping up fish and chips tomorrow. It seemed ages since she had publicly announced the break-up of her marriage and now that story was so old hat. Even the incident of Bertie and the home invaders was vanishing into the archives. But Bethany realised one kind of story never went away – the story with an unresolved ending. She rose each morning with the misery of a missing son on her mind and it remained on her mind all day, sharing space with the misery of the missing Cindy Spratt.

One evening, when she had Lionel and Felicity Spratt to tea, she could see the strain on both. Felicity's 'high' from the home invasion story had soon evaporated under the on-going pain of a missing mum.

'Do you know what I find most difficult of all,' Bethany said, over Weight Watchers' grilled salmon with white bean salad and steamed asparagus. 'Doing nothing.'

Lionel and Felicity agreed. Though they were both doing

plenty in their own way, they said it felt like nothing. They were still at the mercy of others.

'I had a visitor today,' Bethany said, 'a little girl and her mum looking for their missing cat, Comet. They had a picture of Comet that's now all over the neighbourhood. Why don't we do the same for Cindy and Rob? Put up their pictures so people can't move without seeing them.'

Lionel and Felicity agreed. Lionel said he would pay for the printing. They were sure they could co-opt others to help distribute the posters. It would also be sending a message to all those involved that Cindy and Rob were gone but not forgotten.

'Another thing,' Lionel said later, over the Weight Watchers' mango jelly and raspberries dessert. 'A reward. I'll put up ten-thousand dollars for any information leading to the finding of Cindy.'

'And I'll do the same for Rob,' Bethany said. She was sure Paul would come up with half of it. He had been very obliging of late. She knew that he, too, needed to do something for Rob.

Felicity sat with creased brow. 'There is just that one thing about a reward. The drugs bosses might worry one of their own could be tempted by it and do some dobbing in. That might cause them to see Rob and Cindy as dangerous to have around.'

The three of them sat and mulled that over.

'It's a risk worth taking,' Bethany said eventually. 'People fall out with one another, allegiances change. I brought him into the world. I allowed him to go into that other world. I'll now do everything I can to remove him from that world.'

Lionel agreed.

Felicity nodded. She could understand.

Bethany Callendar could sense, like never before, a general feeling of anxiety and uncertainty in her town. She was aware the campaigns of the Forest and Bird Society regarding climate change were responsible for a measure of this, but could not be blamed entirely. She was sure it was the result of many factors coalescing: Cindy Spratt and Rob Callendar missing, the mayor's husband and a prominent rock climber cum hairdresser having an affair, Polly Polson in hospital in Christchurch, Molotov cocktails and a home invasion, a saboteur at the factory... She realised there might be more she didn't know about. Whatever, she felt as though she was overseeing a town wracked with doubt and discontent. She was mayor not of Tumanako but of Angstville.

The home invasion and the celebrated defence mounted by Bertie had the inevitable consequence of a second visit to Hector Dunwoodie by Rowley Rowlands. He was accompanied by Bethany Callendar, desperate for any lead to her son.

'How you going?' asked Bertie when they entered. Then, moments later, 'Polly put the kettle on.'

Bethany's smile faded as her thoughts flitted to Christchurch Hospital.

Bertie realised he was the centre of attention.

'Wave to our visitors,' Hector said.

When Bertie fanned his wings, Bethany and Rowlands could see the hidden warrior.

'Hector, there's no problem about using Bertie to fight off your attackers,' Rowlands said.

'I'm pleased to hear it,' said Hector.

Bethany detected a hint of smugness in his reply. Public perception of Hector had been transformed by the home invasion. He was now greeted in town by supportive waves and claps on the back. He was the infirm crackpot getting on in years who had fought off predators in his own home with the aid of a bird. It was the stuff of legends. The Ancient Greeks would have immortalised him in poetry and song.

'Under Section forty-eight of the Crimes Act, 1961,' Rowlands continued, 'you may use reasonable force to defend yourself. But...' Here he paused, letting the word stretch. Bethany wondered if he, too, had detected a smugness in Dunwoodie. 'Your use of pepper spray worries me.'

Hector shifted uncomfortably.

''Pepper spray has been banned in New Zealand for civilian use since 1984. It can have serious health consequences.'

'So can a blow from a fire poker,' Hector said. "And it's my own concoction.'

'That may be so but I could nevertheless charge you with unlawful possession of pepper spray. What if someone used it when threatened with a feather? I must confiscate your spray and issue you with a formal warning.'

'Do what you have to Rowley,' Hector said magnanimously, with the comfort of knowing he had another can ready for use if necessary. He was confident he knew the difference between a poker and a feather and would use his spray appropriately.

Rowley Rowlands raised another point of concern – why had the home invaders targeted Hector Dunwoodie? Hector admitted he was a small-time user of illegal drugs but stressed that he was now receiving treatment and had stopped using.

The police forensics team had preceded Rowlands to the crime site looking for anything that might help identify the home invaders. Some human flesh on the floor of Bertie's cage was of interest. It provided DNA material and that lead was being further investigated. There was something else that garnered the attention of Rowlands.

'We found the coat of one of your visitors had been ripped and with it, a pocket. On the floor under a chair was a scrap of paper which appeared to have fallen from the pocket. It had a name on it, Bac Nam Nguyen. Can you tell me anything about that?'

Hector couldn't. He could only mumble that Bac Nam Nguyen was a friend from Forest and Bird and made the best fish and chips in town.

'Lovely man with a lovely family,' Hector said.

'Mm,' replied Rowlands, with a thoughtful look on his face. For a moment they sat in silence which might have been uncomfortable for Bertie for he started softly chattering to himself. Then Rowlands threw out a final, catch-all question. 'Is there anything else you can tell me about the home invaders?'

'Only that they were Scum Dogs.'

The information strengthened Bethany Callendar's resolve to forbid the gang insignia in the town. She mentally put it on the agenda for discussion later.

As they drove away, Bethany brought up the name Bac Nam Nguyen. She knew him vaguely from Forest and Bird and she recalled Felicity Spratt's article in *The Tararua Mirror*.

'That family's been through the wars,' she said. 'Well, more Bac Nam Nguyen's parents really. But Bac Nam Nguyen would have witnessed things as a young boy that nobody should have to see.'

Rowlands remained silent, plunged in thought.

Surveillance of Bac Nam Nguyen began the following week. Responsibility went beyond Rowley Rowlands to the district commander.

To the uninformed eye, the widespread drugs investigation in Tumanako was over – the suburbs had been returned to peace and calm and law and order had been re-established. In fact, the probable abduction and incarceration of Cindy Spratt had taken police activity to a new high. And when photographs of Cindy Spratt and Rob Callendar began appearing all over town and beyond, police began receiving a stream of calls which all had to be investigated. When rewards were announced as well, calls tripled. There was even talk in the town of bounty hunters coming in from outside. The police suddenly had to upscale their investigation while pretending they were downscaling.

Since the very beginning, police had wanted to get at the root of the problem – the flow of drugs into Tumanako. Someone was orchestrating the supply but the identity of the drugs linchpin remained a mystery. The Scum Dogs were that person's distributors and muscle. The home invasion had put the name and photograph of Bac Nam Nguyen onto the evidence board at the Tumanako Police Station.

When Bac Nam Nguyen's fishing boat put out to sea, binoculars followed it, and not in a haphazard way. Trained eyes studied its passage and, when it stopped, the eyes peered for an indication that anything had been plucked from the sea besides snapper, trevally, and kahawai, or dropped into the sea, besides discarded catch. Meanwhile, back in his office, Rowley Rowlands pondered the multivarious factors that triggered a policeman's suspicion. Would he have been so interested in

Bac Nam Nguyen if he weren't Vietnamese? What if the scrap of paper from the Scum Dogs gang member's pocket had said Robert Smith or Sylvia Sloan? Might he then have considered something much more mundane like a dental appointment or a shoe to be mended? He, too, had read the article on Bac Nam Nguyen that had appeared in *The Tararua Mirror* and been especially gripped when Bac Nam Nguyen spoke of bad people trying to get Vietnamese people to carry drugs on their return trips to New Zealand. Why would the gangster be carrying the name of Bac Nam Nguyen unless it was something to do with drugs? It was unlikely to be a reminder that four pieces of fish, a pineapple ring and a scoop of chips were to be picked up.

A wire-tap was put on Bac Nam Nguyen's home phone and work phone. The Vietnamese-speaking police officer assigned to the case soon found the phone surveillance discomforting and onerous, especially on early Friday evenings when the orders to the shop made his stomach rumble terribly. Visits between families had him on red alert, straining to recognise if a code was being used. Packages arriving from Vietnam had to be opened and checked. When the family attended classes in Vovinam – a martial art employing grappling, strikes, counter-attacks and use of weapons – the observing officer pondered the need in mostly sleepy Tumanako.

Bethany had requested Rowlands keep her up-to-date but he exercised discretion and withheld from her any mention of the surveillance of Bac Nam Nguyen. He trusted her not to be a tittle tattle but reasoned the fewer people who knew, the better. Recent events had him more than a little rattled. Just when he thought things were calming down, Cindy Spratt disappeared and then a parrot thwarted a home invasion, making international headlines. The way things were going, any suggestion Vietnamese refugees were being harassed by police would have questions being asked in the House.

32

INTIMATIONS OF
MORTALITY

Polly Polson had never considered she might die. Before now. There had been times, such as when hurtling down hillsides on her mountain bike, and driving in fog with her head out the window, death could have claimed her, but she was bullet-proof then. Now, as she lay pale and wasting in the hospital bed, life was measured a day at a time. Sleep came intermittently. She had always enjoyed her food but now her food tray went back to the kitchen mostly untouched.

She was never alone for long. Day and night, there was a procession of staff to her bedside. Nurses constantly monitored her vital signs and regularly took blood. She was on her own treatment plan but was amazed that so many doctors from so many specialties were involved. After numerous diagnostic tests, she had been told she had lymphomas that were slow-growing and could be treated. Thankfully they had been detected early and were not in the organs outside her lymph system. The doctors also said it helped that she was young. But for Polly, lying helpless, dependent on others, each day was interminable. As an only child, she had relished having her own space and ticking off objectives one by one.

For Stephanie Polson, Christchurch had become a second home. Every day she was with Polly. As Polly's treatment continued, Steve Polson flew down every weekend. The doctors spoke with them regularly. They were told there were about sixty known types of B cell non-Hodgkins lymphoma and that Polly had been diagnosed with marginal zone lymphomas. The cancerous cells had originated from lymphocytes, a type of white blood cell that was part of the body's immune system. The B cells were responsible for fighting infection by producing antibodies to neutralise pathogens. Steve and Stephanie were told that, just like other forms of cancer, all types of non-Hodgkins lymphoma could spread to other parts of the body when not treated quickly enough. But the doctors were encouraged that Polly's lymphomas had been found early and that treatment had started promptly.

As Polly lay back on the hospital bed with all the energy sucked out of her, her body at high risk of infection and further complications, Steve and Stephanie inevitably asked themselves where Polly's cancer might have originated. When Steve queried if she could have got it from the factory, Stephanie remained silent. Did she think so but want to spare his guilt? The family already had unspoken anxiety about Rosemary Hurley's spina bifida though Ray Polson had been assured the land leased to the Hurleys had been decontaminated.

Stephanie told him of the telephone call from Patricia Hurley and put forward another possible source of Rosemary's spina bifida and Polly's cancer – the old abattoir in Shambles Line. Steve listened, intrigued, as Stephanie told him what Hector Dunwoodie had said about the chemicals, and of picking up her poppa there sometimes, with her grandmother, and seeing Patricia with her mother picking up her father. No one could say where the cancer originated but for Steve, knowing it might not have been the factory, eased guilt. The agony that could not be eased was the knowledge that Polly had cancer and he and Stephanie vowed to do everything in their power to help her fight it.

Through visits and telephone calls, Polly kept in touch with events in Tumanako and they helped take her mind off herself. The disappearance of Cindy Spratt tormented her. She thought about Rob Callendar as well, and the posters all over town. She remembered him being three or four years ahead at school – his hair, spilling over his collar, pushing the boundary of school rules. And there was the Callendars' marriage break-up to think about. Polly could imagine the field-day the gossip mongers would have had with that. She wasn't shocked that Toni Dalzell was one half of the affair but she was shocked that Paul Callendar was the other.

There were, too, the other patients. Polly had a bed by the window of the oncology ward, providing a long view over greenery. On her first day there, the patient in the bed across from her, Hazel, a slightly built, dark-haired woman in her sixties with a long-time smoker's husky voice, stood at the head of her bed and introduced herself. Then Trevor, seventies, introduced himself from his bed on the other side and Rhonda, fifties, from the bed next to Polly's. A pessimist might have seen them as the four riders of the Apocalypse, signifying the end of times, but Polly soon saw them as the four riders of the Renewal, fighting off their afflictions together. From her chats with them and snatches of conversation from staff and visitors, she quickly gathered what stage they were at in their treatment and she followed their progress. There were others in the ward she had a nodding acquaintance with. Nearly everyone was much older than her and she could see pity for her in some of their faces and the faces of their visitors. There was one young man, Sam, along the other end, who had leukemia. He had lost all his hair but made a joke of that and his gritty, self-deprecating humour lifted everyone.

Polly dared to dream of the future. The psychologist assisted her in this. She realised she was much loved and had many people to live for, besides herself. One morning she vowed to herself to do everything she could to get well but when her lunch was cheerfully brought in and put beside her she could only look at it in dismay. Normally she would have wolfed down the sausage, mashed potato, and vegetables, but she had eyes only for the ice cream and jelly. Her brain was saying 'Eat it for your own good' but her stomach was rebelling at the thought. With a supreme effort, she mustered the energy to have some of the sausage and mash, raising the spirits of her mother when she told her mid-afternoon.

After four weeks of it, Polly could appreciate why people sometimes changed direction after a long stay in hospital. For many, it would be the first time they had slowed sufficiently to consider where they were going. Polly considered her relationship with Daniel and her business studies course. Daniel visited so frequently she was worried she was distracting him from his engineering studies. She felt her illness had drawn them even closer despite the drawn and pale face and patchy hair looking back at her in the bathroom mirror. Daniel's visits, and her mother's, and those of Charlotte and others, gave her something to look forward to every day.

She discovered her cancer brought down barriers. She got the full story of Patricia's battle with pokies addiction and Daniel's admission that he had felt the hypnotic appeal of it himself. She heard of the torment Lionel and Felicity Spratt were going through and the fear they might never see Cindy again. She heard how Melody Gilmour was in trouble over drink-driving and evading a check-point and was worried about repercussions at the school. From a neighbouring bed, she heard snatches of a patient's will being updated. She sardonically reflected there was no point doing one herself – she had almost nothing to bequeath except her mountain bike and a modest bank account.

It was a great day when the whole Hurley family visited. Rosemary was in the forefront and her love for Polly shone bright. Simon and Patricia kept the visit brief and bubbly; they knew that Polly had to harness what energy she had to fight the cancer. Bertie's battle against the home invaders had centre stage with Simon and Rosemary the narrators. Polly listened avidly. They acknowledged their account of it had come from Felicity Spratt's article in *The Tararua Mirror* and left Polly a copy of the article to read at her leisure. They visited the next day as well before travelling home. Rosemary spoke about changing her study from botany to medicine but Polly reminded her how much she loved the natural world. Rosemary said she could always keep that as a hobby.

One day when it was just her mother and her, Polly raised the subject of the factory's chemicals.

'Could they be the cause of my cancer?'

Stephanie looked fraught. The unspoken fear had been aired. 'We don't know. Perhaps.' Then a memory stirred. She was reminded of her conversation with Patricia Hurley and told Polly of waiting with her nanna at the abattoir. 'But really no one knows.' Stephanie looked around her and dropped her voice. 'Where did all these people get their cancer? Was it the air they breathed, what they ate, where they lived, family genes? Whatever it was Polly, the main thing is for you to get over this. One day we'll move to the Mount. I've talked about it with Steve.'

It was Daniel on his next visit who provided a more balanced view of the factory.

'We should be proud of the factory,' he said. 'It's kept the town going all these years. It's well run and it looks after its staff. And let's not forget the wonderful material it works with and the wonderful products it produces. Wood is the only renewable construction material and the manufacture of wood products and structures consumes low energy compared with other options.'

Polly knew of Daniel's serious misgivings about the factory but these were shelved as he defended her family's business.

The pragmatist in him spoke: 'What else would provide those jobs in Tumanako?' And then the committed 'greenie': 'Each tree captures huge amounts of carbon over its lifespan and when it is felled after some thirty years, another tree is planted. Your dad also supports environmental projects outside the factory. He partners with the Cawthron Institute on scientific research. I know one of the projects is to protect endangered birds and another is to research the sediment in waterways from forestry harvesting.'

By the time Daniel finished, Polly felt a lot better about Polson's. She also realised how much she loved Daniel.

◆ ◆ ◆

As day followed day, Polly's treatment plan progressed until she had completed both chemotherapy and radiotherapy and the doctors were able to tell Steve and Stephanie that results looked promising,

A new issue though was vexing staff. The drugs cabinet on the ward was broken into one afternoon and a considerable quantity of drugs taken. It was a rapid and brazen break-in, between the official issuing of drugs by staff. The police were notified and examined the film from the ward's CCTV camera. It revealed a woman at the cabinet but she was masked and could not be identified. They questioned staff about visitors to the ward that day. Besides Daniel, Polly had been visited by Charlotte Hurley, Stephanie Polson and Melody Gilmour who was also visiting family in Christchurch. Police inquiries were continuing.

In the large open room that is a hospital ward where talk inevitably drifts beyond the curtains, Polly heard two staff discuss the theft.

'Fancy someone being as desperate as that for drugs or money.'

She was staggered that a hospital would be targeted. How low could people get? But then she thought of the disappearance of Rob Callendar and Cindy Spratt and could only shake her head in dismay.

33

DO OR DIE

Rob Callendar had decided it was time.

He had had it with the Scum Dogs. The continuing incarceration of Cindy Spratt was the clincher. He feared Cindy's incarceration would end badly, for Felicity as well as for Cindy. The continuing curses and threats against them made his stomach turn. The gang's grudge had not abated with the Molotov cocktail thrown at the car. Mother and daughter were still in the firing line. The home invasion of Hector Dunwoodie and harassment of Patricia Hurley also grated hugely. He had not signed up for his friends to be killed and maimed. Callendar had heard Scum Dogs gang members mercilessly mocking the two members who had been driven off by Bertie and the pepper spray, and he had heard threats of reprisal against Dunwoodie and Hurley for the loss of respect. It was one thing to put him under house arrest for the heat the mayor was putting on, and use him as a P lab slave, but another to kill mother and daughter. He had had enough and was getting out from under.

Felicity Spratt received a text: 'Be at school bus shelter Dome Valley Road 2am Saturday. By rimu tree. No police'.

The timing of his escape was crucial. He had chosen the morning after the Friday night 'Happy Hour'. The gang should be sleeping it off at that time and he would ensure the guard dogs had something to help them sleep as well. He could not afford to fail. The gang did not tolerate loose ends. He would be forever scarred by seeing others trying to break away but failing and could identify where some were buried. He had already taken a huge risk accessing his phone.

That night, when the music stopped and the only sound was the cataclysmic snoring of two of the gang, Rob Callendar rose and crept through the house. First, he threw the dogs some meat heavily laced with drugs. Then he turned off the security alarm and took out his personal copy of the front door key, silently congratulating himself for having it cut earlier for just such an occasion. Then, with great deliberation, he unlocked the door and stepped outside. The chill of the air made him shiver and he had to muffle a cough. At least one other obstacle had to be avoided – a trip wire three metres from the front of the house. If his foot hit that, all hell would break loose. If he had not been looking for it, he would never have seen it. There it was, ankle-high. One high step and it was behind him.

'At least one other obstacle' he had said to himself. Had they planted others he didn't know about? Slowly, slowly, every sense on high alert, he moved away from the house, exercising more patience than he knew he had. Soon he was at a distance from the clan lab and prison, tucked amongst trees on the hill. It continued to sleep, a fortress no longer.

Now he moved quickly. He had brought nothing except his cell phone. When he reached the road, he looked back. A million stars wheeled overhead in the peace of the night. In other circumstances the silence could have been a blessed balm, allowing rest and rejuvenation before the dawn of another day. But he was aware his heart was racing and felt a cold sweat. For the killers in the house on the hill, there was no such thing as the sanctity of human life. His life now depended on Felicity Spratt being at the school bus stop. He pushed on, taking care not to bang into something in the dark and make a noise.

Twenty minutes later, the rimu tree loomed in front of him. He checked his watch again. To his anguish, it still showed half past one. He realised the battery had given out and the watch had stopped. But when had it stopped? Was he late? Had Felicity been and gone? He peered into the dark ahead. To be here at the rising of the sun was to be as good as dead. There was the bus stop and there was the tree but where was Felicity? Would his life end here because the battery of his watch had died? There was no going back. They might already have discovered he was gone.

Then, in thick foliage at the base of the tree, he saw the car. The shrubs almost completely concealed it. He had lived in a world of paranoia so long, another fear struck. What if Felicity had not received his message? What if the message had gone to the Scum Dogs gang and they were waiting for him in the car? It was just the sort of thing they would do. He crept forward and peered through the rear window. There was a driver at the wheel but in the gloom, he could not even tell if it was man or woman. He realised he had to trust. It was now or never. He swung wide. The movement jerked the driver's head around and he could see who it was.

Felicity.

As they drove down Dome Valley Road, his whole body trembled and he had to take deep breaths to calm his heart.

'I nearly left,' Felicity said. 'At two fifteen I began to think you'd put it off.'

Felicity had abided by his wish of no police. He had known that any hint of police and the gang would have been on high alert and he would never have got out of the house. Now she drove, fast but steady, and as the kilometres slipped by and the house on the hill receded ever further behind them, his body gave way, and he slumped half-senseless beside her, head on her shoulder.

She drove him straight to Bethany's house, parked on the street outside, and phoned her. He was barely inside, with a cup of coffee and hot scone in hand, when the police were there, waiting to take him into custody. He offered no resistance. Felicity agreed with Bethany that a police cell was the safest place for Rob and Felicity suspected it might be for her as well. But she had too much still to do.

There was another reason Bethany had summoned the police – she wanted Rob off drugs and believed that would only happen if he were in prison.

Later that morning, Bethany Callendar, Felicity Spratt, and Rowley Rowlands sat in an interview room with Rob Callendar. Callendar, ashen-faced and short of sleep, looked wiped out. Rowlands suspected he could help greatly with inquiries about the gang, but currently there was one subject above all he wanted to talk to him about – Cindy Spratt.

'I don't know where they're holding her,' he said.

'But you know they are holding her.'

'Yeah. They talked about holding the bitch but never said where she was. They were very pissed off about the raids.'

Felicity closed her eyes and lowered her head. Where was her mother and what were they doing to her? She knew very well from her work that not all stories have a happy ending.

After the brief police interview, there was the immediate task for Rob and Felicity of accompanying the police armed offenders squad to Dome Valley Road in a police car with tinted windows. They saw where Felicity had picked Rob up and Rob pointed out the property he had fled from. It was practically hidden from the road, tucked amongst trees on a rise some three kilometres distant. The police raid had a disappointing result – nobody and nothing was there. Rob Callendar's flight had been the signal to strip it bare. The tracker dogs had a field day of sniffing and barking but the only remnants of drugs were slight deposits embedded in the walls, floor, and ceiling.

That afternoon at the police station, Rob Callendar got a whispered threat not to talk. Shortly afterwards, he was formally charged with manufacturing and distributing methamphetamine and other illegal drugs and remanded in custody. Felicity Spratt and Melody Gilmour both testified against him. At trial he pleaded guilty and the judge took that into consideration when sentencing him to only eight years. Felicity suspected the judge might also have felt a measure of pity for him. She winced at his appearance in the dock:

emaciated, pale, and shaky, with darting eyes and anxious expression. She was relieved he was now on a medication withdrawal plan. It would take months of gradual reduction in medication, with his vital signs regularly monitored and his blood tested.

'He could never have got off the drugs on his own,' Bethany said to Felicity. 'If he'd kept going, he would have been dead within a year.' She thanked Felicity again for her part in his escape and enveloped her in a hug. 'I can never thank you enough. Thank God he's now in prison.'

Felicity told Melody Gilmour later that it was sad to hear a mother say that. But that was Bethany the realist speaking.

Bethany became a weekly prison visitor, always finding time amidst her busy weekly round of meetings and consultations to visit the regional prison forty-three kilometres from Tumanako. As painful as it was to see Rob behind bars, she felt for the first time in years she had her son back. On the drive to the prison, she worried what she would see, and on the drive back, she delighted in signs of progress amidst the typical symptoms of withdrawal from opioids: the runny nose, watery eyes, sweating, nausea, and muscle cramping. From her own experience in social services, she urged him to exercise in moderation, drink plenty of water, and do much deep breathing.

Felicity told Bethany she had decided not to visit. She was sure some gang members still saw her as their crusading enemy, whipping up public anger against gangs in general and the Scum Dogs in particular. It would not go well with Rob Callendar if he talked to her. She would keep in touch through Bethany.

Felicity heard that Paul Callendar had also become a dedicated prison visitor, alternating with Bethany's visits. She heard, too, that Paul and Rob Callendar were still getting over the shock of the change in each other's lives. Rob had been astonished at discovering his mother and father had split and even more astonished at hearing the cause. Toni Dalzell was much closer to his age than his father's. For the first time he wondered if he got his wayward streak from his father.

Felicity visited Hector Dunwoodie to show him and Bertie the celebrated article. Bertie took a great interest in the photograph of himself which took up most of the page.

'Flipping hell!' Hector said. 'I didn't think you'd go that big.'

'Bertie was the story and what a photograph he made!' Felicity said.

'Well, rather him than me.'

Felicity had known he would be happy to bask in Bertie's shadow.

Hector was fidgety and restless. Cindy was on his mind.

'I've been wondering if I can trade my help for her release.'

'How do you mean?'

'I can help them with their drugs production you see.' Hector's eyes were shining and his movements were sharp and jerky. Felicity could see he was coming into a manic phase. 'There are all sorts of ways I can help them.'

Felicity looked at him amazed and horrified.

'It's not going to help if you get more involved with them Hector.'

'But it might help free your mother…Not their hard stuff. Just the weed.'

He began striding around. Bertie picked up on his agitation and screamed twice, piercingly.

'I've got this great new organic fertiliser that would grow the crop faster and bigger. And the design for a weed camouflage net that can be dropped at the first sound of a helicopter. There's biogas heating as well that would save them a packet.'

'Hector, they would take you over. You would never get out from under them. In the end they would spit you out.'

He was walking now in a circle, waving his arms at each idea.

'I could provide them with robotic security officers, a spray that would kill scent for the canine patrol, solar power, a better website, urine recycling irrigation.'

She stopped his pacing with a long and heartfelt hug and told him no. The abduction and capture of her mother had taken a great enough toll already.

Later, Felicity received a call from Bethany. Bethany had just come from Rob. He had quietly passed on that the prisoner was being held 'up the gully'. Bethany had already told Rowley Rowlands. Rowlands had been intensely interested but deeply exasperated. In the broken country around Tumanako, there were scores of gullies. The police needed more information. Bethany was instructed to tell Rob to keep his ears open. It looked as though the best chance of a breakthrough might be within the four walls of the prison.

In her contact with the police and the mayor, Felicity also became aware of the police surveillance on Bac Nam Nguyen. She found it impossible to believe he had anything to do with drugs trafficking but being the good reporter she was, she kept a tiny corner of her mind open to the possibility.

34

PASSAGE TO
FREEDOM

After the lead of 'up the gully', maps of the district were studied, drones were sent up, trusted rural dwellers were contacted, postal services were interviewed, and the police armed offenders squad began targeted raids. The result was trauma at dawn for innocent householders near and far, including several individuals and couples who had specifically sought a life of quiet and solitude to escape the frantic pace of modern life and contemplate the meaning of existence. The arrival of furiously barking dogs and heavily armed police officers set pulses dangerously racing and one man – fifties, overweight, a chain smoker – had a heart attack and the rescue helicopter had to be called. Later there was much talk of infringement of personal rights and impending lawsuits and the police cut back the campaign. A much more precise lead would be required before the heavy brigade did their own version of a home invasion again.

The time had come for Bethany Callendar to put her house on the market. She confided to Maia Matenga that it was with mixed feelings and Maia felt deeply for her dear colleague and friend and offered to help in any way. Years of happy memories were going on the market as well as that terrible memory of betrayal. To the person in the street, Bethany Callendar remained the strong, indomitable leader of the town but Maia saw occasional plunges into melancholy and flashes of rage as well.

'I will ask Paul not to purchase in Rawhiti Heights,' Bethany told Maia on arriving back from Tumanako Realty (The least she could do for Lionel Spratt in his time of dire need was to support his business). 'One of us there is enough. Can you imagine what it would be like to go to the gate in the morning for the paper and see his latest bint in her dressing gown next door fetching hers.'

'Isn't he on his own now?'

'So far as I know.' Bethany gazed into the distance. 'As a matter of fact, I think he's still in a state of shock.'

'Not surprising,' Maia said. 'His affair rumbled, Toni Dalzell gone, trusted assistant gone, living in a rented house, son in jail.'

'He's brought it on himself.'

Bethany reflected on how one person's transgression could involve so many others: accomplice, wronged partners, realtor, friends, and, in her high-profile case, the community at large. Yes, the sooner she was in a place of her own, the better.

That evening Bethany decided she and the community could

no longer simply stew in misery about one of their own missing in suspicious circumstances. They had to do more. First, she consulted with Lionel and Felicity Spratt and with their approval, announced a Passage to Freedom to bring back Cindy Spratt. It would be held from ten on Saturday morning to ten on Sunday morning at Kowhai Park. Participants could move in whatever manner they pleased: walk, run, wheelchair, bicycle, e-scooter, mobility scooter (separate lane for the mechanised). The funds raised from sponsorship would go towards the reward for information leading to the finding of Cindy Spratt (Bethany Callendar had already donated ten thousand dollars, with the agreement of Paul Callendar to pay half – after only a momentary pause).

Bethany Callendar had correctly interpreted the mood of the town. The response to the Passage to Freedom was extraordinary. Everybody could do something to help expunge the crippling feeling of helplessness. Even residents of nursing homes turned up to do a circuit or two on their walking sticks and walking frames. Melody Gilmour rallied her school to participate and where the students went, the parents followed. The event gathered its own momentum to such an extent it was in danger of turning from a Passage to Freedom into a carnival and organisers had to turn down offers for free balloons and bunting. The Passage to Freedom spread beyond Tumanako. A four-wheel drive club in the wider district held a sponsored rally, and there was a dirt bike ride, a horse trek, a swimathon, a trampolinathon, and a skateathon.

In an unexpected ancillary benefit, missing persons' cases from years before were resurrected and three were solved. Two of the cases almost certainly were suicide but at least there was closure for the family. The third concerned someone who had run away from crushing debt but was found alive and in a more solvent state than before, though loath to be found and deeply embarrassed.

Regrettably, there were also ancillary drawbacks. A runner, seventies, collapsed at Kowhai Park and an ambulance had to be summoned. As he lay between life and death in the hospital, he might have pondered life's unfathomable chain of events that drew him to that track in the first place. In an adjoining cubicle, a participant from the horse trek who had been brushed off by a branch, might have shared the thought.

The monetary result was pleasing. On top of the twenty thousand dollars from Lionel Spratt and the Callendars, the reward septupled as funds flowed in from the various Passages to Freedom. It was at this point that Rob Callendar, during prison visiting, raised the concern Felicity had earlier voiced.

'When you posted that reward for me, mum, some of the drugs bosses got very agitated.'

'Why?'

'They thought one of their own might be tempted. You know, dob the place in on the quiet and make sure they weren't around when the cops raided. It happened once before apparently. As a matter of fact, I heard two of the guys talking about it doing it themselves. They were going to get a relative to dob in and then the three of them would split the money later.' He shook his head and looked away.

'The gang turned on me you know. Word filtered down that the boss was so pissed off he thought about having me "offed" there and then.'

Bethany shivered. 'I couldn't just sit around helpless Rob. I had best intention.'

'I know, I know. I'm just saying the hundred-and-twenty-thousand-dollar reward will have them worried.'

Within the week, there was evidence the capitalist society was alive and well as bounty hunters arrived from near and far to find Cindy Spratt and pocket the reward. There was, though, one glaring problem – bounty hunters are not legal in New Zealand; they are almost exclusively a phenomenon of the United States of America where they are termed bail enforcement agents or fugitive recovery agents and exposed to legal liabilities. How then would the bounty hunter restrain the criminal or criminals and bring them in? Rowley Rowlands had serious concerns but with the tremendous hue and cry about the missing Cindy Spratt, and his resources already stretched to the limit, he turned a largely blind eye. Were the bounty hunters so different from debt collectors?

Some of the bounty hunters claimed an altruistic motive but Bethany noticed they always had their bank account number handy. One of them had a drone and a long-term plan and assured Lionel Spratt that he would find his wife 'dead or alive', amending that hurriedly to 'alive and kicking' when Spratt blanched and looked as though he would expire on the spot.

With the relief of a mother who had brought a son back from the dead (and knew precisely what cell he was in), Bethany Callendar supported Lionel Spratt to the hilt. She was deeply moved by his devotion to his wife, as was Felicity Spratt, and the three of them were the indomitable spearhead of the Free Cindy Spratt campaign. One of their roles was trustees of the funds raised and they determined that any claim on the monies should be run past Rob Callendar to ensure that if the reward were claimed, it did not go to the gang.

The intensity of feeling in the community gave rise to unprecedented happenings. A seer arrived from Hamilton, complete with exotic name (Madame Suzette) and crystal ball, and established a 'pop-up' shop in the Tumanako Mall where she did fortune telling on the side at ten dollars a head. She told anyone who lingered that hers was an honoured profession and in Ancient Greece had been well respected and highly paid; Greek armies never went anywhere without their seer. A sceptic asked if it was the absence of a seer that had caused Greece to go bankrupt ten years before. 'Quite likely,' she said, unabashed.

Church groups prayed for Cindy Spratt's safe return and there were others, who would never have called themselves religious, who found themselves saying a quiet prayer at reflective moments. The disappearance of Cindy Spratt had brought the community together like nothing else. Everyone was looking at familiar surroundings inquisitively and soberly. Tramping groups, anglers, hunters, and others who ventured into the wilderness looked for Cindy Spratt as much as for bird, trout, or deer. The medical officer of health was concerned that a higher base level of anxiety in the community might exacerbate individual anxieties but also considered the possibility that worrying about Cindy Spratt might take the minds of some off their own problems.

As day followed day and week followed week, there was still

no word from her captors or from Cindy and when Felicity and Bethany next met, Felicity confided her latest nagging fear.

'If they hold her long enough, could there be Stockholm Syndrome? That would make it harder than ever to find her.'

Bethany knew what Felicity was talking about. The bank robber on furlough from prison in Stockholm, Sweden, in 1973. Armed with a submachine gun, he held four bank staff hostage and demanded three-million kronor, a bulletproof vest, a getaway car, and release of his former jail mate. The authorities agreed. As the stand-off continued, some of the hostages appeared to side with the bank robber as a coping mechanism.

'Cindy's too level-headed Felicity. She would never ally with the gang members.'

Felicity looked unconvinced, as if pondering what anyone might do in an extreme situation.

'Who knows?' she finally said.

Bethany thought back to the Stockholm incident. 'Anyway, I seem to remember that was happily resolved. The police finally stormed the bank with tear gas, the bank robber and his freed accomplice were arrested and the hostages were freed.'

Felicity still looked uncertain. She was having weird, random thoughts. Too much had happened to be sure of anything.

35

CARBON-ZERO DAY

Simon Hurley was in his favourite space – leading a demonstration for the Forest and Bird Society. Emphasis at the Commit-to-be-Carbon-Zero Day at Kowhai Park was on solar and wind power. Fortunately, nature had come to the party, providing both sunshine that encouraged people through the gate and a pleasant light breeze that turned pinwheels, spun weather vanes and the blades of windmills, activated puff-mobiles, enabled paper airplanes and kites to soar, and assisted in the main event of the day – the passage of a hot air balloon from Tumanako over the hills to the plain to the south. Prominent in the basket beneath was Toni Dalzell, exulting in the adventure that had the additional advantage of reducing any carping critics to tiny, disappearing dots.

Simon, with hundreds of others, gazed entranced as the balloon swayed briefly above. Toni Dalzell waved excitedly while the other high-fliers had both hands on the basket. Simon became aware of Bethany Callendar to his right, eyes also aloft. Their eyes met and Simon was surprised at the gravity of the face on this day that was celebrating nature's bounty. Then he realised it was the sight of Toni Dalzell that had turned the face of the mayor to stone and that Bethany Callendar probably wished the hot air balloon would keep drifting over sea and desert, mountain range and plateau, savanna and jungle, until it came to earth on a desolate island where no ship passed. They exchanged greetings and Bethany congratulated him on the range of displays and the involvement of so many children. Every child in the town appeared to be present.

'That's down to Melody,' he said. 'She's a whirlwind of energy when she gets going.'

They looked at Melody Gilmour explaining a sundial to a group of children. Neither commented on the recent appearance of Melody's name in *The Tararua Mirror* on a drink-driving charge. A shocking thing, no doubt, for some parents to see and Simon felt embarrassed for her. He remembered the ripe state she was in on the night Hector Dunwoodie hosted the end-of-year Forest and Bird party. He hoped she did not have an ongoing problem.

Bethany Callendar was delighted to see commercial interests had taken the opportunity to promote their products. She shook her head in wonder at a sign Simon Hurley had himself penned: 'The amount of solar energy reaching one acre of land has the energy value of eleven barrels of oil'.

'Astonishing isn't it,' she said. 'All that free energy for us to tap into.'

Simon congratulated Bethany on her Passage to Freedom initiative. For a long moment they were sunk in gloom at the thought of Cindy Spratt somewhere out there.

'Everybody wants to help,' Bethany said.

He knew that was true. He had never seen such a coming together of the community. It had been wonderful really, though sad it had been in such grim circumstances. He saw again those hundreds of people huffing and puffing round the park, breathing in O and exhaling the greenhouse gas CO_2. But that CO_2 was part of a natural cycle and not like burning fossil fuels like coal which released CO_2 which had been locked up for millions of years. The 2500 million tonnes of CO_2 each year breathed out by Earth's 6.8 billion people was only about seven percent of the annual CO_2 tonnage churned out by the burning of fossil fuels around the world.

'A pity there were some motorised fundraisers.' Simon was thinking of the four-wheel drive club. 'Still, they were thinking of Cindy.'

He moved the conversation on to a controversial project he supported – the erection of wind turbines on a ridge above the town. Bethany Callendar was sympathetic but when Simon started on the minutiae of the project, she saw someone just beyond she had to speak to and moved away.

Simon's eye fell on a sign promoting Patricia Hurley's Wildflower Tours and he smiled to himself. Patricia's mantra was becoming, 'Please don't pick. Leave for others to enjoy' and she jocularly asked Simon one day if she said it in her sleep (they were again sharing a bed). The twenty dollars a head had been a welcome addition to the family finances. Retirement homes and schools were supportive and received a heavy discount.

At first, Patricia had been reluctant to promote the tour on this day.

'But Simon, where's the wind and solar power in my tour?'

'Without the solar power, there would be no wild flowers,' he said.

She realised he was quite right, yet again, and agreed to promote the tour.

Wildflower Tours complemented her other activities perfectly. She had become re-energised in her work for Statistics New Zealand and that inevitably meant much sitting down. There was also her recently acquired fascination with addiction in general: gambling, smoking, drugs, alcohol, pornography. Encouraged by her own gambling counsellor, and by Simon, she was enrolled in a university extra-mural course on addiction in all its forms. This also inevitably involved much sitting down as well as a limited amount of fieldwork. She needed the physical exercise leading the tours, and the immersion in nature was a valuable bonus.

Simon pondered the self-destructive forces that drove people to ingest substances that addled their brains and damaged their bodies. Were they the same forces that drove people to pokies machines and penury? Were they the same forces that led to pollution of the planet and the resultant threat to everyone upon it? Was self-destruction always waiting in the wings to be triggered?

He was supportive of Patricia's study of addiction. He reasoned that the more Patricia looked rationally at addiction, the less likely she was to get hooked again herself. Who was to say she might not bounce from the pokies to something else undesirable? So far, he had been thrilled with her progress. It had been fortunate case studies were close at hand: herself for gambling, Hector Dunwoodie for smoking, Paul Callendar for drugs, Melody Gilmour for alcohol. No one, thank goodness, for pornography and he hoped that could be an optional extra.

'Not that I'm a prude,' he said, 'but surely you've got enough without the pornography.'

Patricia agreed she had. Ideally, she wanted a punter on horses and dogs to supplement the course's unit on gambling, but they had not found anyone as open about losing as winning. Where the winning bet was proudly flourished, the losing was more often crumpled and binned. Simon knew from acquaintance with an employee of the TAB that not all ten-thousand-dollar bets came off and he was also aware how fickle was the hand of fate. He recalled his own bet on a greyhound, Mahingar Khan, light years before. The bet was a mistake – he never bet on greyhounds – but that rank outsider won and the multi-bet was looking like a goldmine with only the red-hot Crusaders to go. Then the Crusaders lost to the bottom team.

Simon went in search of Patricia and Rosemary who had left the park and were now at the library. Polly's illness had propelled Rosemary on to a new career path. Botany would now be a recreational interest – her commitment had shifted to combatting cancer. Simon knew she would be up to her elbows by now in the subject, probably paying particular attention to lymph nodes. Polly herself had encouraged Rosemary to maintain her focus on the natural world, knowing how much she loved it, but Rosemary was adamant – she would be an oncologist. Her sights had shifted to the University of Otago in two years' time. This in turn had caused Simon and Patricia to examine their own longer-term plans. Should Patricia move to Dunedin for Rosemary's first year of study at least? Or should Rosemary go alone to develop more emotional independence? Simon worried more about Patricia than Rosemary. His daughter had risen to every challenge thrown at her, but Patricia in Dunedin for a year, away from the routine and constraints of home and perhaps still vulnerable to pokies machines! They had much to think through.

Polly's situation had also impacted hugely on Daniel Hurley. As he visited Polly, monitoring every slight relapse or progression, he looked at his own career path and determined that it would be environmental engineering. Nobody could say for sure what had caused Rosemary's spina bifida or Polly's cancer. But Daniel had been aware of his parents' largely unspoken suspicions from early childhood – a polluted environment. He had listened recently, intrigued, to his mother's reminiscences of the old abattoir and the coincidence of Stephanie Polson lingering there as well. Who could say where malignancies originated? He knew that across New Zealand there were thousands of sites where the number, location and degree of contamination was largely unknown. They included hundreds of former sheep-dip sites where arsenic and the pesticide dieldrin were the two main contaminants. It was just one aspect of the interaction of industry and the environment and he knew, thank goodness, there was at last a great demand for environmental engineers. He would give it everything he had.

◆ ◆ ◆

Simon and Patricia were relieved to hear Rowley Rowlands was keeping a protective eye on Hector Dunwoodie. After the incident with Bertie, he ensured Hector's property was on the mobile patrol route and one of his officers reported that he might have thwarted a retaliatory action. A vehicle had left the scene so rapidly it had fishtailed out of sight.

When Simon visited Hector, his fears were eased on finding Hector relaxed and confident. Hector did not specify what he had up his sleeve in the way of home protection but Simon, for one, would not be making any unannounced visits. There would be alarms no doubt of one sort or another, perhaps a fusillade of ball bearings, a disabling spray, a paralysing ray, a gelatinous substance that glued the feet to the ground, a net that trussed up the unwary like chickens for the slaughter. Bertie, too, was now a seasoned defender.

'How y' going?' asked Bertie.

'Come in come in come in,' Hector said. 'Have a cup of tea.'

It was soon clear that tea was now Hector's beverage of choice. No offer of coffee or elderberry wine. Raymond Proctor had encouraged this and Hector, never one to do things by halves, had begun to build up an array of teas that would have the senses of any tea-drinking aficionado racing.

'I've got more on order from Bhutan, Sri Lanka, India, Cambodia, everywhere,' he said.

Simon vacillated between a ginger or nettle tea.

'Both very good,' Hector said. 'Anti-inflammatory and antioxidant rich. The mint's very good as well. Helps relieve tension and fights bacterial infection. I can't understand why it took me so long to get onto tea. I've set up a microclimate in a pod out the back and I'm starting to grow it myself.'

Settled over a cup of nettle tea, Simon began to feel so calm that he vowed to drink more tea in future. As they chatted, the subject shifted to Hector's wetlands project.

'That's another thing I can't understand why it took me so long to get onto,' Hector said. 'Should have done it years ago, and properly.'

'What do you mean, properly?'

'Cleaning it up systematically.'

Hector led the way down to the site and showed Simon a suction and filtration machine he had devised. It sat on the former abattoir site and at the push of a button, roared into life. Water was sucked from the ground like a Niagara Falls in reverse and passed through a series of increasingly fine filters.

'It removes the harmful particulates!' he shouted above the racket. 'I take the contents to the council landfill for proper disposal!'

As they returned to the house, Simon wished the owners of the abattoir had taken the trouble to do that all those years before.

Later that day the news shot around town that a husband-and-wife bounty hunting team from out of town was claiming the reward for finding Cindy Spratt. They had with them a dishevelled woman in her fifties who bore no more than a passing resemblance to Cindy Spratt. She had been living in a whare in the bush and proved to be a simple soul who had misunderstood their mission and had accompanied them into town thinking she would be receiving a reward herself. The bounty hunters were already counting the money and were so disgruntled at the outcome it took a threat from Rowley Rowlands to get them to take her back home.

36

RED ALERT

Amidst recriminations later, someone remembered that Tumanako did receive a warning about tropical cyclone Ellice.

The cyclone had already caused havoc in Vanuatu and Australia and Norfolk Island was placed under red alert as it approached. Heavy rain and wind warnings were issued across the North Island of New Zealand. Ellice continued to roar southwards and during the next two days intensified into a Category Three severe tropical cyclone with wind speeds of a hundred-and-fifty kilometres per hour. In its path across the Pacific, houses were destroyed by landslides, plantations flattened, boats sunk, water supply contaminated and thousands evacuated.

As Ellice approached New Zealand, states of emergency were declared in the north, east and central North Island. There had already been flooding across much of the island from earlier storms and now residents in vulnerable areas frantically filled sandbags and battened down their houses. Some fled inland. Ferry crossings of Cook Strait were cancelled and many planes were grounded. Civil defence personnel stood anxiously by their posts, monitoring the situation and allocating resources. But when Ellice arrived, the first day of its ferocious winds and torrential rain changed everything. Emergency services in many regions were overwhelmed, with streets too flooded to negotiate, roads and bridges shattered, electricity cut, and means of communication destroyed. In many areas, help could not come from outside – people had to save themselves. Some civic dignitaries began looking for scapegoats.

The wind was bad enough for Tumanako but the swollen Tumanako River running along its western side was catastrophic. The modest stop-bank could not hold the surging waters filled with debris and they spilled over the side for most of its length through the town and breached it in several places. Residents on higher ground looked on in horror as their roof was ripped off and those on lower slopes fled as the sodden land above collapsed against their houses, thrusting them downwards, crushing them. Properties in the lower part of the town were under five metres of water. Power was cut to most properties and phone and internet services were lost. People began to pile into the Red Cross Hall where mattresses around the walls gave it the appearance of a marae.

Bethany Callendar on local radio urged residents to stay at home if they were safe there; otherwise, to evacuate to the Red Cross Hall. She was grateful her own house was high enough to be clear of the flooding. Scarcely any businesses were open. Some homes were beginning to be buried in silt. It was likely the town's water supply was contaminated and emergency message alerts to stop using water were broadcast. The hospital was crammed with the ill, injured, and incapacitated, some more emotionally damaged than physically. Most ominous of all, three people including a firefighter were reported missing, feared dead in flood or landslide.

When raging floodwaters closed railway lines and roads and

took out bridges, Tumanako was completely isolated, apart from helicopter, for the first time in living memory. A radio report from the Coromandel said residents there were becoming accustomed to severe weather events – it was the fifth time that summer they had had a 'one-in-ten-years' weather event.

Though Civil Defence had taken over authority in the district, Bethany Callendar still felt a duty as mayor. She spoke to Rowley Rowlands at Civil Defence headquarters. He was worried, first about locating lost people, and then about looting.

'Incredible isn't it,' she said, 'how an extreme event will bring out the best and the worst. There are those risking their lives for others and those taking advantage.'

He shook his head and muttered his disgust. Bethany realised he had seen it all in his thirty-odd years of policing.

'How many are missing?'

'We can't be sure. There are reports of some swept away. There has just been mandatory evacuation of Poplar, Rimu, and Matai Streets. Some there have taken refuge in an upper storey and some have taken to the roof. It's difficult for rescuers to get access as trees are down as well as roads blocked by flooding.'

Bethany left him to his task of helping co-ordinate the search for missing persons and offered her services to the Civil Defence controller.

'Be on hand please to help get messages to the public,' he said.

And so she sat helpless, in fear for her residents, as the wind continued to lash the town and the rain thundered. At first, she expected her own house to get no more than a drenching, but as the wind shrieked ever more piercingly, the rain teemed, and roofing iron and other deadly missiles began to spin through the air, nobody could be sure they were safe. As she cast her mind over her town, she became especially afraid for the Hurleys right by the river. Their place was sure to be under water and facing the full force of the flood and all the debris it brought down from the hills. There would be forestry slash as well as trees ripped out by the cyclone and parts of bridges and railway lines up country. She went to the Civil Defence lists of those evacuated and scanned them for the names of the Hurleys. There was no mention.

Hector Dunwoodie had also thought of the Hurleys. His own property was high enough to be clear of the worst of the flooding. When it became clear the town had been struck by catastrophe, he donned his wet-weather gear which included a high-visibility jacket, and splashed across his backyard through the howling wind to his amphibulator. Its time had come. It had the shape of a barge above and a vehicle with four-wheel drive below. He started the motor and proceeded towards the Hurleys' property, at first through flood water and then via paddock and road. He was pleased to see Barry Fitzwilliam had taken the weather warnings seriously and got his stock onto high ground. All around were vestiges of the cyclone: toppled trees, sheets of roofing iron, a telegraph pole, a road sign, bits of fence.

As he neared the Hurleys' property, the water surged against the bow of the amphibulator and curled away in waves on each side. At first, he couldn't see the house through the spray and the driving rain, but then the roof appeared and on top of it, Patricia, Simon, and Rosemary, crouching in a tight knot. Rosemary was waving so vigorously that Simon had a restraining hand on her to prevent her sliding down the roof into the raging water. Hector manoeuvred his craft to the leeward side of the house, taking great care to keep the motor running. The Hurleys slid carefully towards him on their backsides and fell and clambered into it. Hector shouted to them above the roar of the gale to spread out to help the balance and to hold on tight to the bench in the middle. Then he turned the amphibulator and went with the current, towards the town, passing over Simon's vegetable garden. The garden and orchard had fed the Hurleys and countless others for years but now they were being torn to bits by the flood water and by more and more silt and debris. It would be a long haul back. Return might even be impossible.

As Hector and the Hurleys passed through the empty main street of town, they gazed in morbid fascination at the water lapping against window sills and door handles. Hector still had to focus with great care on their passage as unexpected currents wanted to take their craft down side streets and into culverts. He steered for the Red Cross Hall, on a rise to the north, and two streets later, the amphibulator was using its wheels and its passengers were disembarking.

Bethany Callendar met them there, with hugs all round and tears of relief. As Patricia led Rosemary inside the hall, with an arm around her shoulder, Bethany turned to Hector.

'People in Poplar, Rimu and Matai Streets are in trouble Hector. Flooding up to the eaves of their houses. Civil Defence are having problems with access.'

Hector's tyres rolled again and soon the amphibulator was disappearing towards the river, once more on a mercy mission.

'I'm not going to say I told you so Bethany.' Simon managed a grim smile. 'Although I did.'

She recalled his banner: 'Humans are responsible for all global heating over the past two hundred years.' Some had scoffed at it. She wondered if they were among the evacuated, or the missing.

Bethany could see Simon was freezing, shivering, and shocked, and ushered him inside the hall towards warm clothing and hot food. Her council had acknowledged there was climate change and had mostly supported the demonstrators, but she had always felt they should have been doing more. Now they were paying for the apathy.

The Polsons' house, on a small lifestyle block on the outskirts of town, was whipped by the wind but missed most of the flooding. Only the basement was awash.

The factory was another story.

Not only was the factory beside the river, it was exposed to the full blast of the gale that roared in from the east. The flood waters, churning with boulders and logs, smashed through the metal gates, turning them into a tangled, grotesque sculpture, and the wind whipped through the lumber yard, filling the air with deadly stakes and palings. The sawmill caved in beneath the onslaught. The power of the raging river was irresistible. The water and rubble smashed into the machinery, tearing it from its foundations and tossing it onto other machinery. Everything in its path was twisted, shattered, or pulverised. The torrents, augmented now by equipment from the factory itself, swept on to the drying kiln, breaking it asunder and leaving it unrecognisable. The thunderous deluge crashed through the CCA pressure-treatment plant, making the water turgid with chemicals. On and on the flood waters rampaged, toxic now, through the planer mill and the showroom. Only the administration department on the second floor was spared immediate demolition, but most of it was left sagging at crazy angles.

No one was there to witness it. For the rest of that day, Steve Polson could only conjecture on the state of his factory. The roads were impassable and the few rescue craft at large were too busy plucking residents from rooftops and patches of high ground to venture anywhere near the tumultuous river. The gale made it impossible to send a drone aloft and so it was that the factory broke into pieces unobserved. Through the darkness of the night, the destruction continued.

37

RESCUE MISSION

With the shrieking of the wind and the hammering of the rain, Felicity Spratt did not at first hear the ringing of her phone. Fortunately, the caller was persistent. It rang again. But when she picked it up, she could not at first make any sense of it. The words came at her staccato. The reception was terrible. As she continued to listen to the broken snatches of words, she finally recognised the speaker.

'Mum!'

Felicity surmised that not only the vile weather but the location was contributing to the shaky reception. As she strained to listen, she could make out occasional words through the static: longwoods...flood...swept away...escaped...gully...love you.

Melody came running at Felicity's shout and craned to hear as well. When the call cut out, they looked at each other and Felicity could see her own hope reflected in Melody's face. Her mother was alive. The phone rang again but cut out almost immediately. In the silence, the howling of the wind and the drumming of the rain on the roof sounded even louder. Felicity knew she could not sit at home and wait to be contacted a second time; there might not be a second time. Her mother needed help now.

Felicity phoned her father. She heard a quiet sob at the end of the line and after he gathered his senses, they talked. When Felicity came off the phone, Melody insisted she would help. They put on wet-weather clothing, put food, water and spare clothing in backpacks, and set off on foot for the Red Cross Hall – the car would be no use on the blocked, flooded roads. There would probably be someone there whom Felicity had to speak to.

◆ ◆ ◆

'The Longwoods?' Patricia Hurley, brought out of her shock and torpor by the question, creased her brow in concentration. 'There are more than one Longwoods. There are the Longwoods to the west over Taihape way, the Longwoods at Gwavas to the east and the Longwoods north of Tumanako, near Kuripapango.'

Felicity remembered that Rob Callendar's call weeks before had said her mother was being held north of Tumanako. That property had been located and raided but Cindy Spratt had been moved. Perhaps the gang had got wind of Rob Callendar's call. The Longwoods mentioned this time was almost certainly the Longwoods to the north, the general location of the place raided.

'Which of them has the most gullies?'

Felicity was dipping into Patricia's unparalleled knowledge of the countryside. She waited while Patricia cast her mind back to the tramping she had done almost every weekend with her parents in the central North Island, and the tramping throughout the region with Simon and Forest and Bird, and ventures in recent years everywhere around Tumanako in search of wild flowers.

'That would have to be the Longwoods near Kuripapango.'

Lionel Spratt, sapped by recent events but energised by the news his wife was alive, contacted Rowley Rowlands. An exhausted and harried Rowlands was delighted to hear she was alive but to Lionel Spratt's dismay, Cindy Spratt was not top priority for the police at that time. There were still people having to be plucked from their homes and from stranded cars and from patches of high ground in danger of inundation.

Felicity and Lionel Spratt talked, but they did not tell Rowlands of their plan as they knew he would forbid it. Lionel Spratt contacted motor dealers in town and, within the hour, the rescue party set off for Kuripapango on two new farm bikes, with spare petrol on board. Felicity Spratt rode one, with Melody Gilmour on pillion, and Toni Dalzell rode the other. Lionel Spratt conceded he was too debilitated to take part.

There would be no school that week and Melody was intent on helping her dear friend. Felicity knew the adventure of the mission was driving Toni Dalzell but she also detected a strong desire to do good. She wondered if animosity to Dalzell in the community, as a marriage-breaker, was driving her in part. Whatever Dalzell's motivation, Felicity was pleased to have her help. Toni Dalzell was fit, strong and gritty.

They motored north at a steady pace, sometimes turning off the damaged road to ride across country and swing back when conditions allowed. Melody Gilmour had map and torch and kept them on track. Fortunately, the rain began to ease shortly after they set off and when they got amidst broken country, the wind dropped to nothing. All along the way, they could see, by the moonlight and the light of the torch, the devastation the cyclone had caused: land slipped away, bridges destroyed or badly damaged, and trees partially blocking the road they were on, leaving just enough room for the farm bikes to manoeuvre past. Once they had had to inch carefully between landslide and cliff-face and once they had to detour over a low bluff. But on and on they continued, occasionally stopping to eat and drink where there was shelter.

Some four hours later they were in the Longwoods area of Kuripapango. But where to from here? Felicity had ensured her phone was charged before leaving Tumanako and she had tucked it into a pocket high on her chest so she would feel and hear it ring above the noise of the bikes. But it had stayed silent. She felt excitement, but anguish too, that her mother might be close by but not able to contact her. There were gullies on all sides. Cindy Spratt's broken phone call had mentioned a flood and something swept away. Cindy herself? The house she had been incarcerated in? Felicity discussed it with the others. They decided they should be looking for a gully where a huge torrent had raged, wreaking destruction. They pushed slowly but steadily on.

As dawn began to chase away the dark, they cruised the area and agreed there was one gully that stood out above all the others as most likely. There had been a shingle road running through it, now partially destroyed, and amongst the debris evident from the road were planks of timber, shattered window frames, and roofing iron. The wind and rain had become occasional showers and gusts. Water was still running through the gully but they could see from the torn vegetation above, how much higher the water must have been, and how much fiercer the wind. The gully must have been a maelstrom.

'Did mum phone before or after the worst of it?' Felicity said, mainly to herself.

They exchanged anxious looks before turning their bikes onto what was left of the road. Toni led the way. Branches and mudslides had to be negotiated and the slivers of roading that remained after most had collapsed into the gully. Skeletal arms of shattered trees reached eerily into the rising sun. No bird song there. When the road ahead dipped, all three looked nervously high and to the right at the huge trunk of a fallen tree poised on the bank above. It looked ready to go at the slightest disturbance. Even as they gazed, a huge log rolled down the bank a hundred metres ahead, crashed into the edge of the road and disappeared with a roar into the gully. They motored gingerly on, glancing nervously to their right all the way.

Felicity realised they were passing what had been dense and flourishing native forest. Gigantic trees, some feeling as old as creation here, had been wrenched out of the ground by the power and the fury of the flood and smashed to pieces. The stream must itself have become a battering ram, a surging, rushing thing of sound and fury, filled with debris, destroying everything in its path and pounding on all the way to the coast. How could any dwelling within reach of the waters survive that? The terrible sound and sight of it would have been enough to stop hearts. Where was her mum when it happened? They rode on, alert and apprehensive.

Soon Felicity, Melody and Toni were pulling their hats firmly down and burrowing deeper into their jackets as heavy rain started. The landscape now took on a Stygian gloom and they had to peer more closely to identify its features. The floodwaters had obliterated so much there was a sameness to the landscape of broken trees and tangled vegetation. Then ahead, out of the rain and mist, high to the right, Felicity saw a dilapidated hut. A hut used by trampers and hunters, she guessed. It was still standing because it was on their side of the creek and high enough to be out of the flood. She pointed in that direction and they left their bikes on the road, hard against the bank, in brush, and clambered up to the hut with their backpacks.

Toni put a hand on the door handle.

'Unlocked.'

That was a bonus. They stepped gratefully out of the rain.

The one-room hut had four bunks, a small table and four chairs. There was a window on the road side and another on the upper gorge side. It was about as basic as could be but for a tramper or hunter wet, frozen, and hungry, a palace.

'This is all right. I've stayed in worse,' Felicity said.

'Fire ready to go too.' Melody looked in appreciation at the neat stack of kindling and logs by the fireplace. She had brought matches in waterproof paper and, with the aid of a tattered magazine in the hut, lit the fire.

They would probably not be able to replace the firewood, but needs must. Toni got their small gas cooker going and they had their first proper meal since they had left Tumanako the day before. There was something else to warm their blood. Some kind soul had left behind a bottle of whisky, about a sixth full. Toni and Felicity drank a nip of it. When Melody declined, Felicity looked at her searchingly.

'I'd finish the bottle and be useless,' Melody said.

As they sat, ate, drank, and dried out, they wondered how Tumanako was faring. They also had a chance to discuss their situation.

'We need a bit of luck,' Felicity said. 'At least we know mum's alive and there's a good chance we're in the right area.'

Melody spread the map on the table. 'This gorge runs a long way before it joins up with other river systems that go all the way to the coast.'

'We saw the smashed remains of one house at the upper end of the gorge,' Toni said. 'With the road through here, it's quite likely there are other places as well, huts or even houses. They could have been holding your mum in any one of them.' She looked around. 'Even here.'

Felicity had a gut feeling her mum had not been held there. The staccato phone message had included the words 'swept away' and 'escaped'. But she felt they were close. The hut was warming up nicely and it would have been easy to lie down and rest for a couple of hours, especially as their stomachs were full of hot food and the rain was tattooing the tin roof. The whisky was also encouraging a rest. But none of that would help her mother.

Felicity was about to rise from the chair when her phone rang. It was her mum again, and speaking amid a burst of staccato, but the call was stronger than before. Melody and Toni pressed close, also straining to hear. When the call stopped moments later, they agreed the only words discernible were 'rock face' and 'down the gully'. Felicity choked back tears. They looked at one another in renewed hope. Her mother was still alive and they might still find her. Felicity felt a wave of relief that the call had come when they were in the hut and wondered if she had missed a call earlier with the noise of the motors and the rain.

It was then she realised the table had moved a fraction to the right, and the empty chair. Then the floor was moving beneath her and the hut was beginning to slide down the bank towards the road and the gorge beyond. Sodden with rain, the land itself was on the move.

38

APOCALYPSE

When Steve Polson saw the factory at first light, it was too painful to step from his car. He gazed on a scene of carnage. Much of the factory had completely disappeared and only wreckage remained. In those hours of turmoil, he had lost his family heritage and income and Tumanako had lost its major employer. When Bethany Callendar visited the site soon after, she contemplated with amazement how rapidly a storm could abate and nature become more normal. She recalled a visit to Tangiwai years before when she had gazed on the river that had torn the bridge apart on Christmas Eve 1953 resulting in the death of one-hundred-and-fifty-one people on a train. It was a slight, meandering stream winding through bush, no longer the rampaging conveyor of death it had been on that night. The Tumanako River was now back within its proper channel and the wind was a mere zephyr, but what devastation was left behind. Two people had been found swept away and drowned, three were still missing, and many homes had been destroyed. Much of Tumanako was a metre high in silt. The town's water supply was contaminated and a state of emergency still existed locally and nationally. Bethany pondered where the town could go from here.

Melody was closest to the door and as the hut gathered speed, she threw herself out and onto the bank. Felicity was just behind. But Toni had fallen onto her hands and knees and had missed the opportunity. Felicity, sprawled on the grass and mud, could only look in horror as the great tide of mud from the top of the hill kept pushing the hut inexorably down the slope. With the weight pressing behind and only a great void ahead, it was certain the hut would crash and smash all the way to the bottom of the gorge. As the hut teetered above the strip of road, on the point of tumbling, Toni appeared in the doorway. She was on her haunches, coiled. As the hut began to plunge, she thrust with all her might off her left foot, landed on the rim of the bank, and scrambled to safety. The hut plummeted onwards, over the road and over the rim of the gorge, smashing and splintering all the way to the bottom. The wave of mud, trees and scrub continued, completely blocking the road. Soon, there was nothing more to come down and the only sound was the splattering of the rain.

Slowly the women collected themselves, and then rose and embraced. All they had was what they wore – the backpacks had gone with the hut. But they were alive. Felicity and Toni checked their pockets and with relief found the keys to the farm bikes. The bikes, they hoped would still be accessible, in the brush by the road, above the mud slide. Felicity felt for her phone. Gone. But then she saw it on the bank.

One look at the mudslide and they realised any further passage down the gorge would be on foot – there was no way they could get the bikes over the blockage. They contemplated their next move.

Felicity voiced the one option she did not want to take. 'We could go back on the bikes.'

'No,' said Toni. 'We've come this far for your mum. Let's go on.'

'We must go on,' Melody said. 'We know she's alive and down the gully.'

Felicity felt a wave of love for her friends. That was the option she wanted as well. But it was not certain they were in the right gully. Was she endangering all their lives on a hopeless quest?

After his first look at his mangled factory at dawn, Steve Polson returned home. The rain had stopped. He passed the occasional vehicle and person on the move. There was a lot to think about but for a couple of hours he moved on automatic, like a zombie, sweeping water from his basement and clearing debris from the property. At least Stephanie and Polly had a house to come back to. Thoughts swirled of his grandfather and father and the business they had built up over decades. He pictured again the tangled and shattered remnants. One storm and one day and night had put an end to all of it. Staff would have to be laid off and most would probably leave town with their families as there would be nothing here for them. Too many eggs in one basket had always been the risk for Tumanako. That had been a burden he and his father had carried. Now the worst had happened and it was little consolation that it had been out of his control.

He was still digesting the shocking extent of the damage when the telephone rang and it was Stephanie, and then Polly. They were fine, they said – Christchurch had not been too badly hit.

'Fine,' he repeated to himself later, saying the word ironically as he pictured Polly in hospital. He did not go into the details from his end. No need to tell them the sawmill and drying kiln were in pieces, the planer mill flattened, the showroom demolished, the CCA pressure-treatment plant shattered and the site awash with toxic material. He simply said, 'The factory's gone.' There was little Stephanie and Polly could say after that. The factory had been the reason for their life in Tumanako. They could only be thankful Steve was still alive and not one of those he said were dead or missing.

Later that day, Daniel Hurley telephoned.

Felicity, Melody, and Toni set off walking down the gorge. Soon the rain stopped once more and the mist cleared. Felicity glanced both sides of the gorge for a rock face. If her mother had been in a house anywhere near the road, it was almost certain the flood would have washed it away. The damage line of broken vegetation was metres above the road. The house would have floated for a while before disintegrating, and anyone in it would have been drowned, crushed, or tossed somewhere high. She knew of occasional miracles of salvation from the floods elsewhere but here in the gorge she had seen close-up the truly awesome, destructive power of the cyclone. With land on the move, the effects had not finished yet. Felicity had to wonder, too, what condition her mother would be in after such an ordeal. If she were exhausted, cold, and starving, how long would she last on a rock face? Cindy Spratt was fifty-five and not an outdoors person but Felicity did take some comfort from her mother's quiet determination and from her love of family. She knew that Cindy Spratt would be surviving as much for her husband and daughter, as for herself.

It was Melody who saw the man first as he came round a bend far ahead down the gorge on a horse. Fortunately, he was looking down, helping his horse pick its way through the fallen rocks. At her warning, they dived onto the bank. The vegetation was thick and loose and they were able to press themselves deep into it, out of sight. Soon they heard the hoofbeats striking pebbles and Felicity risked a peep through the leaves as he passed. His hat was well down over his face. He was riding with his stirrups long and his legs splayed out in front. Horse and rider seemed too preoccupied to be looking at their immediate surroundings. The glimpse of a rifle strapped to the side of the saddle caused her to gasp and avert her eyes. Felicity realised that in about forty minutes he would come to the massive mudslide over the road. What then? Would he turn back or would he negotiate a path above and continue? Would the farm bikes still be concealed after that last heavy burst of rain? When he was gone, they slipped out and around the bend and proceeded quickly on.

Perhaps it was because they were coming down the gorge with a long view that Toni spotted Cindy Spratt where the rider had missed her going up. She was high on a cliff face on their side of the gorge, on a ledge. There was, as well, a thick clump of vegetation to her side which would have obscured her from the rider. She was sitting with her back against the cliff.

'Look! There!' Toni shouted.

Cindy Spratt was too far distant to read the expression on her face but the slump of the body indicated fatigue and weakness.

Felicity gazed in mixed relief and fear. Her mother! Free from captivity! But in

such a perilous situation, high on the narrow ledge of a cliff-face. The man on horseback was

probably searching for her.

Toni's trained eye took it in and she surmised what had probably happened.

'The flood would have carried her down the gorge. She might have been holding on to something. Maybe a door or plank of wood. And when she came to a stop, she clambered up the cliff face as far as she could and got stuck.'

Cindy Spratt had seen them and was waving. They hurried further down the strip of road until they came to the flat area at the base of the cliff. It was covered with rocks, big and small, and even as they looked, a small rock broke away from the cliff and rolled and crashed some thirty metres to the bottom. High on the cliff-face, they could see the flood-line, with stunted vegetation above and scoured rock below. Already, Toni Dalzell was determining her route to the ledge.

'Are you sure Toni? Mightn't it be better to wait for help?' Felicity followed the line of Toni's gaze. Where Toni might have seen hand and foot holds, she saw only flat rock.

Melody was struck dumb at the very thought of climbing up there.

'How would you get her down if you did get up there?'

Felicity appeared to have voiced Toni's own thought, for Toni put her hands on her hips and stood undecided.

'I would have to go first and guide her down.'

'If she fell, she'd bring you both down.'

Toni nodded in agreement.

Then Melody spoke. 'How exhausted and weak is she? She might just fall off anyway.'

She saw Felicity shudder and muttered, 'Sorry.'

As Felicity gazed on her mother crouched high on the ledge, she remembered how conflicted she had felt when her father was incapacitated and at his most tyrannical in the car, all but driving the car for his wife from the front passenger seat. Where her mother would shy away from confrontation, Felicity would embrace it when appropriate and resolve issues one way or the other. The passivity and silence of her mother had drawn out her empathy, but, at the same time, deeply frustrated her. Once again, Felicity realised she was looking on helplessly while her mother shrivelled, at the mercy of the situation. But then, for the first time, Felicity understood a truth: her mother's patience, grit and endurance had been at the heart of the family. Cindy Spratt had been the one holding the family together, holding the office together, keeping things going day to day while her husband lambasted others with his opinions and glad-handed his way around town. Her absence had exposed a truth – Cindy Spratt had really been the most significant force.

◆ ◆ ◆

Since Felicity, Melody, and Toni had left Tumanako the day before, Lionel Spratt had waited on tenterhooks for a phone call, but there had been nothing. It could be the weather or the terrain, he told Bethany. But Bethany could see the fear in his eyes. His wife and now his daughter were in peril, out there somewhere in the wind and rain with God knows what happening. They could see Rowley Rowlands and the police had too much on their hands to help. Reports were still arriving of people who needed to be rescued and people who were missing. Finally, they both departed the Red Cross Hall for their houses to catch what sleep they could.

As dawn broke, Bethany sensed the worst was past. There was only the occasional gust of wind and when she ventured out once more, she saw with relief that the river was back within its banks. The destruction of the factory, though, had deeply shocked. She checked in with Civil Defence and with Rowley Rowlands. The bags under Rowlands' eyes and the drawn face told their own story. Checking for survivors was still top priority. She heard that Hector Dunwoodie had distinguished himself. All night the floodlights at the front of his amphibulator had pierced the darkness, illuminating people stuck high on roof or shrinking patch of land as he continually traversed the worst-hit areas, picking up survivors and, sadly, the corpses of Tom and Edith Beckingsale. But as the morning passed, the focus of the police changed from recovery of people to prevention of looting and it was then that Lionel Spratt and Bethany Callendar approached Rowley Rowlands and told him of the phone call from Cindy Spratt the previous day and of the mission of Felicity, Melody, and Toni.

'Bloody hell!' he swore. 'Of all the stupid, bloody things I've heard, this takes the cake!'

When he calmed down, he realised Lionel and Bethany had done him a favour in not mentioning it until then. Now, this matter that he would have shelved the day before, became a top priority. Four more citizens needed help: Cindy Spratt, whose disappearance had traumatised the town, and Felicity Spratt and her two friends, who had ridden into the cyclone. He made two phone calls, one for a helicopter, the other to the armed offenders squad.

Toni could not help herself. She took off her all-weather jacket, boots and socks and readied herself for the climb, flexing her arms and feet. How she would have loved to have her climbing shoes but at least her bare feet, hardened over the years, would be much better than the cumbersome boots. Cindy Spratt's voice came faintly from above, with a note of alarm to it, like mother bird protecting her nest. Head craned back, Toni studied her route once more and then stepped forward.

The zing of a bullet past her head stopped her and for a second froze them all in place. They turned to see the rider in the distance, now off his horse on the road and looking at them. In his long coat, hat, and moustache, he could have been the villain in a Western film. Felicity raced to the nearby cluster of large boulders, Melody and Toni on her heels. Felicity looked around. The only things they had to fight with were the fist-sized rocks at their feet. How long could they hold him off?

39

KICK OF LIFE

Cindy Spratt looked on with horror. She had seen the man on the horse appear on the road, look in the direction of Felicity and her friends, dismount and reach for his rifle. She had shouted to warn them but they hadn't heard. The shot had made her convulse and lurch forward and she had nearly toppled off the ledge. She recognised him as one of the two who had been holding her prisoner, awaiting word what to do with her. He had been away on his horse when the flood roared in and smashed the house into pieces. Her other 'minder' had gone under the water and not come up and that was the last she had seen of him. She wasn't sure if this one had seen her. Yet.

Small hope. Next thing she saw him look up and point the rifle directly at her. She shrunk as much as she could. There was a blast and a bullet zinged off the cliff a few metres to her left. Then another blast and a bullet zinged off the cliff to her right. Small stones rattled down the cliff-face. The ratbag was tormenting her. She was at his mercy, a sitting target. She made herself as tight and small as she could, clenching her ankles. As he approached the cliff, holding the rifle loosely by his side, she could see Felicity and the other two – was it Melody and Toni? – crouching behind huge boulders away to the right. She could see that in moments, the women would be in his rifle's line of fire. Then the man disappeared beneath her. She had one option left.

She uncoiled, moved to her right, braced herself against the cliff, put her foot on a large rock that was already loose, and pushed with all her might. As she pushed, she was aware she might bring down the ledge itself and her with it. The rock shuddered and then jerked free, crashing and bounding down the cliff-face, starting a thunderous avalanche of stones, earth and boulders roaring to the ground and cascading far out towards the road. A great plume of choking dust rose skywards. It was as if Cindy was in the middle of a sandstorm. Her ears, eyes, and mouth filled with grit, making her weep and gasp. The ledge trembled but only a section to the right collapsed.

As the tears continued to roll down her cheeks, the rocking stopped, the thunder turned to silence, and the air began to clear. Within a minute it was all over. She risked a look over the edge. Where the man had been, there was rubble metres high. The predator had become the victim. To the right, she saw Felicity emerge into the silence, followed by Melody and Toni. They looked at the great pile of earth and stones where dust was still rising and walked further out from the cliff-face, looked up at her, waved repeatedly, and embraced in deep relief.

As Cindy lay back, breathing in gasps, blinking amidst the dust, she saw the three women confer, taking care to stay out of range of any loose stones that might follow the others. They were looking at the cliff and shaking their heads – it was obviously now too unstable to climb. Felicity then passed something to Melody, the three of them exchanged more waves with her, and then Melody and Toni departed back up the gorge leaving her alone with Felicity, though with fifty metres of cliff-face between them. How she would have loved to scramble down and embrace her daughter, but she dared not attempt to descend. It was the floodwaters that had carried her most of the way up to the ledge, weakening the cliff, and she sensed that any more movement could collapse the remaining ledge and send her plummeting.

◆ ◆ ◆

As indomitable as Cindy Spratt had proved to be, Felicity had to question whether she could survive another night on the ledge. She realised Cindy must be frozen, hungry, and exhausted and one wrong move would be the end of her. Melody and Toni would scarcely have made it out of the gorge. But Melody had Felicity's cell phone and key to the farm bike and Felicity prayed the worst of the cyclone's effects in Tumanako were over and help could be summoned.

Some two hours later, as light began to fade and Felicity began consigning her mother to another night on the ledge, there was an unfamiliar thump, thump, thump high in the distance, coming closer, and then a Bell 412 helicopter was hovering overhead. The sight caused Felicity to stagger and nearly fall to her knees. Melody's call had got through! A spotlight helped illuminate Cindy as a new fear struck Felicity – would the down draft destabilise the already fragile cliff? She could feel the force of the whirling blades even as she stood back from the cliff. Would her mother perish during the very act of salvation? Cindy Spratt remained huddled, unable to gaze at the dazzling light.

A crewman was descending. His feet hovered on the very edge of the ledge. As Felicity watched with her heart hammering in her chest, Cindy Spratt stood and was enveloped in a harness. Together they rose until they disappeared inside the helicopter. The helicopter circled slowly above and then swooped down onto a relatively flat piece of ground nearby. The rest was like a scene from a James Bond film – two helmeted men in black holding guns emerged first at a crouched run, checking the perimeter, and then two paramedics hurried to Felicity who by now was on her knees. Soon, she was sitting in the helicopter with an arm around her mother.

The phone buzzed in Melody's pocket. She stopped riding and signalled to Toni who pulled up beside her. It was Rowley Rowlands with the news that a helicopter had picked up Cindy and Felicity. He instructed them gruffly to pull over and wait for the police to arrive. Elation, though, chased away fatigue and they decided to carry on and meet the police along the way.

In the early morning of the second day after Cyclone Ellice, Bethany Callendar stood on the site of her future house and gazed over her town. In earlier times, the site would probably have housed the hospital, the winds helping clear tubercular chests and the elevation protecting it from pestilences in the swamps below. Now, it would be floods it was escaping from. From one side of town to the other, Bethany could see the ravages of the cyclone's wind and water. Neither the stopbanks nor the town's drainage system had coped and boats still navigated some streets. Hector Dunwoodie's distinctive amphibulator came into view, patrolling a flooded street on the river side of the town. She knew he had turned it over to a grateful Civil Defence after that frantic first night and they now proposed to buy it.

'Every town by a river should have one,' she had heard the Civil Defence chief say. 'I can't think why we didn't have one before.'

Bethany had smiled knowingly to herself – not every town had a Hector Dunwoodie.

She watched as the amphibulator lingered by the Hurleys' property and her heart sank. That magnificent vegetable garden would now be covered by a metre of silt. Simon would have to start again and she doubted it would be by the river. She had spoken to Patricia and Rosemary at the Red Cross Hall and they were putting a brave face on it.

So many thoughts mingled; such a mix of grim and joyful. Two poor souls had drowned – the Beckingsales, an elderly couple who lived near the river – and so many houses had been destroyed by flood or landslide. Red stickers would be needed on others. Polson's was virtually gone and, with it, the jobs of most of the townspeople. But the three missing had been found alive and there was the wonderful news of Cindy Spratt's rescue. Bethany had felt such relief at that and she could barely imagine the relief of Lionel and Felicity. As for her own family, she had telephoned Paul and he had said he was all right and they both knew Rob was safe – sometimes it was an advantage to be locked up well out of town, dry, fed, and watered.

She had already held informal discussions at the Red Cross Hall with town councillors. They agreed they would have to look afresh at house sites and at forestry slash. The slash had choked rivers, battered down bridges and been a significant factor in the flooding. Roads and railways as well as bridges would have to be repaired and made as 'future-proof' as possible.

They were surprised to hear that the leader of the Hub of Truth Church blamed pornography, abortion, and gay rights for causing Cyclone Ellice and claimed that Tumanako had one of the highest rates of pornography consumption in New Zealand. They wondered at his source of information. Bethany shuddered to think what councillors Peabody and Rudge would make of the claim.

She also met with Steve Polson at the factory site. They embraced and she patted him twice on the back.

'So sorry Steve. The extent of damage is incredible.'

He grimaced. 'Unfortunately, my staff can't work from home, Bethany.'

'Can you do anything for them?'

'I'm not sure how much. I'm putting in an insurance claim.' He ran a hand through his hair, and winced. 'I can provide alternative work for some of them, away from the factory site. Some of them might take redundancy. Some might get a benefit from Work and Income.'

He turned and looked at his shattered factory. 'There's a force majeure clause in the employment agreement.'

It was Bethany's turn to inwardly wince. The force majeure

('act of god') clause provided for an employer to avoid the performance of their contractual obligations when an event outside their control meant the business could not operate. In other words, the employer did not have to pay employees if work could not be provided.

She waited for him to elaborate.

'I don't think anyone could dispute that the event was beyond my control. Or that the event prevented the performance of the contract. It's up to me now to try to lessen the effects for the staff. I will need to consult with them.'

That was what she wanted to hear and what she had expected to hear. Steve Polson was a good man already suffering from the illness of his beloved daughter and now the destruction of his business. She knew he would act in good faith and do his best for the staff. She didn't ask about the rebuilding of the factory or retention of the site. That was in the 'too hard' basket. Looking at the nearby river and at the numerous breaches in the top of the stop-bank, she had to question whether that site was now viable.

Bethany Callendar knew the future of her town largely depended on Steve Polson's decisions over the next few weeks.

'There is one thing within my control,' Bethany said. 'Bring in extra counselling staff for staff, families, and others. This has been a huge upheaval for everyone and we need to look after everyone's mental health.'

Stephanie and Polly Polson had been rivetted by the news emerging from Tumanako. A phone call from Steve had quelled their fears about him but they pondered the implications of the damage to the factory.

40

INTO THE LIGHT

L ionel Spratt was waiting at the hospital. Cindy said later she had wondered who was the patient and who was the visitor. He was haggard, pale, and gaunt and she had had to look twice to believe it was him. He and Felicity embraced, he kissed Cindy, and then she was whisked into the hospital for a check of her vital signs. While Felicity and Lionel waited, Felicity recounted the events in the gorge. When she saw her father tremble, she cut it short and focused on the rescue. Medical staff insisted Cindy stay overnight despite her protestations, and it was not until the next day she returned home. It was there that Rowley Rowlands and a detective interviewed her in the presence of Felicity and Lionel and then alone. She provided a description of the two gang members who had held her captive. She said she had not been tortured or otherwise interfered with. It was clear the house had been destroyed and that one of the gang members had died under the rubble and the other had almost certainly drowned.

Over the succeeding weeks, Felicity observed a striking change. Her mother left the curtains of the house open long after darkness had fallen. When Lionel at first went to close them, she asked him not to and he obliged. It was as if she was inviting the outside world to look in and declaring she had nothing to fear. The incident reflected a change in their home dynamics, with Lionel overtly appreciative of Cindy's presence and alert to her needs. Another change as well – Cindy was moving out of his office and taking a clerical position with the town council's social services. Felicity was grateful her father's new-found consideration was not unduly tested by a twisted ankle from a fall or a swollen foot from gout that might put him in the passenger seat of the car. She revelled in their palpable love of each other and was delighted when they pencilled in a second honeymoon in Hawaii.

Tumanako began slowly to pick itself up. At least in part, for its major employer was gone. Bethany Callendar presided over a ceremony to remember Edith and Tom Beckingsale. She also initiated an awards ceremony to honour those who had distinguished themselves during the disaster. Hector Dunwoodie received such attention and such hearty applause, he couldn't get off the stage fast enough. Several said he had saved their lives. Bethany took advantage of the occasion by presenting the reward for the discovery and the recovery of Cindy Spratt. The recipients were Felicity Spratt, Melody Gilmour, Toni Dalzell, and the Rescue Helicopter Trust. Toni Dalzell felt it discreet to be absent, and peeked at proceedings from the back of the hall. All three women donated their share of the money to the Rescue Helicopter.

Bethany felt curiously unsettled at the awards ceremony without Paul by her side. She found herself unconsciously looking around to check his aberrant behaviour but he was nowhere to be seen. She reached for another glass of wine to help relax herself and afterwards got Maia Matenga to drop her home – the last thing the town needed was the name of the mayor in the court news of *The Tararua Mirror*. Later, she was pleased to hear Paul had been visiting Rob at the prison. She was pleased, too, to learn that Rob had commenced studies towards a degree in forensic psychology and that a senior prison officer had said he was giving his fellow prisoners valuable insights into their behaviour.

Felicity Spratt flung herself back into work at *The Tararua Mirror*. Fortunately, the newspaper office missed the worst of the flooding. Staff were rushed off their feet with the welter of news to report and there was heavy demand for the newspaper from outside town as well. Readers were drawn to the disaster like bees to nectar. Felicity's rescue mission to find her mother was still raw and real and a part of her wanted to bury it and expunge it from her mind. But after the awards ceremony, encouraged by the urgings of Colin Trainor, she wrote the story and the circulation of the newspaper rose yet higher.

Felicity's series of articles on drugs dealing in Tumanako already had her in the sights of Julie Frobisher, editor of the *National Observer* in Auckland. Felicity's first-person narrative of the rescue of her mother now had Frobisher reaching for her phone and making an offer Felicity could not refuse. Before departure, she decided to wrap up her series on personalities of Tumanako with a profile of Marjorie Flett. The interview, though, was a damp squib as Flett's stories were just gossip, some of it libellous, and Felicity had to ditch the idea. Marjorie Flett was not too dismayed and continued to reward the gossip of others with cups of tea and ginger biscuits.

Felicity was able to write about one final twist in the drugs-dealing story. Undercover police identified the contact for the drugs entering Tumanako. It was the thin and wizened bar man at the Club Hotel. The connection went all the way back to Asia and the Golden Triangle. The bar man had fed the police the name of Bac Nam Nguyen to mislead them. Bac Nam Nguyen was himself soon in the news in two respects. Horrified at the amount of plastic in the ocean after the cyclone, and at the death of a whale that had ingested plastic which got stuck between its two stomachs, he organised a 'plastic fishing tournament', and funded the prizes for the most plastic recovered. He also won a national award for his fish and chips.

The cyclone and the rescue of Cindy Spratt was transformational for Melody Gilmour and Toni Dalzell. Both were prompted to uproot themselves and venture into new territory. Gilmour took a year's sabbatical and became a contract gardener, with the intention of returning to teaching with renewed vigour, and Dalzell became crew member and hairdresser on a Green Peace vessel sailing the world, including Antarctica.

Daniel and Charlotte Hurley initially felt disembowelled at the news of the damage to their parents' property, but a long telephone call brought a measure of relief. By good judgment many years before, Simon and Patricia already owned five disregarded acres of higher ground some twenty kilometres out of town. Simon had already begun to establish a tree nursery there; he would now establish a market garden. Hector had already given him seedlings of the auber and other exciting plants. The catastrophe of the cyclone had not surprised Simon – indeed, he had expected it – and now that it had occurred, he was more energised than ever in promoting the green cause. They began to build at their out-of-town property and determined to make it carbon-zero. Hector Dunwoodie had shown them the way. They intended to eventually run 'Green House' tours. They were thankful for Patricia's job with Statistics New Zealand. The cyclone, ironically, had boosted the workload as a great wave of new data had to be processed. Patricia was also leading wild-flower tours and conducting part-time gambling cessation courses. Life was busy for the Hurleys.

The heroic work of Hector Dunwoodie during the cyclone garnered national and then international attention. The televised coverage of his rescue mission lingered in people's minds. Extraordinary that a man in his sixties with bipolar disorder should rise to the occasion as he had. When journalists probed further, they discovered the story of Hector and Bertie the parrot thwarting the home invaders. Then an American journalist visited Hector and was staggered to find the exoskeleton and a host of other inventions and innovations, besides the famous amphibulator. Comparisons were made with Thomas Edison. Soon, a medical technology company whisked Hector to Rochester, New York State, United States of America, accompanied by Bertie who proved a smash hit in his specially designed enclosure in their foyer. The chairman said a genius must be catered for and gave him a contract that ensured a comfortable future. Bethany Callendar assured him there would always be a place for him and Bertie back in Tumanako.

Steve Polson had precious days with Polly and Stephanie in Christchurch. Her doctors' reports were encouraging. Steve had always tried to shield her from his business concerns, especially since the cyclone. Her health was more important to him and Stephanie than anything. He under-estimated, though, her strength and resilience. She preferred to face problems head-on, with no obfuscations. Daniel and Charlotte had kept her up-to-date on events at Tumanako.

One afternoon when it was just Steve and Daniel at her bedside, she came straight to the point.

'Will you start up again dad?' She looked at him without expression. 'Or pack it in?'

Steve Polson looked at her and then at Daniel, and spoke slowly and reflectively. 'I've talked it through with Stephanie and she agrees. The factory's too important to Tumanako to pack it in. The town needs the jobs.'

Polly reached out a hand and put it on his.

'But we can't go back to that site,' he said. It was a flood plain until they built the stop-bank. It's too risky now. The same thing or worse could happen again.' He shook his head, as if trying to clear it of images of his smashed factory. Then he looked piercingly at Daniel. 'And we must do things differently. Do those things you and I talked about before.'

He turned back to Polly. 'The cyclone's taken away a lot but it's also given us the opportunity to do things better.'

He got up and looked over Hagley Park that stretched out of sight. 'We can do it much more efficiently, and cleaner. No need to damage the environment. Or people.'

When he turned back, Polly and Daniel could see his zest from years before had returned. His face was alight and there was a sharpness in his movement.

'I'm thinking of a tidy, compact operation on the other side of town. I've got an option on land there. With new technology and good operating practices, we'll produce timber with minimal waste and a low carbon footprint.

Looking sometimes over the park and sometimes at them, he explained his vision.

'Every time we fell a tree, we replant. We rail the logs as much as we can. At the sawmill, a loader puts each log on to a conveyor belt. The bark's stripped off and sold as garden mulch and bark. A Transverse High Grader scans the log and sends it to the saw that will get the best boards out of it. Most of the left-over chips and pieces is turned into sawdust and that's burnt to provide steam to power the drying kilns. All in all, there's less trucking, a hundred percent use of our lumber, and no burning of oil for power.'

Daniel was nodding. He said he had other ideas as well he wanted to run past Steve.

'What about the chemicals?' Polly asked.

'Instead of the copper chromium arsenic to treat the timber, we'll use copper-organic preservatives and organic fungicides and insecticides. They're environmentally friendly. For wood coating, we'll use the new water-based products rather than solvent-based.'

'There's potential for related business as well,' Steve said. 'Wood chips from the sawmill and a blend of ethanol and water can be put into a pressure cooker that breaks the wood down to lignin. That can be used as biofuel and turned into biopolymers as well for plastics that can be composted. GreenChem at Marton is doing it already. Imagine if we could run the trucks on biofuel instead of petrol.'

The news that the Polsons wanted most of all to receive, came the following week. Polly was declared clear of cancer. Polly was with Stephanie at the time, tears flowed, and they embraced for what seemed forever. Steve was told in an emotional phone call and then Daniel and Charlotte. Within a day, the news was around Tumanako and there was much weeping of relief and joy, and many broad smiles. Rosemary eagerly awaited Polly's arrival back home. Rosemary was by now fully committed to medical study and would begin at the University of Otago the following year. Polly would take the remainder of the year to recuperate before resuming her studies at the University of Canterbury. Patricia would divide her time between Tumanako and Dunedin. She told Simon he didn't have to worry about her playing the pokies – she wouldn't have time.

The great day came when Polly was discharged home. At first, she was worried that every ache meant the cancer was returning but gradually she banished that fear. The Cancer Society put her in touch with another cancer survivor in Tumanako – a woman in her thirties – who told Polly of her depression after discharge and when the same thing happened to Polly, she was not taken by surprise. Stephanie ensured that Polly shed her workaholic habits and focused on getting completely well. A physiotherapist helped devise an exercise routine and Polly was soon a familiar figure again in Tumanako, walking, swimming, doing light weights at the gym, and doing yoga. One of the best bonuses from her point of view was that, within weeks, she was starting to taste food again and enjoy her meals. From time to time, she thought of the other patients and prayed they were well. She never heard the outcome of the drugs theft.

A mystery in the town remained unsolved and Rowley Rowlands, for one, believed it would probably always remain so. The identity of the saboteur. At one time Hector Dunwoodie had been top of his list, and then the other firebrand 'greenie', Toni Dalzell. Stephanie and Polly Polson had floated briefly into the reckoning, suspected of wanting Steve Polson to close the factory and move away. Even Felicity Spratt's name had been floated – desperate for a scoop. Could it have been a disgruntled employee? Was it a random troublemaker? Whatever, Steve Polson made it clear he wasn't interested in pursuing the matter. He was intent on creating something new, lasting, and good at Tumanako. He also made it clear the Polsons would be spending more time in future at rest and recreation in Mount Maunganui. All work and no play...

Bethany Callendar decided to stand for one more term as mayor at the urgings of several people she respected, including Steve Polson and Frank Hamilton, the widower at the helm of the Waitaki District Council with whom she had become close through frequent telephone calls. Bethany remained on friendly terms with Paul. They wished the best for each other and were united in their support of Rob. Bethany was pleased Maia Matenga would stand again for council; her drive as well as her aroha was needed.

Tumanako slowly lurched back onto its feet. As the new town began to take shape, Alison Peabody and Trevor Rudge urged visitors not to 'stop and take a break' but to 'step into the future', with the slogan: 'A dash of yesteryear with the technology of tomorrow'. One morning Bethany felt strangely exhilarated. The feeling seemed paradoxical as her town had been devastated, her marriage shattered and her son imprisoned. But as she thought of Rosemary, Polly and their parents, Felicity and Hector, Melody, Maia and others, it was a feeling she could not shake. Finally, she recognised it as hope – for Tumanako, for everyone in it, and for the world beyond.

ACKNOWLEDGEMENTS

My thanks to family and friends for the constant support, to Sean Monaghan of the Palmerston North City Council for his assistance, and to pixabay.com for the images.

BOOKS BY THIS AUTHOR

The Rugby Quiz Book (With Craig Mcfarlane)

Fancy That!

Black Jersey Silver Fern Tom Ellison

New Zealand On Foot

New Zealand Adventures By Rail

The Good Citizen

Group Tours Unveiled

Billy Wallace

The Walking Frame War

Of Three Families